THE
INNOCENCE WITHIN

Here is a story unusual in its characters and
as various in its settings as a travel film.
George Blake does not wholly desert his beloved
Firth of Clyde nor cease to cast a shrewd eye
on the changing fortunes of the industrial
middle-classes. In this tale, however, he views
the scene mainly from below stairs, taking as
his hero a little page-boy who, by dint of character and integrity, returns at length to meet
his former employers as an equal, distinguished
in his own right. It is a long journey in time
and space from the house of Ardyne and back
again, and little Jimsy Bell is in the West Highlands, Ceylon, Hollywood and New England
before he sees the familiar Firth again, having
been a liner steward and a film actor on the
way. His adventures are various and colourful
but never grotesque. George Blake has never
ranged more widely nor written a story in such
bold yet acceptable outline, and his eye for
character is as unerring as ever.

GEORGE BLAKE

THE
INNOCENCE
WITHIN

COLLINS
ST JAMES'S PLACE, LONDON
1955

PRINTED IN GREAT BRITAIN
COLLINS CLEAR-TYPE PRESS: LONDON AND GLASGOW

CONTENTS

CONTENTS

CHAPTER ONE

Little Boy Lost

THE BEDROOM corridors of the great railway hotel seemed to be stuffed with afternoon silence. Somewhere in the bowels of the Northern Grand a vacuum cleaner whined faintly as a waiter in shirt sleeves swept up crumbs and tobacco ash after a business men's luncheon, of which the considerable cost would be duly claimed against Income Tax as "promotion expenses." Now and again the whuff of a passenger engine starting up under the glazed arches of the terminal station, or the more cheerful toot of a pilot engine, might have caught a sensitive ear. But the sounds were familiar notes in a subdued and calculable diapason. Here was approximate peace in the heart of a city.

The Northern Grand was living up to its advertised claim to be "the quietest railway hotel in the country. At any moment of the day you can rest and forget in cushioned silence." The carpets were thick along those upper corridors, the lights subdued; the dead doors of locked bedrooms rather suggested that the establishment was really a monastery of which the superiors did themselves extremely well. Ambiguous placards, hanging on door-handles and reading PLEASE DO NOT DISTURB, wore the air of redundancy.

On the fourth floor, however, at the end farthest away from the lifts, three young people played an absorbed game, using the thick pile of the carpet as their fathers might the turf of a green on a seaside golf-course. Indeed, their implements were a couple of battered golf-balls. Down on their knees and beautifully absorbed, they bowled them in turn towards a circle of pennies laid out some five yards from a join in the carpet they had chosen as a base-line. The game was to roll one of the balls at least within the circle of coppers; to get both within the fairy ring was triumph.

They were quiet as they had been enjoined to be. They were beautiful in their raptness. They were as creatures who had somehow been orphaned by the esteemed peace of the Northern Grand at a period of afternoon when more fortunate children would have been tumbling about a lawn or exploring the pools of a rocky seashore. The faintly-lingering, jaded burden of cooked foods, even on this fourth floor, was as a miasma, poisoning the innocents.

Of the three, one was a girl in her early teens, an eager creature in the gipsy mould, wearing a kilt in the Robertson hunting tartan below a sensible grey pullover and above short-socked ankles and sandalled feet. Dark locks fell around an eager, freckled face and over sharp, brown eyes as she knelt, hands on knees, to watch the run of the balls as delivered by a boy, slightly younger but also dressed in the kilt. This was a fair-haired lad and so delicate and pink of feature that one, recognising them as indubitably brother and sister, might wonder why the girl was so like a spirited boy and the boy so like a tender girl.

"Good shot, Billy!" the gipsy child hailed her brother's effort. "That last one was nearly one to you."

"It *is* one to me," the boy claimed petulantly. "It's in."

"It isn't. The ball's just lying against the penny."

"It isn't. It's more than half-way over the penny. It's one to me."

"But it isn't, Billy, really."

"But it is, isn't it, Jimsy?"

The fair boy started to sniff, tears forming on his long lashes, but before the question could be answered the bedroom door numbered 449 opened violently inwards. The playing children were suddenly aware that the rising tones of their dispute had disturbed an adult, a guest. He was a bulky, ageing man in a dressing-gown of blue towelling, hemispherical over his stomach. The players observed the immediacy of his bare feet and contorted toes, the threat of a cropped grey moustache smearing his upper lip.

"Do you young devils," barked this ominous stranger, "think this is a public park?"

The gentleman had had a bad overnight journey from Birmingham and had solaced himself perhaps a thought too freely at the industrial luncheon in the chamber below. Not unreasonably he pointed to the placard hanging to the handle of his bedroom door, asking loudly: "Can you not read?"

"Of course, we can read," retorted the girl with the Spanish look, but rather more in confusion than impertinently.

The indignant stranger glared at her, and then he suddenly turned from her piquant face to challenge that of the young person who had been referred to as Jimsy, referee in the dispute between Billy and his sister.

"And what the devil are you doing up here?" he demanded to know. "You should be down in the hall, shouldn't you? Wait till I ring the manager."

The bedroom door was viciously slammed on three frightened and bewildered faces. The small group of young people was frozen within a shared sense of critical calamity.

"That's the sack for me," said Jimsy.

He stooped to pick up the pennies that had formed the target of their primitive ball-game. The green trousers of the hotel's uniform tightened round a plump, almost female, bottom. When he stood up he pulled down the tight jacket of a page-boy with its row of useless, spherical buttons down the front. His face was round, fresh and pleasant; his black hair had been assiduously combed and pressed down with the help of a good deal of cold water. This page-boy was most remarkable, however, for the maturity of his bearing in relation to his physique. He stood no higher than Billy. The ordinary observer would have classed him as a dwarf and guessed his age to be anything between seventeen and twenty-four years.

"I had better be going," he now said quietly, and his speech had the Highland intonations of those who have lisped in

Gaelic before they have been tutored in English. Then he added anxiously: "But here he comes."

There was no way of escape. This end of the fourth bed-room corridor was a *cul-de-sac*. And what the page-boy saw approaching was the figure of the floor-manager on his after-noon rounds, in his uniform of black jacket and striped trousers, plump and pasty of face in the way of those who live almost entirely in terms of central heating and eat perhaps too well.

The floor-manager bowed to the hotel's honoured guests—the fair, pink boy and the girl with the air of a gipsy. Then he turned on the young person in the much bebuttoned jacket.

"Go and report to the hall porter at once. Then come to my office when your shift is over."

The dark girl protested with spirit: "But it wasn't his fault. We asked him up to play."

The door numbered 449 opened again, and the man in the blue dressing-gown, his belly ballooning it outwards, was shouting:

"Is there any hope of peace in this ruddy place of yours? I've been trying to get you on the phone, and even your blasted operator seems to have gone to sleep. Why should a blasted little bell-hop spoil a man's rest? Cushioned silence, my foot!"

The floor-manager bowed towards the angry man from Birmingham and spoke in the ingratiating accent of the German-Swiss *hotelier*, pointing to the marionette figure of the page-boy disappearing at a trot along the depressing length of the corridor:

"I apologise, m'sieu. It is most unfortunate. It will not happen again. You see: he is gone. He will be dismissed, promptly, for the breaking of our most strict rule."

"And ruddy high time!" said the occupant of Number 449, again slamming his door shut and heaving himself on to his bed, wishing that these blasted Scotsmen wouldn't dish out so much neat whisky.

"Now I tink, mam'selle, m'sieu," the factotum returned to

the kilted sister and brother, "you return to your sitting-room, Number 464, not so? You have no doubt a book to read, a game to play. Allow me . . ."

The plump man bent down to pick up the two golf-balls that had been left on the carpet and rose to present them, with another bow, to the dark girl. He was taken aback to find that she had braced herself, her hands locked behind her back, to do battle like a terrier.

"Did I hear you telling that gentleman that Jimsy is to be dismissed?"

"Oh, shut up, Beth!" implored the weak boy called Billy.

"It is a pity, but——" The floor-manager shrugged his padded shoulders.

"I won't shut up," the girl protested. "Billy and I were making all the noise. Jimsy told us again and again and again to keep quiet. And then that rotten old man over there . . ."

She pointed to the door of Number 449 and, being female and weak after the first burst of the volcano of outraged loyalty, started to sob.

The floor-manager's voice was creamy, reassuring. "It is a little thing. Come, mam'selle. Let me switch on the radiator in your sitting-room."

"I don't care. I'm going to tell my Daddy."

"Oh, shut up, Beth!" pleaded Billy, also starting to sniffle.

"_Alors!_" exclaimed the floor-manager, relieved to feel that another small crisis in a life of recurrent crises had been decisively subdued.

2

Within the sitting-room numbered 464 of the considerable suite their father invariably hired on their visits to the Northern Grand the children called Billy and Beth were imprisoned, and so they felt. It was a pleasant enough chamber, if rather in the manner of a fashionable surgeon's waiting-room, and the array of glossy weeklies on the central table and a light hanging

from the ceiling high above it could not do away with the
institutional air. The early darkening of a wet afternoon,
continually shot through with blue flashes from the tramway
cars, made their segregation to these young people peculiarly
forlorn.

Mummy was, of course, lying down. Mummy was much
addicted to lying down, especially when Daddy brought them
all to live in the hotel while he watched the progress of The
Case through the courts. She had made of herself the figure of
a martyr to what she called sick headaches and was a great one
for sending out to the chemist's for the specifics that had most
lately been recommended to her or had caught her eyes in the
newspaper advertisements. Indeed, Jimsy Bell had just delivered
a bottle of her newest fancy—a proprietory article called
Soothex—when he had been caught up in the floor-game with
Beth and Billy and was thus in danger of dismissal.

A sense of guilt, of their own responsibility for the plight
of the small page-boy, lay upon the lonely children as, in that
characterless hotel sitting-room, they sought to pass the time
until Mummy should cease from lying down or Daddy return
from the Courts. The vivid, black-haired girl called Beth
resumed an attack on a jigsaw puzzle of great complexity, a lot
of trees in it. The fair boy bent over the pale-green pages of a
periodical called the *Dynamo*, given over to stories of a pseudo-
scientific nature. Every now and again a heavy tear would
drop from his blue eyes to make a dark-green mark on the
pale-green sheets.

Beth ignored these signs of her brother's distress. When he
was in mental trouble, as he so often was, Billy shed tears in
this silly, uncontrollable way. You wished he wouldn't. You
wished he could be much more of a man. But, being female,
you were terribly sorry for him: you wished you could help
him.

"Oh, shut up, Billy!" she protested nevertheless. "What's
the good of blubbing?"

"It wasn't Jimsy's fault," her brother wailed.

"I know that perfectly well. Don't be such an ass. Look

here," she said, rising from before her intricate problem in pattern, "I'm going downstairs just now. And if Mummy or Daddy come in before I come back, don't say a word. Do you understand, Billy?"

"Yes, Beth. I'm not to say a word."

"Promise. Cut your throat."

"Cut my throat."

Surveying the length of the corridor from behind the gingerly-opened door, Beth found it to be empty as usual. She slipped out with the agility of an eel and ran its length, hastening to get to the stairs before Daddy might come bouncing out of the lift. Her flight downstairs was headlong, but a small miracle of grace and sureness of foot; and when she reached the mezzanine floor, the palm lounge crowded for afternoon tea, suburban ladies raised their heads and ceased their chatter to exclaim: "What a pretty kid!"

Elizabeth Ferguson Ferrier was in fact hardly a beauty as yet. The small freckled face under the raven-black hair cut short in the mediæval manner was, rather, piquant with its high cheek-bones. Her nickname at school was Monkey. The charm lay in colouring and carriage: the little head held so proudly on a slender neck, the virgin body upright and slim, informed by what seemed a poise of personality, in which candour and vehemence were fortunately blended.

The child, always watchful for the sudden appearance of her father—who might, she knew well, halt his progress upstairs for a drink in the lounge while Mummy was safely away lying down . . . the vivid child almost ran round the corner into a busy corridor of kiosks, lavatories and telephone cabinets and, ignoring an old and adoring friend, Joey in the cloakroom-bookstall, pushed her way through a white door marked DIRECTION—STRICTLY PRIVATE.

A young man with silky, flaxen hair, the unmistakable apprentice *hotelier* in black jacket and striped trousers, rose from behind his desk as if to protest against the invasion of the tabernacle, but he was professionally quick to recognise the daughter of one of the hotel's most profitable patrons, M.

Ferrier, *le forgeron*. He spoke in fact with the thick accent of the German-Swiss, bowing:

"Is there something I can do for you, mademoiselle?"

"I wanted to see that other manager, the gentleman who looks after the fourth floor," Beth announced breathlessly.

"But impossible, I fear. M. Renoir is now off duty. Can I help—explain?"

"Could I see the manager, then?"

The young man smiled, as if a candidate for ordination had asked to see the Pope before taking his vows.

"That also, I fear, is impossible. He is with the chairman at this moment. If you will explain, mam'selle, I shall be honoured to help."

Beth suddenly realised the impossibility of her task, the humbling littleness of her ignorance and innocence as against the carefully built-up aloofness of the catering trade.

"No, it's all right, thank you," she stammered, the lump of emotion in her gullet. "I'll see Daddy when he comes back. Thank you very much."

However automatically, she dropped a funny little curtsey and fled from the scene of a repulse. Knowing that she was in the mood to blub, the very weakness she deplored in Billy, she nevertheless found time to look down the wide well of the main stairway and saw that Jimsy Bell was still in his proper place beside the head porter's desk in the entrance hall, a comic, attractive, diminutive figure, the white gloves of his office folded rigidly under the shoulder strap. Thus slightly re-assured, the girl turned and tore up the stairs, her tempestuous passage flustering a puffy member of the Scottish peerage who had been taking a cup of tea with Miss Valerie Mainwaring of the *Hoity-Toity* company at the Prince's in her suite on the second floor.

The private sitting-room was empty on her return to the securer heights of the fourth, and a murmur next door told Beth that Billy was with their mother, probably snuggling in beside her on her emergence from the process of lying down. Billy was always Mummy's Boy just as she was, by a family convention she dimly resented, Daddy's Girl. By now, she was quite sure, her soft and pretty brother would have told the sad story of Jimsy Bell to Mummy, throwing off his sense of responsibility for the loss of their playmate, so odd in his physical make-up as to be as enchanting as a new toy.

Her own concern remained profound. Guilt and pity made a formidable mess within her young mind, and she was perhaps even more seriously daunted by the frustrating outcome of her first encounter with organised authority in the person of the flaxen-haired young man in the office labelled DIRECTION.

She took up the pieces of the jigsaw puzzle again but could not recover her interest in it: perhaps just a young girl of high spirits who had failed to get her own way. Thus she was sitting at the table, her head between her hands and her eyes sightless over the formal array of the pieces, when her father entered in his invariably noisy way to disturb her.

"Hootsy-toots, Bettypet! " he cried in greeting.

He was a man much given to phrases and catchwords in a sort of facetious shorthand, and Beth promptly drew the inference that Daddy was to-night in one of his good moods, The Case going well. She was lifted from the chair into his arms like a baby, and she discerned that he had been drinking and smoking a good deal throughout the day. He carried her to the armchair before the radiator and set her down on his knees with a plump and kissed her.

"Well, had a nice day, Bettypet? " he asked.

"Quite nice, Daddy. But——"

She was female and had an acute sense of rhetorical advantage. Now she could cry a little and with effect, and to her father's waistcoat she confided the shameful story of Jimsy Bell's degradation. He heard it out with the judicial gravity that had so impressed him in the Courts.

"Hm! " he summed up. "He's an odd little fish that. Shouldn't have been playing during working hours, and with hotel guests. But don't cry now, Bettypet. Kiss the tears away. There! Your little friend won't suffer. We might even take him with us to Ardyne. Trained servants aren't easily come by these days. I'll see your mother."

He was an impulsive and even foolish person, given when in the mood to spoiling his children with extravagant gifts. For him the page-boy was not a human being, only rather an amusing toy who would be comically decorative about the big house of Ardyne.

"Oh, Daddy!" was all that Beth could gasp in her wonder at the bold brilliance of this solution of a human problem.

"That's all right, darling," he said as he put her down, mightily gratified by his own awareness of power. "Now we'll see what Mummy's doing."

It was characteristic that he made no mention of his only son. When he entered the double bedroom the pretty boy rose from before the picture book he had been reading on the floor beside his mother's bed and seemed to run for the door, his passing acknowledged with a "Hallo, Billy!" that was almost a dismissal. The father bent down and kissed the woman who lay in studious *négligée* on one of the twin beds.

"Had a good rest, dearie? Oh, that's a pity! Has that boy been disturbing you? . . . He was in blubbering to you about the page-boy business? I've just had it all from Beth. Oh, well, if they feel it was their fault I'll talk to Capaldi this evening. We could do with a lively boy about the house at Ardyne if you insist you can neither get nor keep women servants."

Mr. Ferrier's dialectical processes were apt to follow short-cuts and imply weakness of mind in his opponent, and to his demonstration of power—"A fellow's got to be master in his own house"—the woman on the bed could only oppose her own acquired technique of langour and resignation within a private world of physical suffering. If Festus, for such was her husband's unusual Christian name—if Festus had made up his mind that this funny little boy was to be taken to Ardyne as a sort of toy for the children there was nothing more to be said, for opposition only hardened her husband's inclinations into determinations and she was too lazy to frame even a comment.

Elaine Ferrier had been pretty in her day, if never beautiful,

and was still so in her middle forties. It was striking to see
how extensively she had transmitted her pink fairness to her
son, just as her husband, though now greying in the hair and
the eyebrows that jutted out above high cheek-bones, was
manifestly a near progenitor of vivid, dark-haired Beth. She
slowly swung her long and slender legs off the bed and asked:

"Are you dressing to-night, Festus?"

"Don't think so. Just a quick bath and into another suit.
There's nobody coming, is there?"

"Unless Ketron brings in a friend."

"Ketron!" repeated Festus Ferrier, thus seeming to dispose
of his older daughter by his first wife. He started to peel off
his jacket.

"Weren't you going to do something about that page-
boy?"

"Oh, damnation, yes! Well remembered, dearie. I'll run
down now and see what I can fix up."

This was an excellent opportunity of nipping into the
American Bar and getting Charlie to mix one of his extra-
specials. It was also in the man's small but complex mind that
he would enjoy exercising his influence on the hotel manager,
Capaldi, a sad delusion in respect of one who had battled his
way through the hotels of Europe for three decades on end.
Elaine Ferrier dropped all her garments, save a gossamer vest,
to the floor and stepped out of the silken pool.

"I wish this Case of yours was finished," she said. "I want
to get home."

"Only a day or two now, dear. Only a day or two now."

Meanwhile, a tall young girl, beautifully dressed in the
adult mode for all her mere eighteen years, wearing on her
brilliantly contrived fair hair a fetching little hat that any
other woman would know had cost her guardian the best part
of twenty guineas, brought a whiff of the out-of-doors into
the private sitting-room.

"Hallo, kids!" she tolerantly greeted her stepmother's
children, busy again with their small amusements at the table.

"Hallo, Ketron!" Beth greeted her heartily. She thought

that Ketron was beautiful. "Do you know what happened this afternoon? Listen . . ."

The young eager girl babbled her tale of Jimsy Bell, the floor-game and the floor-manager. She ended breathlessly:

"And Daddy has promised, almost, that he'll come down with us as a page-boy at Ardyne."

"Oh, my God!" said her stepsister coldly. "The sight of that little twerp about the place will be just too sick-making."

Ketron Forrester Ferrier, so like her stepmother in so many ways, was passing through a fashionable phase of intolerant boredom. Beth was happily distracted from more tears or an explosion by the knock of the floor-waiter, a kindly man with children of his own in Savoy, wishing to clear and lay the table for the evening meal the young people would share after their baths.

3

A river steamer backed out of the terminal pier at Oliver's Bay, turned in a flurry of water aerated the colour of lime green by the action of its own paddles, and then shot off with the acceleration of an arrow in a northerly direction across the Firth. It headed for a low-lying island some six miles away, aglow and inviting in the flawless sunlight of a fine summer afternoon.

Of the little ship's complement at least three were indifferent to the sparkle of the day as seen from on deck and to the blue, alpine loom of the mountains on a large island in the outer estuary. Like all children, in age or spirit, they were happier to hang over the rails that guarded the well of the engine-room below decks and watch the gleaming cranks turn round and round and round.

"You would think they were punching their way to get on," said Beth Ferrier.

"I," said her brother Billy, "like the little ones at the side that rub their faces together."

"These are the eccentrics that control the valves," explained Jimsy Bell.

"Gosh! You seem to know everything, Jimsy," cried Beth in the frankest tones of admiration.

"I'd like to be an engineer," he replied.

The Chief Engineer of the *Countess of Airlie* regarded the young people sourly from behind his levers at the after end of the pit in which his machinery turned in its appointed way. He had no feelings of romance towards double diagonal compound engines. If they worked, they needed constant attention with long-spouted oil-cans and tubs of grease; if they broke down they could be a fair b. He also objected, while admitting that his engines were the show-piece of the ship—he objected to children climbing up the railings above them and chipping his fresh white paint, chattering loudly and ignorantly at the same time. Now Beth had climbed so high in her eagerness to behold the mechanical marvels below that she seemed in a fair way to falling into the churning welter of moving metal parts below.

"Here, youse!" cried the Chief Engineer, jerking a thumb upwards. "Away up on deck and get your Mammy to shut your traps with a bun. Or do you want me to get the captain to ye?"

The young people stood back in the alleyway, each face wearing the baffled and slightly sullen look of children reprimanded in the midst of their most instinctive play.

"We'd better clear out," muttered Jimsy Bell, more experienced in life than the other two and more fearful of it; and at that moment a band of music, in the waltz called *Sobre les Olas*, started to play on the promenade deck above.

"Yes, come on." cried Beth. "There's the band."

She started running aft and turned in a whirl of tartan skirt to dart up the companionway like a young roe-deer, Jimsy Bell small and quick behind her and, in the wake, Billy clumsy and half-sobbing in his congenital inability to understand and master one of those new sets of circumstances in which his sister, Beth, was apt so suddenly to engulf him.

The band was a modest but reasonably competent trio of fiddle, cornet and harp, the latter played by a grey elderly man, his sightless eyes uplifted like those of a saint blinded by the glory of a divine revelation. The faintly pathetic group was already surrounded by all the juvenile passengers, but Beth wriggled like a trout through the ring and took up a prominent place beside the harp, her brown eyes entranced by the sure play of the blind man's fingers on the strings. Hanging back, Jimsy Bell muttered to Billy, dependent by his side:

"I must go up and check the luggage."

"Don't go away, Jimsy," protested the pretty boy. He felt safer with the servant than with his sister.

"Just stay where you are for a minute or two. I won't be long."

He had been specifically charged with the care and counting of the luggage.

"I want you to act as our courier when we're travelling, what we used to call a bearer when I was in India," Mr. Festus Ferrier had instructed him grandly. "Look after our tickets. Find an empty carriage and keep it. Keep our luggage round you. Sit on it if you have to. And always, *always* keep your eyes on Mrs. Ferrier's dressing-case. Valuable—and she sometimes forgets it. Understand, Bell?"

On this first day of his service with the family the responsibility would never leave his mind at peace. He could still quite literally tremble to relive the panic into which he fell when, two days before, the cashier at the Northern Grand had handed him his books and his last pay packet. He had stood by the hall porter's desk to work out the last hours of his first job, running his messages automatically but frozen in his spirit by the awful consequences of dismissal—reporting to the Welfare people in Glasgow, getting a row from an inspector, perhaps being cast out utterly, at the best sent back to the Exchange with a black mark against him.

The circumstances of his life had made this unusual youth acutely aware of his dependence on official charity; he was burdened always by his own conscientiousness. Ah! It was wonderful to have been so suddenly, strangely, freed from the shadows of the prison-house, to be sailing across the open Firth towards the island and the big house of Ardyne, favoured servant of a rich family! Even so soon, however, a tickle of concern had started to work in his mind. It was going to be difficult to be at once the impetuous Beth's toy boy-friend and the humble, obedient servant Mr. Festus Ferrier would require for the satisfaction of his personal dignity and the smart adornment of his big house.

Here, meanwhile, was the luggage, ranged neatly about the base of the funnel. The large consignment for the Ferriers of Ardyne had the distinction of Crown jewels amid the humble pieces about it, and women among the day excursionists were turning over labels and standing back to admire and reckon the cost of the articles. Three trunks of a matching motoring set in green, four large suitcases of the finest pigskin, an array of zip-fastener bags loosely packed with the irrelevant impedimenta of every female passage through this world, and his own case in fibre, strapped to compensate for unreliable locks— it was all in order, and Jimsy Bell cocked himself up on the funnel casing, his short legs dangling above the treasures in his care.

He saw himself stared at by the ruder passengers about him. He heard a small girl cry "Oh, help, Maw! What a funny wee man!" It was a condition of his living, and he had learned to keep the personal dignity he so deeply cherished. He knew that his status as a man in miniature could be exploited on the stage; he could be a comic in his own right, tumbling a few cart-wheels, singing a pathetic orphan's song and duly passing into the protection of a strapping principal boy. You had to learn to accept much as an oddity in the ordinary world of vulgar folk, even if you knew that it was with the kindliest sympathy that most people, especially the mothers, stared at your neat body, bright face and jet-black hair. But even their amused affection was an intrusion.

Soon the cornettist, the youngest of the instrumental trio, was moving among the people with his collecting bag in jaded black velvet, jingling the coppers in it while his colleagues sawed and plucked their way through a rendering of the Mascagni *Intermezzo*. Beth was inevitably at his heels, always savouring new experiences, Billy at hers. She stopped at the sight of Jimsy cocked above the luggage and cried in her embarrassingly clear voice "Oh, Jimsy! I haven't got even a penny for the collection."

Jimsy groped in his trouser pocket, found a sixpenny piece and passed it to his young mistress, who dropped it into the velvet bag with a careful regard for the accuracy of her delivery. The young cornettist glanced at Jimsy with a smile, these two passing strangers exchanging a flashing signal of understanding as between those who must work for poor livings and accept subservience as a condition thereof.

"Oh, help!" Jimsy cried in sudden alarm. "Your mother's dressing-case," and slid off his perch.

"She's got it herself," Beth declared. "I saw her with it in that beastly cabin place."

"Yes, she carried it on herself at Oliver's Quay, now I remember."

Jimsy found himself breathing heavily as a consequence of shock. He had been brutally reminded of the weight of his responsibilities and of his own fallibility.

"I wonder," speculated the dark girl, raising her bright eyes to a platform before the funnel, "if the Captain would let us up beside him. It must be an awful lark up there."

4

The second Mrs. Festus Ferrier looked on sea passages, salty breezes and oily smoke from a ship's funnel as barbaric intrusions on the comfort she required of life. Even on this enchanting day she had a rug over her knees as she sat with her husband at a corner table of the small lounge bar and sipped a glass of stout which, though she much disliked its taste, she believed to possess body-building qualities. Festus Ferrier had armed himself with a bubbling glass of whisky and soda and, four minutes after the steamer had left the mainland pier, raised it blithely, his eyes rejoicing in its beady promise, and cried:

"The first to-day! Your health, dear. Ah, that's good! Now, I was going to tell you about The Case. Didn't want to say too much with the children around."

The Case had become this limited man's obsession, providing him with agreeable illusions of importance and of himself as a doer of public duty; but it was in fact a shabby enough litigation. It concerned the terms of his father's will and a claim to certain holdings in the family firm now known as Ferrier Foundries, Ltd. It was another of Festus's illusions that he was really fighting the case—against his own younger brother and his co-directors—on behalf of his spinster sisters, Millie and Florence, now retired to Bath. His overhanging eyebrows twitched as, across the small, liquor-ringed table, he declared his passion in the matter to his wife.

"I don't care what happens in the Outer House, though I think we'll win. And if that blasted brother of mine appeals I'll fight them again. I'll take Finlay and the rest of them to the House of Lords if I have to, by God I will!"

"Quite right, Festus," agreed Elaine Ferrier, but a little listlessly. She could not understand the ins-and-outs of The Case any more than could most lay readers of the Law Reports in the *Scotsman*. It had the mere virtue of keeping Festus interested and of allowing her a week in Edinburgh now and again. She secretly felt, for critical thought was almost beyond her, that it was all a bit silly.

"Finlay was always a twister," her husband went on. "Even when we were all kids in the nursery at home. . . ."

Festus Ferrier could not have known it, but two of the leading figures in The Case sat at a window of the Old Club overlooking Princes Street and up to the portentous loom of the Castle on the Rock. Both fine-featured men in the conventional dark clothes of their profession, they sipped at long glasses of the club's very good dry sherry. They were them-

selves dry of manner, almost aridly detached in their pro-
fessionalism.

"And what is Winnie-the-Pooh going to make of our little
argument this week, Joe?" asked Neil Maudslie Stobs, K.C.,
senior counsel for the defenders, Ferrier Foundries, Ltd. He
referred to a lately-appointed Senator of the College of Justice.

"Oh, he'll sit on it for a fortnight, I suppose," replied J.
Jardine Shanks, K.C., who had conducted the case on behalf of
Festus Ferrier and his sisters, pursuers.

"You made the best of it in your speech yesterday, old boy,"
said Stobs, K.C., on a cold sort of cackle. "It was a cracking fine
display of how to make bricks without straw. We'll get the
judgment eventually, you know. And is it proper to ask, now
that Winnie has reserved judgment, what sort of person your
client really is?"

"Oh, Festus!" laughed Shanks, K.C., but carefully. "I've
known him most of my life. His old father's place marched
with ours at Barnlee. . . . No, all the guts were in your man,
the brother Finlay. I think the old father made the mistake in
the first place. His first-born, Festus, having scaled the heights
as a public schoolboy, couldn't possibly go into an iron foundry,
and if you'd known the awful old go-getter his mother was,
you'd understand."

"But my Finlay went in and took charge."

"Yes, Neil," agreed Shanks, K.C. "But only after the old
man realised that Festus was futile. They got him a job as an
assistant with Maclaurins in Calcutta first of all: all the
influence and all the money in the world behind him, and he
fluffed it. Not sufficient brains: not enough guts. So your
Finlay was bunged into the foundry as an apprentice, even
hounded into taking a Science degree, and is now Chairman
of Ferrier Foundries, Ltd."

"And still your Festus can afford to follow up a fairly
expensive case?"

"Festus," laughed Stobs, K.C., "was shrewd only in choosing
two wives with packets of industrial money behind them.
Really, and in confidence, old boy, expensive litigation is just

about the last possible expression of power left to him—of mere personality, if you like. Of course, he'll appeal."

"Ah, well!" observed Shanks, K.C., dryly. "It's fair enough. Hard-working men like you and me have to make a living somehow."

He rose from his chair and pressed a button set into the wall and, pointing to the empty glasses, said:

"Better have the other half before we go down to lunch."

Mr. Stobs's client continued, in the lounge bar of the river steamer, to harangue his wife on the progress of The Case.

"Our man's final speech was terrific. I must say that Neil Stobs can fairly lay it on. The other fellow, Shanks, is pretty good, of course, but you could see he's just trying to make bricks without straw. Winnie-the-Pooh "—Mr. Ferrier had avidly absorbed the slang of Parliament House—"reserved judgment, of course, but all the legal chaps think he'll come down like a ton of bricks on our side, and leave my beloved brother shivering in his shirt-tails."

"I certainly hope so," observed Elaine Ferrier with what might have been a subtlety of ambiguity. With almost blissful vagueness she added: "Not Finlay in his shirt-tails, of course."

A bell clanged in the engine-room, and Festus jumped up from his swivel-chair.

"Turning into the bay now," he announced. "Get your stuff collected, dear. I'll run up and see that the boy knows where he is with the luggage."

Jimsy Bell was still at his post above the collection of fine travelling gear arranged about the funnel casing, but now he was considering with lively interest the approach to his new home. The ship had swung round a northern point of the island into a crescent bay with, at the head of it, the long breast of a deep-water pier, a clock-tower above the buildings of a snug fishing harbour, and the frontages of shops, hotels and boarding-houses strung along the length of an artificial promenade.

In that first photographic glimpse Jimsy noted the concourse of yachts and small naval craft close-gathered at moorings off the pier but clear of the steamer fairway, and he appreciated that this was the perfect harbour of refuge from the prevailing sou'-westers of the wide outer Firth. His eye delighted to see how, in the Highland idiom, so familiar to him, villas and cottages had been built to rise above the tower of a castle ruin, and scale the steep slopes about the harbour, so eccentrically, so whimsically defiant of plan, you wondered how the households contrived to get their coal delivered and how the housekeepers could be patient enough to carry their shopping baskets up and down paths so steep and tortuous.

But he was quick enough to slip off his perch at the approach of Mr. Festus Ferrier, his wife feebly struggling with wraps behind him. Studiedly nonchalant as ever, Ketron had materialised from whatever part of the vessel had sheltered her during the voyage. Beth was at hand, alert, Billy close by her side.

"Now," said Mr. Ferrier, surveying his possessions. "Got everything here, Bell?"

"Yes, sir. I've just checked it again."

"And where is madame's dressing-case, eh? Dammit, boy, didn't I tell you, the very first thing. . . ."

Mrs. Ferrier was heard to utter an apologetic "Oh!" Ketron protested: "Really, Mummy!" But Jimsy Bell had already darted away and tunnelled a passage through the crush of passengers massing to disembark and so below to the smoke-room bar. The fat steward in charge handed him the missing article.

"There ye are, son. She's aye lossin' something, that yin. She'll loss her ruddy head one of these days," said the steward, speaking out of experience.

Jimsy Bell was rather proud to carry the case in fine crocodile leather back to his new mistress and assure her: "Here it is, ma'am. Shall I carry it ashore for you?"

"Of course you will," said Festus Ferrier, vehemently turning on his wife. "Didn't I tell you to leave everything with the boy? That's what he's paid for, isn't it? Littering the whole damn' place with your odds and ends. . . ."

Embarrassed, Jimsy had another of his photographic glimpses—of Ketron pretending to be interested in a refined way in the crowd on the pier, of the unhappy look on Beth's face as, from under her long, dark eyelashes, she considered the face of her father, reproach and shame subtly blended in the expression. Billy sniffed and moved closer to his sister. Elaine Ferrier just stood still, an experienced actress in many a scene of the sort, perhaps rather pleased by her ability to create one at any moment.

"Well, here we are!" declared Festus Ferrier, almost jovially recovering his command of the situation. "There's Jamieson on the pier with the brake. Just wait here and let these people get off first. Won't be long now. Sure you've got everything, Bell?"

At length the disembarkment of the Ferrier family was complete. There were salutes from the officers on the bridge and at the gangway of the river steamer and a great touching of forelocks by the deck-hands who carried the heavy stuff ashore to the waiting vehicle and were duly tipped. This, Jimsy observed with appreciation, was a very large shooting-brake on a Rolls-Royce chassis. He gathered that his new employers were people of consequence as well as wealth.

It was all the more surprising that the driver of the brake was a saturnine man in working clothes and perhaps in his late forties, an old tweed cap scrugged down over his right eye. This, to Jimsy's concern, he did not remove or touch as the ladies approached to settle themselves down on the benches behind the driving-seat. Indeed, he seemed to receive the Ferriers with a sort of contemptuous hostility. His face was lean, and his thin lips curved upwards at one corner, a stain of nicotine spreading thence towards his right nostril. The butt of a half-smoked cigarette was tucked behind his left ear.

The appearance and bearing of this person induced in Jimsy Bell a first, faint tremor of concern as to the circumstances into which he had been so suddenly and strangely dragged, but he happily decided that this Jock Jamieson was a spare driver hired from some local garage. His interest turned to the swift passage of the brake out of the harbour area and along a built-up esplanade, above which tier upon tier of villas and terraces in solid sandstone rose on the steep slopes of this northern butt of the island. The brake swung round the point the steamer had passed some twenty minutes before, and Jimsy felt that, with Jock Jamieson's violent wrench of the steering-wheel, a new world burst upon his understanding.

Now the shore road, narrowing and running southwards above weedy rocks, served only a long succession of houses, each in its own considerable domain and so large and eccentrically varied that Jimsy thought of them as castles. It was not within his knowledge of social history that these mansions, some of them wondrously eccentric in their architectural styles, had in fact been the dream-castles of Victorian industrial magnates, building largely, lusciously and competitively along a pleasant stretch of estuarine coast. But there, stretching southwards, lay the Firth, shining in the afternoon sun, the inner islands all lighted green: the Firth immemorial, showing in its constancy and beauty the obsolescence of man's creations along its shores.

Jock Jamieson's dirt-ingrained forefinger flicked the trafficator lever on the steering-wheel to the right. The brake turned in between two large sandstone pillars that carried the enormous weight of gates in ornamental ironwork and climbed the curving rise of a drive. It stopped before a flight of steps, generously planned to lead up to the front door of a large house in the manner of Norman Shaw.

Jimsy was quick to jump out through the near-side door and ceremoniously turn the handle of the one behind for his new master to descend.

"Here we are then, Bell," said Festus Ferrier genially. "This is Ardyne. All set to work hard and make yourself useful? Good! . . . For God's sake, Elaine, don't forget your confounded dressing-case again! *There!* On the seat behind you."

5

The domestic staff of Ardyne sat down to supper about eight o'clock that evening. They arranged themselves about a deal table in a large old kitchen, of which the most pleasing feature was a modern cooker, brightly enamelled in cream, the effect of modernity oddly offset by the ancientry of the dresser and of a grandfather clock which, with rustic pictures in colour on its face, announced in lovely cursive lettering that it was the creation of Jos. Fulton, Kilwinning, 1798.

Jimsy Bell had come a little late to the feast, having been called to recover and take to the drawing-room the evening-bag his mistress had somehow left on her dressing-table. (He was learning rapidly that Mrs. Ferrier's environment was eternally littered with possessions forgotten.) He had helped Lorna, the house-tablemaid, to lay the table, serve the family dinner at seven, and then clear away. Finally he had washed his face till it shone and used plenty of water and a comb on his sleek black hair.

"Help the blind!" cried Jock Jamieson at the sight of him. "Here's Wee Georgie Wood, the pocket wonder."

Jimsy had already come to understand the status of Jock. He ranked as chauffeur-gardener, but the gardener in him prevailed over the attractions of the more courtly office. Even at the supper table he continued to wear the dirty tweed cap pulled down over his right eye, defiantly, and Jimsy wondered what curious amalgam of ignorances and emotions moved him to do so. Himself, he was neatly dressed in the uniform of servitude he had carefully thought out—white jacket, navy-blue trousers, a black bow-tie under the wings of a stiff collar. Jock Jamieson's thin lips curled more wryly than ever at the sight.

"Posh wee guy, aren't ye?" he observed, but not unkindly, swallowing soup with the noises of a drain in a rainstorm. "Another willing wage-slave."

"I've got my job to do," said Jimsy stoutly.

"Aye, and ye'll get plenty of jobs in this house!" cackled Jock, dropping his spoon with a clang on the empty plate. "Page boy! Ye'll be footman and vallay and ladies' maid and hall porter and scullerymaid and the man that carries in the coal if ye don't stand up, here and now, and tell that mug upstairs where he gets off. One man, one job: the policy of full-employment—that's what Labour has done for you, ma lad."

"Yes. Changed days, changed days!" quavered old Mrs. Munn, the cook. "I've seen the time when there were eight servants in this house, the butler and the shover, and every one of five girls as smart as a new pin in a fresh wrapper in the morning and a neat black dress and a well-laundered apron, and a cap forbye, after lunch. And just look at her——"

Mrs. Munn pointed the butt of her knife at the girl called Lorna. This was a sullen, sallow young woman who chose to go about her work in a print overall, bare heels showing through holes in cheap stockings, and, Jimsy had noted with concern, in bedroom slippers down at the back.

"They can like it or lump it," Lorna defended herself through the handicap of a nasal polyp. "D'ye hear what that Ketron tried to put over on me? 'Could you rinse out thae nylons for me?' sez she. Sez I, 'Ye've bags of time to rinse out yer ain nylons,' sez I. The impertinence!"

"Good for you, Lorna!" cried Jock in high approval. "One man, one job. Full employment and nae exploitation. And that, Wee Georgie Wood"—he turned genially on the new-comer—"is a lesson for you."

"Yes. But——" Jimsy demurred.

"But what?"

"If you don't like your employment, and if you don't like the conditions, why do you stay in it? If there's full employ-ment, you can go to another job."

Jock Jamieson, a Woodbine now increasing the area of the stain above his upper lip, smacked the table in delight.

"There's a good yin!" he cried, addressing himself to Mrs.

Munn at the head of the table. "He's got the right dialectic in him, this wee chap. Have ye studied the dialectical materialism, chum? No: all right. But since ye've asked me a fair question, I'll give you a fair answer."

"It'll be a lot of the old blethers," observed Mrs. Munn indifferently, pouring out cups of strong tea from an aluminium pot. Jock ignored her.

"I stay here, young man," he earnestly addressed the little page boy, "juist in order to witness at close quarters the collapse of one bit of a rotten system. Rotten. I'm no' mindin' a capitalist as such," he allowed, stressing the second syllable, "if he does a bit of work. We workers can meet him through our unions or with the strike weapon, if need be."

Jimsy noticed how Jock's prose took on the sing-song rhythms of the practised speaker for sentimental Socialism.

"No! The class-war is best conducted in the workshop and the factory. But when you take a pudden like that yin in the drawing-room. . . . Never done a hand's turn in his life. Living on capital. . . . The man's juist a parasite on the backside of society!"

"Langwidge! Langwidge!" Mrs. Munn made a protest against this violent peroration, but only automatically, as it seemed to Jimsy Bell.

She had made it many a time over a period of years. Jock had first heard the locution on the lips of a Left Wing orator at the Mound in Edinburgh one Sunday evening and had been so taken by the justice, pungency and even poetry of it that it had become the keystone of all his postprandial orations. He had long enjoyed the attentions of a purely female audience and it was a new experience for him to be challenged by a diminutive page boy.

"That's all very well," Jimsy heard himself saying. "But what's the use of staying here if you're so strong about it as all that? You said yourself the real war is in the workshop and the factory."

The light tenor voice was clear and careful in its Highland intonations.

"That's one for you, Jock Jamieson," observed Lorna with heavy satisfaction.

"Not at all! Not at all!" protested the chauffeur-gardener. "Fair argument: the right dialectical method. Wee Georgie Wood's got the hang of the thing. I'll make a good Socialist of him yet." He rose and patted Jimsy's black head as he went towards the door. "Now I'll away down and see how my hot-house fires are gettin' on."

Jimsy discovered that he was expected to help Lorna with the washing-up. Mrs. Munn, as he had perceived earlier in the day, was too old and worn for her appointed task and given to plump down in a basket chair, and with her skirts pulled up and her thick legs apart, enjoy all the heat from the patent cooker, her slow mind no doubt brooding on the complexities of life as she had found it.

The scullery was a long chamber with a cold stone floor, a builder's afterthought that ran out in red brick to be imprisoned in semi-darkness by a congeries of low-browed outhouses. As Lorna washed up and Jimsy dried the many dishes of two meals, the silly girl sang a crooner's song with the refrain

I'll be close to you to-night
In spirit, at least . . .

and the implication made Jimsy Bell feel very unhappy as he built up a pile of dried dinner plates on the black tray. He had lived long enough to realise that his own oddity as a man in miniature could too easily arouse the inquisitive instincts of one sort of woman. He would wake up early in the morning thinking of this as the unhappiest consequence of his physical inheritance, as the crudest threat to the self-respect he was obliged by his very oddity to cherish.

Lorna, having finished washing-up, flicked a dishcloth from the rail and fell to helping Jimsy with the tinkling masses of cutlery. She still enunciated her fatuous song, and Jimsy became aware that she was edging her heavy body against his until, in an idiotic consequence, he was almost pushed round the corner of the drying-board at which they worked together.

"You're awful shy," suggested Lorna, leering with her stupid eyes.

"I want to finish this and get to my bed," said Jimsy curtly.

"Get to your bed? What's wrong with mines?" She took the wet dishcloth from Jimsy's hand and added in her slattern way: "Mines is just three doors along the attic floor. Me— Oh boy, Oh boy!—I'm just a big bag of love."

Earlier in the evening Jimsy had learned from one of Jock Jamieson's asides that Lorna was to be regarded, in his Scots phrase, as glaikit—soft and irresponsible to a point just short of positive mental deficiency. The knowledge helped him little when, at length and with a good-night salute to Mrs. Munn drowsing before the patent stove, he sped upstairs to his room in the attic.

It was a bare but tidy chamber, with an iron bedstead, a narrow chest of drawers and a small mirror on top thereof. Jimsy started to unpack his fibre case, placing each piece of his small wardrobe in the drawers with the precision of a woman. He laid out his four pairs of shoes and decided that to-morrow he would give them all a good brush with the appliances he had brought in a tight tin box. He set up his own miniature alarm clock on the top of the commode by his bedside.

He had locked his door, the ominous threat of Lorna's approach always in his mind. He was well-placed in his new job now, he knew, but he was still not easy in his own mind; and when he slipped into bed at length, having set the clock for an awakening at six in the morning, the happenings of the day and their implications kept churning and churning about within his mind. Jock Jamieson was a gasbag, but Jimsy ruefully considered the literal truth of his charges against the demanding nature of Mr. Festus Ferrier as a boss.

It was difficult for one who was anxious to please in return for a decent wage, but there passed through his mind the cine-picture of all that had happened since he first crossed the threshold of Ardyne seven hours before. He had served tea in the drawing-room and had then been called, by Festus Ferrier himself, to be a playmate for Beth and Billy at French cricket on the lawn. He had pressed Mr. Ferrier's evening-dress trousers, rinsed out two nylon shirts, and been warned that, to-morrow, the whole wardrobe should be gone through with necessary repairs and replacements in view. If perhaps out of the goodness of his own heart, he had peeled the potatoes for Mrs. Munn. Then all these dreary chores he had shared with Lorna. Full employment was the phrase, indeed!

As he turned over in his restlessness his eyes opened to see the beam from the lighthouse on the Lesser Brunt swing across one wall of his attic room, and the apparition strangely comforted him. Jimsy lay and listened to the slow crash of small waves on the beach a hundred yards below and then, with delight, to the whimper of shingle disturbed to protest by the backwash. This was his familiar world again: the world of a strange childhood spent by the shores of the restless western seas.

CHAPTER TWO

Early Morning

THE AIR of the May morning was keen after a touch of late frost, but the inner Firth stretched quiet as a mountain lake towards the mainland hills. The sun was up above them by now, throwing clear golden beams of an uncannily pellucid light on the slopes of the islands. The white pillars of three lighthouses seemed to be ancient monuments to storms that could no longer afflict this enchanted arm of the sea.

Having moved cautiously across the side-lawn by the northern gable of Ardyne, the time being just after six o'clock, Jimsy Bell paused on the terrace of the big house, and the sense of wonder held him for a measurable space of minutes. He had been brought up by the sea, and it was one of his private mysteries, but he knew that that glassy patch of enclosed tidal water, only faintly catspawed as yet by the breaths of early errant winds, could within an hour be a dangerous boil of dirty grey seas. He saw against the green of the mainland the absurd shape of a puffer laden deep with coal for the Isles and knew that it might within a short space of time be bucketting, nose under, in treacherous Hebridean waters. Inward-bound, a big Lamport & Holt freighter, a bone of white in her teeth, surged proudly towards a quiet anchorage in the Deeps off Garvel, but there were crusts of salt on her funnel to show how she had been buffetted on the passage across the Bay.

Jimsy had planned to come out early, while all the others in the big house slept, in order to have a careful look at the physical body of the new world to which he had attached himself. His first impression that the big house was not un-handsome was confirmed when he looked up to see how its architect, building for an Edwardian industrialist, had made handsome use of the native sandstone. He saw again that the mansion stood agreeably on a high terrace, the noble view of the sea wholly commanded, the small commerce of the shore road screened from view by a line of poplars beyond what, on a lower level, appeared to be the garden area.

From the level of the lawn a flight of steps led down a steep embankment and, a very odd figure in the early morning, the neat diminutive person of the page-boy—curious and intelligent withal—picked its way to see what sort of garden Mr. Festus Ferrier maintained. Jimsy turned to appreciate the play of the morning light on the strong front of the house. He paused to notice for the first time that the mansion commanded a shallow but natural bay, protected by two small islands, hardly more than reefs about two hundred yards each in length. In the lee of the southerly one there lay at moorings what the lad re-cognised as a diesel-engined motor yacht of some twenty-five tons, and he studied its beauty of efficiency with a knowledge-able eye.

From the bottom of the steps his small feet traced a track across a stretch of frosted grass to the verge of what had once been an acre of good kitchen garden and was now nearly derelict, the shaws of last year's potatoes still rotting where they had been cast aside, and only a strip of the purple earth turned over for the new season's growth. Smoke was still wavering from the chimney of a long conservatory, however, and Jimsy had the feeling of life still struggling to exert itself through near-ruin.

He was peering through a pane of glass to see what the hothouse contained when footsteps on the path behind him brought his head round to see Jock Jamieson approach, the tweed cap always at its challenging angle over one side of the thin, wry face.

"Hullo, young fella-me-lad!" was his cheerful greeting. "Lookin' for work at this time of the morning?"

"I was looking at the garden," Jimsy half apologised.

"And what d'ye think of the magnificent demeen?" Jock asked sardonically. "I mind the day when the head gardener here had two men and a boy under him. Now His Nibs upbye thinks I'm goin' to cultivate a half-acre of vegetables and grow flowers and pot-plants for the house as well, never mind drivin' his ruddy cars. He can take a runnin' jump at himself. You watch your step, son, or you'll get more jobs fitted on to you than a platoon of sodgers could manage in a day. Stick you up for the dignity of labour; one man, one job."

It did not seem to Jimsy quite the time of day for a political discourse, and he evaded Jock's comic vehemence by asking if there was anything to see in the conservatory. His friend melted, his personality seeming to change in a flash from the basis of bitterness to that of sentimentality.

"Anything to see! Come you in here, Jimsy ma lad, and I'll show you sumpthin' worth seeing."

Unlocking the conservatory door and quickly closing it behind his guest, Jock waved a hand to indicate a shrub that, beginning to burst into pink flower, had been trained to cover yards of a whitewashed wall.

"My goodness!" Jimsy admired it sincerely. "What is it, Jock?"

"Did you ever see the like of that? No, you never did," Jock asked and answered the question rhetorically. "Bougainvillæa, son. The old chap that built the house up there brought it from India, and it took, but it's one man's work to keep it in life. A glory, eh? By God," he swore earnestly, "if that bush was to die on me, I'd walk out straight and put myself into the water! And him, His Nibs, is always at me to cut down on the firing!"

There were many other wonderful things to see—all the pot-plants for the house with all sorts of fancy Latin names and especially what Jock called "ma calceoleeries. Some grand strains there, toppers! They'll throw blooms as big as your fist." If a little bewildered, Jimsy began to understand the attitudes of his colleague. Here was his life, here the love of his heart. To have to drive cars as a sideline was a murky intrusion on devotions. One man, one job.

"Well," said Jimsy at length as he insinuated himself towards the hothouse door through the barrage of Jock's enthusiasms, "I suppose I'd better get up and see what's doing in the kitchen."

"Man, it's just past seven!" protested Jock, producing a fat silver watch from his waistcoat pocket. "If old Ma Munn can pull up her breeks and get into the kitchen by eight it'll be a bloomin' miracle. As for that Lorna . . . But what would you expect when His Nibs comes to life about nine and his missus lies till twelve? Come on, we'll go down and see if Lachie's comin' in for his milk."

Slightly bewildered by the reference, Jimsy followed Jock through the protective grove of poplars, over a low wall on to the shore road and so down a wooden jetty to the water's edge. A varnished dinghy, obviously from the motor yacht in the lee of the southern island, was charging shorewards, its passage dispersing a great concourse of gulls rolling and bobbing on the smooth wavelets of the bay.

"Is that yacht ours?" the small page-boy asked eagerly.

"It's no' yours and it's no' mines," returned Jock sourly. "It belongs to the honourable, ruddy Mr. Festus Ferrier. Juist a piece of swank. He's that feart to get his feet wet, it's a sensation if the boat's out once a fortnight in the season. But that, my little man," he painfully sought to reproduce a mincing middle-class accent, "is the *Ron*, our yacht."

"*Ron's* Gaelic for a seal."

"Mebbe it is. I call it the Sailor's Home. But Lachie's a decent old chap. Here he's comin' in now."

Instinctively, Jimsy was down at the edge of the water lipping the slats of the jetty to take the length of fine manilla rope the occupant of the dinghy, casually shipping his oars, as casually tossed ashore. Just as carelessly the small youth gave it a couple of half-hitches round a tiny bollard. A large man in a blue jersey and rubber boots stepped out of the rocking craft and considered the person of Jimsy with tolerant interest.

"And where did you learn that trick, little man?" he asked kindly.

"On the pier at Mallaig," responded Jimsy cheerfully.

"*Am bheil Gaidhlig agaibh?*" the question was urgent.

"*Tha, pailteag!*"

Then the two of them were at it in the old tongue of the Celtic West. Did Jimsy have the Gaelic? Yes, plenty. They rattled out their affinities until Jock Jamieson made a moaning protest.

"Here, youse two, this isny the Mod. Have a heart and speak the King's English."

"Chust a poor Sassunach," said Lachie Macdonald, winking to the small page-boy.

This was the old Highland joke, of course. The Saxons, including the Lowland Scots, were inferior in their apperceptions to the folk of the western fringes; it was the joke that sought to laugh off their own defeat and defeatism. But it was a pleasant and harmless one among friends; and Jimsy rejoiced in this encounter with a new friend: a man of the West and the western seas.

"Well, I suppose we'd better get up to the Big House," suggested Lachie Macdonald at length. "Tell me, Jock—has the laddie with the milk come yet?"

"Ask Wee Georgie Wood here," suggested Jock Jamieson at his most jocular. "He's the boss now. Page-boy, vallay, skivvy, chief cook and bottle-washer already. Next week he'll be the shover-gardener and then he'll be skipper of the *Ron*. That's the dole for you and me, Lachie. You watch this wee block."

"Always at your blethers, Jock!" said Lachie tolerantly. "Never heed what he says, Jimsy."

Jimsy Bell followed Lachie up the steps to the terrace on which the big house stood, the ashlar now taking real warmth from the morning sun. On the lawn was young Beth, slim and long-legged in her tartan skirt.

"Hullo, Jimsy!" she called to him. "I want to ask you something."

"What's that, Miss Beth?"

"Can you stand on your hands?"

"Yes, of course. That's easy."

"Show me."

"The great thing," Jimsy proceeded to demonstrate, while Lachie watched with a tolerant smile as he turned the corner of the house, "the great thing is to get your hands well planted on the ground, your fingers splayed out and your wrists ready to take the strain. The rest of it's just balance and keeping your head. Like this——"

The small man then plunged down at the lawn, as it were, and threw his body upwards, his legs apart and slightly hanging backwards above the head stretched outwards a foot or so above the grass. To demonstrate the ease of the manœuvre he took to waggling his legs in the air.

"See, it's easy," he remarked with a touch of vanity as he returned to his feet.

"Golly, I wish I could do that!" cried Beth fervently.

"Anybody can do it. Then you'll learn to do this."

Jimsy was showing off a little, but it was not without some artistic warrant. Again he made a dive at the lawn and in a trice was whirling its length like a teetotum in a brilliant series of cartwheels. From the other end he turned to come back at speed in the same eccentric way and jump triumphantly to his feet in front of his young friend.

"Oh, Jimsy! I wish I could do that," she cried.

"Yes. But you'll have to learn to stand on your hands first."

"Right! Watch this."

The vivid child thereupon made her own awkward plunge at the grass, tried to heave her body upwards, and then stuck, her neat little bottom in the air but her legs floundering behind her.

"No, no!" Jimsy scolded her with professional impatience. "You've got to spring right up and take a risk. You won't kill yourself if you fall over."

"Right," agreed Beth, breathing heavily. "This time."

The second effort was more successful. The pluck of the

young girl forced her towards the alarming point of balance, but at the top of the arc of unaccustomed motion she started to wobble.

"Keep your wrists stiff," Jimsy shouted. "Spread your legs apart. Oh, help!"

Beth's frame had started to sag, and the page-boy's automatic interest was to step quickly forward and seize her ankles and so hold it in the erect position. Then their small palace of enchantment fell into shards at the crack of a shocked, self-righteous voice from an upper window of the house.

"Beth! What do you think you're doing?"

They were as innocent as the May morning these two. In the course of the gymnastic exercises Beth's skirt had fallen down towards her torso, but her underwear was strictly functional, and Jimsy had lived too long among young females in a crofting community to be interested in the erotic symbolism of feminine garments. The voice from above was that of Ketron, leaning from a casement window in dressing-gown, lace cap over her hair.

"I'm going to tell Mummy," she shrilly threatened her half-sister and then, turning her tongue on Jimsy, "you get away to the kitchen and get on with your proper work. You'll hear about this."

Jimsy paused for just a moment as he turned the corner into the path leading to the back premises and saw in a photographic flash the picture that was to be at the back of his mind all his life—the picture of Beth, a proud slip of a thing, standing on the lawn with her head boldly raised and shoulders braced, her hands folded behind her curved back, shouting defiance at her half-sister:

"Tell-tale-tit! Tell-tale-tit! I'm not frightened of you."

As he helped about the kitchen and dining-room to prepare for the service of family breakfast Jimsy Bell knew the gathering of fear within him. It was such a puzzling and alarming circumstance that, within the space of a day or two, he had offended against two codes of social behaviour in company with Beth Ferrier. He was worried for the child herself, but a more profound concern troubled him so much that even Mrs. Munn scolded him for being clumsy with the dishes.

It had seemed to him in the early morning that, with Jock Jamieson and Lachie Macdonald, he had entered a community more stable, more friendly, than that provided by the Northern Grand Hotel. It distressed him to think, as he went actively enough about his duties, that he had been overtaken by the conflict of codes Jock kept talking about; and the brightness of his first morning in Ardyne was darkened.

2

He let the blades of the bright-varnished oars float on the water above a patch of white sand and watched the rock cod and saithe swim across it in the shadowy vaults of the sea. Behind him, in the bows of the boat, Beth hung over the stem and likewise peered down into these mysterious depths. Billy Ferrier was in the broad seat at the stern, rapt in the illusion that he was fishing with a length of string and a rag of coloured wool Jimsy Bell had fashioned for him, to keep him quiet.

It was mid-afternoon over the Firth, warm, quiet and so calm that even the tidal water seemed to bear on its surface an oily sheen. The sails of a few early yachts were white blobs on the expanse of the estuary between island and mainland, but even the passage overhead of a great flying-boat making for its base in one of the little lochs of the Outer Firth could not break the illusion of stillness, of time halted. For Jimsy Bell it was a wonderful return of the illusion of interest and contentment that had been upon him in the early morning of the same day. The return of the mood of security seemed in the nature of a miracle.

He had been along the shore road after breakfast on one of his appointed tasks: fetching the newspapers and mail off the early steamer from the booth in the hamlet of Ardyne Bay that was at once the General Stores and the Post Office. He was far from whistling like a normal lad on a morning so fine, and as he made his way back towards the big house and saw the figure of his master, Mr. Festus Ferrier, standing on the roadway outside the main gates, he thought with concern of his sin of having held the legs of Miss Beth apart while she had tried to stand on her hands.

"That you, Bell?" he was greeted coldly. "Give me the papers. Something I want to talk to you about."

"Yes, sir."

"Can you handle a boat?"

"Yes, sir."

"How did you learn to handle a boat?"

"When I was a boy in the Highlands, sir. My—my people fished off shore, and I was always in and out with them."

"Well, see that skiff on the buoy up there?" Festus Ferrier jerked his head. "Get her in and bring her round to the jetty. I want to go out to the yacht."

His master's manner was at once so morose and abrupt, Jimsy felt that some sort of punishment still awaited him. It was almost as if he was to be taken out to sea, thrown overboard and drowned. He ran up the beach to a cove beyond the jetty and hauled the boat in on a running-line, and his eyes rejoiced in her fitness—twelve feet of the best out of Smith's at Tighnabruaich, the light varnish shining after Lachie's spring overhaul. Pushing off and bending to the oars, Jimsy found her as nimble and tractable as a polo pony under his practised hands, and he was so pleased with his situation that he showed off a little: turning the dainty craft off the tip of the jetty, backing her in and, with a fancy shipping of his starboard oar, bringing her alongside so featly that Mr. Festus Ferrier had only to step directly into the sternsheets.

"I see you can handle a boat all right, Bell," his employer allowed.

Jimsy's approach to the motor yacht was equally confident and expert—a neat little check as they came to the small companionway hanging by the vessel's side, another nippy shipping of the port oar this time, a hand out to grasp a chain and pull the obedient shell of the boat against the platform at the foot of the ladder.

"Wait there," his master instructed him. "I won't be long."

The lad hitched the boat's painter about a silvered stanchion and let her drift with the tide. He could relax under the forenoon sun in the sternsheets, thoughtful merely to hold out an arm and fend his charge off the gleaming white side of the *Ron*. He was content merely to worship with his eyes the loveliness of this rich man's toy. These eyes took in the perfection of the flare inwards from the slanting stem to the grace of the bellowing curve amidships. They considered the fitness of the navigation chamber under a stub of yellow funnel for the exhaust from the diesels. It would be wonderful to be up there with the wheel and the engine controls at your hand. See how beautifully Lachie had the brass and copper of the fittings polished; watch the play of light reflected from the idly-moving sea on the yacht's green underside. . . .

"Have you fallen asleep there, Bell?"

"No, sir."

Jimsy jumped to pull on the painter and bring the boat alongside. Lachie stood at the top of the ladder and raised his cap to authority in the act of departure.

"I'll let you know when I want the yacht, Macdonald. Perhaps Sunday if this weather holds. Take me back to the jetty, Bell."

The little fellow rowed his master ashore, again performed his act of expert oarsmanship, and was up on the landing-stage like a monkey to hand Mr. Festus Ferrier to a safe place on dry land.

"Just tie her up here. She'll be all right, won't she?"

"Yes, sir, on this rising tide."

"Something I was going to say to you, wasn't there?"

"Yes, sir." He awaited sentence, and it was queer that the Master should seem so strangely distracted.

"Oh, yes! What I was thinking of, Bell. Plenty of time on your hands. What I was thinking of was you could take my son and daughter out in the boat in the afternoons and give them some lessons. Rowing, feathering, getting a boat ashore —you know the sort of thing. Pay special attention to my son."

"Yes, sir."

"No going outside the islands, of course. You understand that?"

"Yes, sir."

"Carry on."

And here they were, the young people, idling in mid-afternoon within the shelter of the northerly islet of the two that protected Ardyne Bay from two prevailing winds.

Jimsy Bell had discovered that the education in oarsmanship of Master Billy was going to be a difficult task: so difficult that it had him fascinated. You could take Miss Beth, give her the two oars, sit on the after thwart and, pushing to help her with the weight and movement of the paddles, cry "Arms well forward, wrists together, dip, slow back, *out* and wrists up. Forward now and wrists down. . . ."

"But I want to learn to feather my oars the way you do."

"Better leave that for a day or two. Come on now, Master Billy, and have another try."

"I don't like rowing," pleaded the pretty, soft boy.

"Don't be a sap. You know what Daddy said."

It saddened and confused Jimsy Bell to see how feckless a young person of his own sex could be in the performance of an ordinary manly exercise. The sheer lack of physical strength was understandable; it was the complete lack of will and instinct that baffled him; and why should the girl seem to be born to it? Billy's wrists appeared to melt under the weight of a single oar. He caught crabs at great depths. He was to be seen trying to row ahead with the curve of the blade turned the wrong way. Finally, and with a wail, he contrived to shoot his oar, as it were, through the jaws of the rowlock and started to weep as he saw it floating away.

"Oh, shut up, Billy!" Beth implored, while Jimsy unshipped his own oar, leapt into the sternsheets and started to scull the boat after the missing implement, using as a fulcrum a semicircle cut into the sternsheets.

The performance of inshore seamanship was dexterous, beautiful in its efficiency of control over a given situation.

"Oh, Jimsy!" cried Beth. "I'd love to be able to do that."

"You'll learn," he grunted, leaning overside to recover the missing oar while Billy continued to weep over his own most recent failure in a complex world.

Then they were resting in the lee of the island, the boat rocking gently in the oily wavelets of the hot afternoon. The heat and the peace of it had them in thrall after exercise. It was such a peace as might have lasted into the chaotic beauty of a sunset over the island peaks, but the youngest child of Festus Ferrier was not to be held entranced by the nihilism of loveliness about him. He quite suddenly lost the illusion of being a fisherman and quaveringly cried:

"I want to go home."

"Oh, don't be a sap!" Beth protested. "It must be more than an hour till teatime. Let's land on the island, Jimsy."

"I don't know that your father would like that."

"He'll never know. Come on and we'll look for treasure."

Billy was still sniffling as Jimsy Bell eased the boat into an indentation of the beach that had once been cleared of rocks: probably in the days of the herring fishing, he surmised. Beth was first over the bows and tore away on long legs towards the bracken above the tide-mark of wrack on the shingle. Jimsy lifted the sobbing boy ashore and patiently promised him that he would show him something uniquely interesting. Billy complained at the hardness and slipperiness of the stones under his soft feet, but the little servant was patient with him and at length found a rock pool, its walls encrusted with whelks and limpets, a hermit crab about its affairs in a miniature drift of sand under eight inches of pellucid water.

Billy ceased to cry as Jimsy patiently explained the nature of this small acquatic world and, in the manner of those imperfectly endowed, became absorbed in the business of tearing the whelks from their moorings on the rock. From the other side of the islet came the bright, light, clear voice of Beth crying:

"Cooee, Jimsy! Come and see this."

He felt it safe to leave the absorbed little boy and run through the fringe of bracken to where Beth had made her glad discovery on the other side of the islet. This was but the sort of glorified reef he knew to litter the western coasts of Scotland by the thousand: impossible of cultivation, too small for even a wintering of Blackface sheep, just a breakwater and a basking platform for the occasional grey seal. What Beth had come upon was a tiny dell through which water from a spring ran down to the sea and in which a proliferation of wild flowers were concentrated as in a rock garden.

"Look at those lovely little yellow things!" she greeted Jimsy. "They're like beads on a cushion."

"Tormentil," he explained. "You'll find it all over the place. But it's nice, growing through those pads of heathery turf."

His eyes turned from the enamelled flowerlets and considered the area of the sheltered place.

"There's marsh orchis down there by the mouth of the wee burn. And you'll see the flags out in July."

"Flags? Nobody has flags out here."

"Wild iris," he chuckled. "Yellow flags, they're called. . . . See the funny little butterburs. . . . No, you're standing on them."

"These little velvety things?"

A wail of distress from the other side of the islet broke into their confidences, and Jimsy guessed that Billy's precarious grip on self-control had been disturbed in an encounter with the hermit crab.

"We'd better get back," he suggested anxiously to Beth.

"I suppose so," she agreed as they set off. "But where on earth, Jimsy, did you learn all that stuff about flowers and things?"

"Oh, if you've been brought up in the country and by the seaside—well, I suppose it comes natural, Miss Beth."

"But I've been brought up in the country and by the seaside and don't know a thing."

"It all depends, I suppose," he glossed over the thought that had immediately occurred to him; but the bright girl was not to be put off, saying:

"Do your Mummy and Daddy live in the country?"

"I haven't got a Mummy and Daddy," he replied, curt in his embarrassment.

"Oh!"

The girl had the delicacy to leave it there, and then their joint business was to comfort Billy, lift him into the boat and promise him that Home and Mother were not far off now. He was approximately happy in the possession of a limpet he had managed to knock off the rock-face with a stone.

Jimsy rowed slowly back to the jetty, again showing off a little the lovely quality of his oarsmanship—the quick clip of the blades into the water at the end of the slow pull-through, the easy slithering of these same blades along the smooth surface of the water as he feathered. He was prolonging for himself the loveliness of the day that had started with brightness in the early morning and now, as the westering sun put a touch of gold into its lighting of island and sea, was drawing to a close in a bliss of security and companionship.

3

Lord Milnathort's courtroom was the smallest in Parliament House, and known to junior members of the Bar as the Hencoop. As the junior judge of the Outer House of the Court of Session, His Lordship, formerly plain John Grant, K.C., must make do with a forum which, beyond the long Bench and the fine oak panelling behind the judicial seat, had space only for two tiny side galleries for the accommodation of Jury and Press respectively, the hooded witness-stand in between, and, beyond this small pit, only four benches for counsel, solicitors and such members of the public as might be interested in the cause now about to be disposed of.

None of the latter was on hand this morning, the habitual

idlers about the courts having crowded as one man into the ampler First Division courtroom to hear the Lord President dispose of a Greek millionaire's attempt to interdict the marriage according to Scots Law of a runaway daughter to a motor car salesman: the climax of a hue and cry to which the newspapers had devoted much eager and romantic attention and a great deal of space. Maudslie Stobs, K.C., and Jardine Shanks, K.C., were more profitably employed elsewhere and had left their juniors to decorate the front bench in their stuff gowns and report on Winnie-the-Pooh's conclusions. At the extreme left hand of the second row sat Festus Ferrier and, at the extreme right, his brother Finlay, separated from each other by their respective solicitors and a clutch of seedy law reporters. A few briefless junior counsel lounged against the walls on both sides.

The drab setting and the apparent lack of public interest in The Case intensified the agitation that possessed Festus Ferrier. On a morning so bright that not even one electric light was burning in the chamber it seemed to him a sorry anticlimax to the drama of that thundery afternoon when Maudslie Stobs and Jardine Shanks had hammered out their closing speeches while a reading-lamp threw a circle of light on the white foolscap of the judge's notes. His face worked; the lips were continually wetted by a serpentine tongue and the bushy eyebrows rose and dropped as if mechanically operated. He glanced sideways along the bench towards his brother, so much fairer and bulkier than himself, and was horrified to see him share a joke with his solicitor. Dashed nearly contempt of court, Festus thought, and damned offensive. Always was a lout, Finlay.

The whispering and rustling were stilled at length by the opening of a side-door behind the Bench and the cry of "Court!" The robed officer carried in the mace and placed it ceremoniously in the bracket behind the judge's chair while Lord Milnathort followed in the maroon robe faced with crimson crosses befitting a Senator of the College of Justice at the hearing of a civil action. He was a hollow-cheeked, white-

faced little man, and his mien was grave as he bowed right
and left to the Court before taking his seat and indicating to
the others within the chamber that they might resume those
from which they had respectfully risen at his entry.

"This case," he began primly, "is of a character familiar to
all whose avocations bring them into contact with the day-to-
day working of these courts."

It was easy to see and hear how His Lordship had come by
his nickname. He had a trick of speaking through puckered
lips in a mild voice that had, nevertheless, an agreeable hint
of his origins in Fife behind its primness.

"It concerns," His Lordship went on, "the destination of
valuable holdings in an industrial concern founded by the
grandfather of the two parties chiefly concerned, duly developed
by their father and, with certain valuable subsidiaries, ultimately registered under the Companies' Act as Ferrier
Foundries, Ltd. The pattern is, as I suggest, familiar, but this
litigation has one unusual feature.

"We encounter in these courts continually the case of the
oldest son of a family, in the highest position of responsibility
in a business, possibly the architect of its ultimate prosperity,
being sued, and thus called upon to disturb his reserves if not
his working capital, by younger brothers and or sisters eager,
for no doubt sound personal reasons, to realise their inherited
holdings. In this instance the Chairman and Managing
Director of the defending Company is the younger brother
while the pursuer is the older brother who, on his own ad-
mission under cross-examination, admits that he has no skill
in the trades of the concern and has contributed nothing beyond
the loan of his capital holdings to its prosperous development."

"Blue look-out for your man, Bill," whispered one of the
juniors in the front row to his neighbour. "A level ten bob
on our chap."

"However that may be," the gentle voice went on, "the
issues so ably presented to me by learned counsel on both sides
are complicated here by the somewhat unusual testamentary
dispositions of the father of both the pursuer and the principal

of the defending Company, the late Fergus Ferrier. . . . Apparently a family," His Lordship permitted himself a small judicial joke, "which relies considerably on alliteration's artful aid in its domestic nomenclature."

Lord Milnathort paused to let the appreciative titter pass like a puff of morning air over the court; and Festus Ferrier began to wonder when the old ass was going to start talking sense for a change. Himself a man incapable of detachment and without subtlety, he could not understand the legal affection for the nuances of the Law as distinct from the imperatives of Justice. This gittering blighter on the Bench could surely cut the cackle and say who was right and who was wrong. That crack about his never having taken an active part in the business was damned cheek and damned unfair; that was how the old man had arranged it. He was aware, however, of a sinking of the heart and of the fidgetiness of his own person. He wished he could control the blinking of his eyelids and the tensing and flexing of his eyebrow muscles. These benches were confoundedly hard on the bottom.

His Lordship was not to be denied his hour of authority. His discourse embraced an admirably succinct outline of the Scottish laws of inheritance. There was much emphasis on the rule laid down by the Lord Justice Clerk in the matter of *MacWhattie v. MacWhattie* 1902. The testimony of actuaries on both sides was acutely analysed, and Lord Milnathort animadverted on the subtleties created by the acquisition of subsidiaries by Ferrier Foundries, Ltd., since the death of the testator, Fergus Ferrier, in 1928. At length, drawing fine, white fingers across his forehead, Lord Milnathort approached his peroration.

"I cannot refrain from observing that this is a case in which, as it seems to me, a trifle of commonsense and a willingness to submit the matter to arbitration might have avoided the expense of protracted litigation and saved the time of these courts. That apart, and after the most anxious consideration of the many and complex issues put before me, I have no hesitation in finding for the defenders."

The little figure in maroon robes rose, bowed slightly and disappeared offstage, the mace before him. His going seemed to leave a sort of vacuum in the courtroom.

"Does that mean we've lost?" asked Festus Ferrier of his solicitor, his voice as empty as that of a disappointed child.

"I'm afraid so," said Mr. Quintin Wright curtly enough. "Shall we move out now?"

The solicitor shepherded his client through the swing doors, along the corridors and into the vastness of Parliament Hall where, under the high, dark, vaulted roof that had once sheltered the Scottish Estates, the wigged advocates paced up and down in two's and three's discussing their professional affairs and, no doubt, their golf handicaps. Under the waxen-hued bust of an eighteenth century jurist Festus Ferrier turned suddenly on his adviser.

"I can only say that you legal chaps have made a ruddy mess of this business," he snarled.

Quintin Wright had long known of his client that passion was apt to be substituted for reason in his conduct of life, and he simply said "It is a disappointment, no doubt, but this is hardly the time to discuss it." He looked into the face that had gone so white and anxiously asked "Are you feeling quite well, Ferrier?"

"Of course I'm feeling perfectly well, just damn'd angry. God, I could do with a drink!"

"My car's outside. I'll drive you down to the Northern Grand."

They were about to move away when the touch on his arm caused Festus Ferrier to swing round with an upward hitch of his shoulders, as if a blow had been struck. It was his brother Finlay, holding out a hand and saying quietly:

"I'm sorry, Festus. Couldn't we have a talk about it all some day soon?"

"You go to hell!" was the reply, so vehement that two ageing K.C.s, discussing the culture of roses, involuntarily broke step and halted a moment to stare at the author of such unseemliness.

"Oh, very well! " said Finlay and turned away.

Quintin Wright did not like the look of his man at all when at length they settled down in the hotel lounge. Two large whiskies sucked down while he himself had the best part of a small dry sherry still in hand; a cigarette lit the moment after the last had been crushed in the ash-tray half-smoked. . . . Little enough perhaps in the case of a man bitterly disappointed, especially a man utterly without a philosophy of life. . . . There was more than that, however—that twitching of the face, a shaking of the hand reaching out for the glass, and mutterings apparently addressed to the world at large.

"Wanted to shake hands, did he? Wring his ruddy neck. . . . What blasted fools ever put that old nannygoat on the Bench, piffling through a hole in his silly face? . . . And they call it Law! "

Quintin Wright, an old-fashioned gentleman of 67, was disturbed and distressed. He thought of this blood-pressure business that was all the go nowadays and that other new-fangled thrombosis affair.

"When is your train, Mr. Ferrier? " he asked.

"Oh, don't you start fussing about me now, for the Lord's sake! I can look after myself." Then he quickly regretted his outburst. "Sorry, Wright. A bit on edge. Rather a shock this morning. . . . My train's at two-something. The porter'll know. Gets me home about six. Want to have a rest and do a bit of thinking. I'll be quite all right."

As he left the lounge Mr. Quintin Wright glanced back to see his client stretch an arm upwards to press the bell and summon the waiter once again, and he was unhappy to think that Festus Ferrier had perhaps suffered more than rather a shock that morning. A difficult man: headstrong and not very wise.

4

A thin drizzle was falling in the West, but Jimsy Bell whistled cheerfully as, in an oilskin coat flapping open, he made his way along the east breast of the inner harbour at Brendan.

He had enjoyed a busy and amusing afternoon. After his first few weeks at Ardyne it had become a loose rule of the household that, along with Jock Jamieson and on every Thursday afternoon, he should go into the seaside town in the shooting brake, and attend to odds and ends of shopping.

It was conveniently assumed by Mr. and Mrs. Ferrier that this made a pleasant break for their two manservants, their day off; but the mere business of moving in and out of the stores was enough for Jimsy. He enjoyed it all the more when, as now, the narrow streets of the seaside townlet were thick with holidaymakers moving in the slow aimless way of all city-dwellers on vacation, all of them—young couples in love as well as trailing families—inevitably finding a haven under the bright lights and among the laden, coloured counters of Woolmark's: as if the Brendan branch of Woolmark's could somehow differ subtly in atmosphere and stock from any other of Woolmark's thousand branches throughout the British Isles.

Jimsy always compiled a careful list of his commissions. It might start with the brand and shade of Miss Ketron's latest fancy in lipstick and end with a pair of Mrs. Munn's old shoes to be collected from the crippled cobbler in the Castlegate, but it had come about that the indolence of Elaine Ferrier was so gratified by the competence of the new page-boy that he usually had great household orders to bestow on gratified shopkeepers as well—groceries and the odd cases of spirits and beer from Mr. Addie, who still called himself an Italian Warehouseman; fish to be chosen from the slabs of Miss Carmichael's cool emporium on the Front; fruit from Lennie's and, inevitably, a selection of the newest patent medicines for the mistress, the package neatly sealed with red wax on white paper at the hands of P. Skirving Deas, M.P.S.

For the man in miniature, however, there was more than amusement in these weekly outings. They ministered sweetly to that profound need of his being: the maintenance of self-respect in the face of a physical disability nearly comic. If he was just "Jimsy" to such as Miss Carmichael, a rough woman with raw arms and bleeding knuckles, he was "Mr. Bell" to P. Skirving Deas, M.P.S., a newcomer most anxious to keep up the old connections and attract the new. He was trusted; he had been given a position, if only through the Ferrier family's casual impatience of detail.

So his movements were buoyant as now he swung down the quay to where he knew he would find Jock Jamieson, closeted with Calum Blue, her skipper, in the tiny wheelhouse of the battered puffer with the noble name of *Thane of Cawdor*, unloading gravel. Jock was the first to spot his approach and pointed with his blue-enamelled mug of black tea.

"Here comes the pocket wonder," he chuckled affectionately. "Here's oor Wee Georgie Wood."

"He's a smart one, that," allowed Calum Blue, who might have been full cousin to Lachie MacDonald of the *Ron* but was also a man physically remarkable in having three separate sets of russet moustaches growing out of the sides of his nose, his upper lip and under his lower lip simultaneously, so that he was known in the coasting trade of the Highlands and Islands as The Full-rigged Ship.

"He's smart, all right," Jock Jamieson agreed, "but he's just a bit too dashed willing. That lot down there," he jerked his head in the general direction of Ardyne, "would fit all their dirty work on to the wee chap, and him that keen to do his best. No! One man, one job—that's what I've always said."

"I've heard you," observed Calum dryly.

Jimsy jumped to the deck of the stumpy craft with only a tap of his foot on the gunwale and reached up to open the wheelhouse door. In so doing he waved to Peter the engineer at the winch and to two dim figures shovelling gravel into a hopper in the vast belly of the little ship.

"Come in, come in, Jimsy!" cried Calum hospitably. "Can you find a corner for yourself? You'll have a dish of tea? Where's that mug of Peter's, the one without the handle? You can use your hankie, mebbe."

Though obliged to stand stiff upright in a corner of the pentagonal eyrie, the hot mug awkward to handle between chest and mouth, Jimsy Bell was happy in a new way. These two grown men were of his own sort; their accepted simplicities and the very dirt and smells of the *Thane of Cawdor* offered a blessed realm of escape from the imperatives of domestic service in the big house. He was helped to feel a real man among real men.

"What's this you've been buying, son?" asked Jock, pointing to a neat parcel in brown paper Jimsy had laid on the glass top of the compass. "A box of chocolates for the girl-friend?"

"No, books."

"Books! The only books worth readin' are the seed catalogues and the *Communist Manifesto*—Marx and Engels, ye ken, yon was a couple of boys! Mind ye," Jock prepared to launch out, "I'm no' away out on the Left Wing. Ye might cry me juist a wee thing Left-of-Centre. But the *Manifesto*—boy!"

"Give me the *Oban Times* and the *People's Friend*," interrupted Calum with a wink to Jimsy, "and you can keep your *Manifesto*."

"Yes. And look here, Jock; there's a lot of stuff to be collected at the shops. We'd better be moving."

"Food for the rich man's table and a hell of a lot of crumbs for the likes of us," observed Jock sententiously. "We'll be back soon, Calum. Time for a snifter before His Nibs comes off the boat."

The skipper stood at the door of the wheelhouse to watch them overside on to the quay.

"And when will you be coming on that voyage with us, *Seumas og*?" he cried to Jimsy in the Gaelic. "We could be doing with a good cook."

"Some day, Calum," Jimsy replied in the same tongue. "But when will they be giving me a holiday, worthy man?"

"Youse two and your Hielant blethers!" muttered Jock as they crossed the quay to where the shooting brake was parked against a granite wall.

They were back within twenty minutes, the rear compartment of the vehicle fairly loaded with goods, and Calum was waiting for his crony to accompany him to the bar of the Brendan Arms at the pierhead for what he delicately called a "refreshment." This was common form, and Jimsy stayed in his place by the driver's seat, automatically reminding Jock that the boss's steamer would be in at 5.25 and that he must study not to be late.

"The times that nyaf has kept me waitin', he can wait for me once in a while."

This was also common form, one of Jock's rhetorical flourishes, and Jimsy was glad to be left alone with his neat little parcel in brown paper. He unpicked the knot in the fine string with the delicacy of a surgeon and then knew the special sort of joy that comes to those who love and reverence books: that of opening in privacy what was only glanced at in the shop.

The first of his purchases was a slim, flat volume with cardboard covers in a horrid yellow and entitled *Simple Bookkeeping for Caterers.* But this was personal, utilitarian, to be studied later, and he pushed it into the recess in the dash; and then, his neat fingers working as with something precious, he opened its chubbier companion, the little Oxford *Flower Book for the Pocket.* In this he almost lost himself, brooding on the palely-tinted plates, rehearsing the fascinating names of flowers he had seen and never been able to put a name to— centaury, persicary, periwinkle, woundwort, fennel and even samphire. But this was not his own, this was for a fond and private purpose. He closed the small book unwillingly but hurried to wrap it up again with its grosser companion before Jock should return to guffaw at and befoul a pretty secret.

The latter returned betimes, his breath and clothes exhaling the malty, sawdusty reek of any Scottish pub.

"Better push up to the pier now," he said. "I wonder how His Nibs got on with the great Case? What's the betting he got a flea in his lug?"

Jimsy knew the answer as soon as the gangway was down and a deckhand from the steamer had hurried to hand him the master's cases. Festus Ferrier had the look of failure on him, the pallor of his face apart. He uttered not a word of greeting and forebore even from the familiar, scolding yelp when Jimsy, arranging the luggage along the floor beside his seat, accidentally pushed a suitcase against his leg. Not a word passed within the brake until, before the front steps of the big house, the master came out of a sort of sour abstraction to command the page-boy: "Run and see where your mistress is. Tell her I want to see her in the morning-room at once."

The bush telegraph, even if speeded by vague and unreasonable loyalties, works fast within any domestic establishment. Within half an hour of his return Mrs. Munn in her kitchen bewailed the fact that poor Mr. Ferrier had lost The Case and would thus, for some time to come, be an ill devil to live with; and Lorna could add the picturesque detail that Billy, and even Beth, were crying sorely over their supper in the day nursery. Only a little later on she could return from clearing up that meal with the news that the mistress was taking to her bed and wanted nothing to eat, wished only to be left alone.

If he had cared to expand the tale, Jimsy could have told how, as he laid the customary salver of drinks on the table by his master's chair, the silver legs of the tray had screeched a little on the polished surface and how Festus Ferrier, visibly starting in his seat, had violently blasphemed, almost shrieking, "For Christ's sake, boy! Don't make noises like that."

About the supper table in the kitchen the servants sat as a jury, hearing first a spate of further evidence from Lorna.

"It was fair murder at dinner the night," she made the best of the story in which she had figured so intimately. "There he was, glowerin' at the tablecloth and jerkin' them eyebrows of his up and down till you'd think he'd have a fit. Not a word to Miss Ketron, and her juist watchin' him and rollin' her bread into wee balls. Did he speak to me? Aye, if you can say ' Take it away ' is speakin' civil to anybody. I doubt if that lot's et a plate of soup between them. If you ask me," Lorna concluded shrewdly, "he's no' in this world juist now, the master."

Jimsy sought to bring the crisis within measure by observing "He's had a real shock, of course."

"Aye, and he asked for it," said Jock Jamieson truculently.

"It doesn't matter," Jimsy stuck to his point. "If you had a case, right or wrong, and you worried about it, and you lost it, you'd have a shock."

"Aye! " crowed Jock, dialectically triumphant, "but I wouldny have a case that was wrong. I wouldny go to the High Coorts, chasin' my brother. Democratic arbitration— that's the ticket. This is juist the kind of mess a' thae dawmned, greedy capitalists go in for when they're scrabbling for money, money and mair money."

Mrs. Munn would have none of this, declaring "Ye're a great man to talk, Jock Jamieson, and the good God alone knows how long I've had to listen to you. But Jimsy's right; you're only kicking a man that's down, poor soul. Wait you till he's better, and then go and tell him to his face what you think of him."

Jock soon retired to his conservatory and its greedy furnace and, having duly helped with the washing up, Jimsy Bell hung about uneasily. It was the unhappy condition of his service with the Ferrier's that he never knew how soon or how late the bell might not summon him to find and fetch the master's copy of the *Glasgow Herald*, frequently mislaid, or, as it might be, to run up and bring down the box of chocolates Miss Ketron always required to have near at hand. This evening the silence of the morning-room queerly strengthened his feeling of a brooding crisis about him.

By a service passage he reached the billiard room, a period

piece musty from disuse. The cues in the racks had warped, and the balls were scattered as Beth and Billy had left them after one of their games. Jimsy found two reds in a pocket and rolled them experimentally, his eagerness of concentrated interest in such things delighting in the geometrical patterns so exquisitely produced. He must have spent half an hour in this absorption before he realised that it had suddenly grown dark outside. Yes: the drizzle had turned to heavy rain battering in squalls against the windows, and the scudding clouds would be low over the Firth.

And still no call from his employers, a most unusual circumstance. He slipped back to the hall and listened outside the morning-room door and heard only the ordinary, reassuring plangencies of a palm court orchestra on the Light Programme. Dare he enter and ask if anything more was required of him or might he now retire? No: another half-hour. He climbed the stairs to his attic room, switched on the light, drew the curtain in the dormer window and picked again at the string about his little parcel of books.

Simple Book-keeping for Caterers; that was important and interesting but must await the right time for study, paper and pencil beside him, and he placed it on his tiny chest of drawers. But *A Flower Book for the Pocket*—here were wonder and fragrance and all the delightful mystery of his secret intention. He sat on the edge of the bed and gingerly turned the pages.

"Bell! Bell! Bell, where are you?"

The cries started far downstairs and came nearer, nearer as Ketron Ferrier, panting and sobbing, came running towards his door. He slipped the book under his clothes in the top drawer.

"Miss Ketron, what on earth?" he stared at the pretty, distracted face.

"It's Daddy, it's Daddy!" she wept miserably. "Something's happened to him. He's dying, he's dying. I'm frightened."

"Have you rung for the doctor?" Jimsy was abrupt.

"No. I didn't think. I'm frightened. Oh, Daddy!"

"Better ring at once. Say it's urgent. I'll go downstairs."

He raced to the ground floor, taking the shallow steps three
in a leap, and found in the morning-room that Mrs. Munn
and Lorna had already assembled, like spectators before a booth
in a fair, to consider the person of their employer in his
extremity. Festus Ferrier lay back in his chair, his mouth
slackly open; his eyes seemed very dark and frightened under
the bushy eyebrows. Jimsy ignored his fellow-servants and
advanced to the master's side, asking kindly "How do you
feel, sir?"

Festus Ferrier pointed the quavering forefinger of his left
hand to the loose mouth to indicate that he was incapable of
speech, then to his right hand and arm to suggest that the
power had gone from them.

"Better give the poor soul a drop of brandy," said Mrs.
Munn as if speaking of one quite beyond consciousness.

"No," said Jimsy decisively. "Wait till the doctor comes.
He'll be here in a minute."

Dr. Robertson, a youngish, fair man, followed Ketron into
the room within a few minutes.

"Well, Mr. Ferrier, what's all this? . . . I think you'd better
leave us alone now."

Mrs. Munn, Lorna and Jimsy removed themselves from the
fascinating scene, but Jimsy lingered outside the door he had
been careful to leave slightly ajar. He listened to the doctor's
commentary and could imagine the slack, assenting nods of
the patient's head.

"No power in your right arm? Try to twiddle your fingers.
No. . . . You don't feel you can speak? But that will come
right. . . . Let's try your legs, Mr. Ferrier. Yes, stand up if
you can. I've got a good grip round your waist. Fine! Now
it's into bed with you as quickly as possible. A good rest, Mr.
Ferrier; something to put you to sleep. . . ." Jimsy could
imagine the doctor turning to Miss Ketron. "Get these women
to fill at least a couple of hot-water bottles and get a bed ready.
I'll get your father upstairs."

Ketron did not see Jimsy bunched in the corner outside the
door. He stepped into the room and said boldly:

"Can I help you, doctor?"

"Yes," said Dr. Robertson turning his head with a smile. "Good lad. First of all, run down to the hall and fetch my case from the table, then bring a bowl of hot water to Mr. Ferrier's room. Oh, there's a washhand basin? Good."

So Jimsy Bell, the only sound man in a household of far from efficient women came to assist in the bedding of his humiliated master. They stripped the clothes from his person, so sadly incapable of protest, and Jimsy noted and admired the doctor's technique in this business; they pulled the pyjamas over his nakedness; they levered him on to the bed, face downwards. Then Jimsy, fascinated as ever by a specialised skill, saw the flash of the needle, the sure puncture of the buttock and the swift emptying of the syringe. He carefully ordered the bedclothes about their patient.

"You'll be all right now, Mr. Ferrier," said the doctor. "Lie quiet and don't worry about anything. Somebody will be up to sit with you, and I'll see you first thing in the morning. I'll have a word with Miss Ferrier."

Ketron had largely regained her accustomed poise of elegant languor and told how Daddy had come home with the burden of disappointment upon him and then, more vividly and with recurring distress, how he had sat with her after dinner, neither reading nor speaking nor listening to the wireless.

"Just staring, and his eyebrows working. There was a funny twitch about the corner of his mouth. And the next I knew he was waggling his hand at me."

"Yes?" said the doctor. "Your father's had a slight shock, you know. It's highly localised, and I really don't think it's serious. I shouldn't be surprised if he has his speech back to-morrow. He should rest well to-night with the drug, but he may be restless. I'd like somebody to sit up with him."

With an exquisite understanding of the forces at subtle play in this unhappy household Jimsy Bell saw poor Ketron Ferrier exposed in the weakness that had been imposed upon her by the man she was now being invited to nurse. She was afraid of

responsibility to a point beyond the power of affection to reach;
she was fated to a nearly complete incapacity in affairs.

"I could sit up, sir," Jimsy put in modestly.

"Yes," the doctor turned on him with another smile, "that's
the idea. You can ring me any time, but there should be
nothing to worry you."

So Jimsy Bell settled down in the sickroom in his new
capacity of night nurse. He sat in a deep chair under the
subdued glow of a reading-lamp that cast just sufficient light
to let him watch his patient's face and yet not disturb him.
He had on his knee his *Simple Book-keeping for Caterers* and a
writing-pad, in his hand an industrious pencil. The thought
of losing sleep did not irk him in the least. He rejoiced in the
opportunity of quiet study, and perhaps he was a little vain of
responsibility.

Festus Ferrier lay quiet in his affliction. At first he seemed
to be staring blindly at the ceiling, and you might think in
foolish alarm that he was dead, but the hollow eyes closed at
length, and the master of Ardyne snored rather horribly. Now
and again he tossed under the bedclothes as if in nightmare
and emitted sounds that were more like a whinnying than
anything articulate. Then the drug-induced peace would come
over him again and Jimsy could proceed with his study of the
arts of bulk-buying and the calculation of overheads, while
the deep chime of the grandfather clock in the hall below
relentlessly sounded the measure of every man's life—twelve,
one, two, three.

Then it was dawn on this morning of midsummer, the
light filtering even through a thick cotton blind and a pair of
heavy red curtains. Jimsy yawned and, feeling the stiffness in
his bones, rose after a glance at the sleeping man, sidled in his
house slippers between the curtains and pulled the edge of the
blind aside.

The rain had stopped and the cloud-ceiling was breaking
up to reveal ragged patches of blue and enchanting banks of
oyster-hued cirro-cumulus above the mainland. A naval
frigate was slipping up from the sea on its mysterious occasions

and outwards round the Riccar Light came an antique tramp riding light, probably a Greek.

It was the same old Firth this early morning; and yet, in the clarity of mind which so often comes of fatigue, Jimsy Bell knew in his bones that it was not for him the same Firth he had looked out on from his attic window only twenty hours before, but he did not go on to consider that the essence of change might be in himself and his circumstances. For he was suddenly aware of a sickening emptiness in his belly and wondered if he dare leave his patient and run down and seize a clutch of biscuits and make himself a cup of cocoa.

CHAPTER THREE

Thunder in the Air

KETRON FERRIER stood at the window of her stepmother's
room, her lovely person arrayed in a dressing-gown of
shell-pink satin over a pale-blue nightdress in silk, her
feet warmed by mules at once copiously furry and elegant.
She conversed over her shoulder with Mrs. Festus Ferrier who,
although it was already eleven o'clock on a brilliant morning
of July, still lay abed in garments fully as frivolous and
expensive as those of the younger woman.

"There he is now," Ketron reported.

"Is he properly wrapped up?"

"Yes, he's got a coat and scarf on, and there's Bell with his
chair and the rugs."

She could have added that Jimsy carried also an armful of
illustrated papers, a small table and a table lighter, a box of
fat cigarettes and, over one shoulder, a pair of binoculars in a
leather case. In his capacity of invalid Mr. Festus Ferrier
needed a lot of attention.

"He's made a wonderful recovery," breathed Mrs. Ferrier
piously.

"Yes, when I think of that night . . ."

"Oh, let's forget it now for goodness' sake!"

Yes, the memory of crisis and fear, like that of pain, is
blessedly transient; and restoration to health confers on all
within the house of sickness the agreeable feeling of having
partaken in an act of positive virtue. The Ferrier women were
at one in agreeing that the man of the house had given them
a fright which, if not positively wilful, had best be forgotten.

"I don't suppose you had time to speak to him—about

Brian, I mean?" Ketron asked shyly, turning to the bed in the knowledge that her blush would not be seen.

"My dear child! All those weeks of fussing about that awful Case; you know he couldn't think of anything else. And now this business. But I'll speak to him soon. He seems so awfully much better. I hope he'll have the sense to forget The Case. . . . By the way, have you got the new *Vogue* in your room?"

"Yes, I'll bring it up. There's a smashing Hartnell tea gown —midnight blue taffeta with a wide, deep collar and long gauntlet cuffs in *café au lait.*"

"Sounds lovely, dear. . . . I think I'll get up now."

Ketron moved in her gliding way towards the door.

"I'll have to go into Brendan this afternoon and get something for the kid, I suppose," she announced with resignation.

"Oh, dear, yes! I forgot. I expect Daddy will give her money from us both. It saves trouble."

"Yes, but I was an ass," complained Ketron, "and promised her a tennis racket. What a bore!"

Festus Ferrier was meanwhile enjoying his status of convalescent in his chair on the sun-warmed terrace. He believed himself to be in the nature of a medical miracle and counted it an act of considerable virtue in himself; "always was as fit as a fiddle," he asserted frequently to Jimsy Bell, now of necessity his confidant. ("Good little chap," he had confided in Dr. Robertson. "Knew the moment I saw him that he had the makings of a first-class servant. Catch them young: that's what I've always said.") As the doctor had foretold, he had recovered his power of speech, if hesitantly, on the first day, and he had then improved on the suggestion to stay in bed for a couple more by resting in the security of his room for a week.

Dr. John Robertson had more than one patient, some of them quite seriously ill, and his mood was impatient as Jimsy met him at the front door on the eighth morning.

"And how's your patient to-day, Bell? Not up yet?"

"I think he ought to get up, sir, in this fine weather. There's just that funny twist about the right-hand side of his mouth."

"Touch of what we call Bell's palsy—but don't talk about it. That should come right. The thing is to get him on his feet. Better come in and hear what the drill is to be."

Dr. Robertson was professionally brisk as he rested his arms on the end of the bed.

"You're all right now, Mr. Ferrier; strong as a horse. Bell will give you your pills three times a day until I tell him to stop, but you must make a job of it by getting up and getting the muscles working again. Two or three turns up and down the terrace and then a chair in the sun. More walks every day until you won't want to use the chair at all.

"You're a marvel, really," the doctor added with professional cunning, "and now you can forget all about it. Eat plenty; go as easy as you can on drinks and smokes. Above all, start living a quiet, normal life; and don't worry, just don't worry about anything."

As now he sat in the noon sunshine Festus Ferrier perceived that issue coming up like a mist between his eyes and a brilliant photograph in the *Yachting Monthly*. That damned Case! The memory was like weevil in the mind. There were the hours of sleeplessness when a fellow felt the pounding of blood in the head and, biliously hating the image of his brother, thought of harsh and obliterating things to say to him. Mustn't think. Been damned ill. That brute Finlay's fault. So difficult to forget, to falter in the battle for justice. Mustn't start trembling, however; start up that awful feeling of helplessness again.

"Bell!" he called his attendant, absorbed on a garden seat nearby in *Simple Book-keeping for Caterers*.

"Sir?" Jimsy was at his side almost in one leap.

"Bell, yes. Something I was going to say. Just a moment. . . . Ah, here they come!"

Beth came running round a corner of the house, Billy panting but faithful in her wake. The girl's face was alive with colour and eagerness.

"Hullo, Daddy! Are you feeling quite well now?"

"Yes, yes, Bettypet." He put his arm about the child's small waist and sought to match her cheerfulness. "Much better, anyhow. What have you been doing this morning?"

"Playing in the wood. It's scrumptious in there. Will we be allowed to build a hut, Daddy?"

"Of course, you'll be allowed to build a hut, dearest. Used to have a grand hut in there when I was a boy." And Jimsy noted the wistfulness that memory and the presence of his vivid daughter brought to the sick man's eyes. "But that reminds me. What was it, Bell? Ah, yes. . . . I haven't seen you giving these children their rowing lessons lately, Bell."

"No, sir," agreed Jimsy, tactfully evasive.

"How are they getting on?"

"Billy's rotten," declared Beth with the cruelty that too easily marches with honest candour.

"I'm not," protested Billy, the tears starting to flood his blue eyes.

"I think the oars are a bit heavy for him as yet, sir," Jimsy hurried to explain. "He'll come on all right."

"I should hope so," said Fergus Ferrier. "And that's quite enough from you, Beth. But there was something I was going to say. . . . Oh, yes. I'd like to see you using the boat a bit more. Got to learn to handle a boat, you know."

"Can we go out this afternoon, then, Daddy?" cried Beth agog.

"This afternoon? Why not?"

"I'm afraid, sir," Jimsy demurred. "Miss Ketron said she was going in to Brendan this afternoon, and perhaps I'd better be on the spot."

"Oh, drat it! Ketron can be an awful bind sometimes."

"But to-morrow, Bettypet," her father promised her fondly. "A treat for the big day. You might have a picnic on the island."

"Oh, super, super, super! A picnic, Billy."

"Can I have kola?" asked Billy, interested now.

"Certainly you can have kola. Anything you like. But run off now, you two, and have your lunch. I'm tired. These rugs,

Bell. Better help me inside. Young children can get you down, can't they?"

There it was, as Jimsy believed only he and the doctor knew. Festus Ferrier grew tired easily, a man back on at least the second line of his physical defences. He could go so listless and remote, fumbling in movement and speech. It had all changed since the day, a year ago it seemed, on which Lord Milnathort had acidly repelled the master's pleadings.

It boiled up into something near a quarrel with Jock Jamieson over the supper table in the kitchen that night: the chauffeur-gardener in his inveterate tweed cap like a jockey, as Jimsy saw him in a flash of illumination, riding his worn hobbyhorse to death.

"I see His Nibs is back on the map again," Jock had begun truculently. "It'll no' be long before he's bossin' about the place as if he'd won his bloomin' Case instead of losin' it."

"I don't think so," Jimsy remarked quietly.

"Oh, aye! You're always at the horse's mouth these days. Well, give us the dope."

"There's nothing you can't see for yourself. He's slowing down; he gets wandered in the mind. Yes, Jock; I'm at the horse's mouth if you like to put it that way, but I'm telling you that the boss is a sick man."

"It's what I said! It's what I said!" Mrs. Munn suddenly intervened oracularly. "Drap doon deid, that's what he'll do. Mebbe at the table wi' his heid in a plate of my good broth."

"I don't think so, Mrs. Munn," Jimsy laughed.

"You see, Mrs. Munn," said Jock, heavily sarcastic, "the wee chap knows better nor us. Mr. Ruddy Ferrier's handy wee friend; a real friend of the family. How do, old boy? Jolly fine morning. He's in a fair way to being nothing more nor less than a ruddy parasite."

Jimsy disciplined himself to keep his temper, but his retort was curt.

"I'm trying to learn a job, that's all. Do you hand him back his wages? He gave me a good rise last week, if you want to know."

"Aye, aye! The fancy man." But the comment was feeble, and Jock, muttering something about his preparations for the Brendan Flower Show, quitted the field while Mrs. Munn slopped with a sigh into her chair before the kitchen cooker.

"I suppose you'll be above helping me with the dishes now?"

This was Lorna at her games, and the embers of anger that Jock's truculence had stirred in him glowed again.

"Why?" he asked sharply.

His ungraciousness was born of a disgusted distress. It pained him to be so sensitive to the poor girl's crudity of approach, in which a pathetic self-knowledge of weakness and a sort of lazy lust were in conflict: Lorna the lost one, carrying tales from above stairs to those below and from below to above; Miss Ketron her confidant on the upper level, her reward Miss Ketron's numerous pieces of cast-off finery and illustrated periodicals.

"You fairly stuck up to Jock to-night," she said ingratiatingly as they started together on the cutlery.

"Oh, Jock talks a lot. It's just a bad habit," Jimsy dismissed at once the episode and the girl's attempt to insinuate herself with him. "There you are," he added, throwing the last sheaf of forks on the tin tray. "I'd better go and see that Mr. Ferrier is all right for the night."

Festus Ferrier had been installed in the dressing-room off his wife's bedroom. This arrangement permitted him the twin illusions that he was fit to look after himself without that confounded boy reading his confounded book under the shaded lamp, and that, should he require attention, Elaine was within call. The nightly process of bedding him down was apt, however, to be prolonged and fussy. Out of the remoteness that would come over him with the normal fatigues of the day he could turn in this ceremonial hour to a nice, nervous interest in his own unique condition and the drugs and techniques that had been prescribed for its improvement.

This was one of the difficult nights, one of those on which

the man who had lost The Case alternated between explosive irritability and genuine weariness.

"Didn't I tell you, Bell, to put that lamp nearer the edge of the table? And that isn't the book I was reading. . . . Oh, yes, it is; thought it had green covers. . . . A bit fuzzy about the head to-night, Bell. So don't forget to give me my pill or the doctor will have something to say to you. . . . I've had it? When? Well, if you say so. Can't remember. . . . Only know I'm damned tired."

There was a last-minute hitch about the position of a hot-water bottle, and Jimsy had forty minutes of it in all before he could climb to his attic room. He also felt tired in his mind, at least, with the bleak feeling that his small row with Jock Jamieson had wastefully reduced the sufficiently small group of friendly souls about him. From under the garments in the top drawer of the chest he took the small oblong of the flower book in its tidy wrapping and, within his hand a ball-point pen he had bought in the same shop that happy afternoon, sat down on the edge of his bed.

The door opened, and he looked up to see Lorna standing there. She wore a purple flannel dressing-gown, its fastenings so arranged as to show that there was only a shift between it and her nakedness.

"What do you want?" he asked, his voice shaking a little.

"Kidding on you don't know?" she teased with a heavy peasant smile that, even in his state of concern, made Jimsy think irrelevantly of prints he had seen of the Mona Lisa.

"Get out of here."

"Come on and be a sport."

"Get out of here or I'll shout the house down."

"Ach, ye useless wee nyaf! Ye're only fit to play footy-footy wi' that cheeky wee moll of yours."

The doric insults came at him with the effect of a fusillade of sharp stones. There followed them a gush of the filth in words the unhappy girl had picked up as the by-blow of a ploughman on a mountainy farm, all the earthy abuse she had endured from the man's lawful, resentful wife, like the dark overflow of a byre emptying itself into a midden by a pipe much used by rats.

Jimsy rose and advanced on the young woman, his face white.

"Get out."

"Aye," she triumphed, "and now I ken ye're no' a man at a'."

She disappeared. It was surprising somehow to be alone again, almost disappointing in a vague way. Another position lost: Jock and now Lorna; and only the frail and tenuous relationships with the Ferriers left. He sat down on the edge of the bed again and poised the new pen, if with a shaking hand. On the brown paper he wrote the legend long cogitated:
With respectful compliments, from Jimsy.

2

Interesting parcels were already heaped about Miss Beth's breakfast plate when Jimsy, slipping downstairs early, invaded the early morning emptiness of the dining-room and took the little book of flowers from its hiding place in his armpit under the white jacket of his servitude. He placed it at the bottom of a pile of grander oblongs and hurried away.

The children ate together at half-past eight, and Lorna was given to running late with the service of their porridge and boiled eggs, but on this special morning, driven by a profound need to have what she would have called a good look at the presents, she slipped into the dining-room even before the eager child had dressed herself on such an exciting morning.

Lorna's handling of the parcels was thorough, speculative; her heavy hands must weigh and shake each one; her eyes laboriously deciphered the inscriptions. In her turn she hurried out of the room, and when Beth had come storming down, Billy at her heels, to pounce upon the collection, the house-tablemaid was ready with a glib, surprised:

"Man, that's a grand pile of presents you've gotten the day! And many happy returns, Miss Beth."

It was her business about nine o'clock to take Miss Ketron her cup of morning tea; and she repeated herself, saying: "Man, Miss Beth's gotten a grand pile of presents the day!"

"Oh, she's always spoiled," Ketron almost yawned.

"I see there's one from Bell. I couldn't help noticing." Adding innocently: "It was on the top of the pile."

"And what business," the young lady of the house became almost vivacious, "has Bell got giving Miss Beth a present?"

"That's what I was wondering," said Lorna.

Ketron's sense of social irregularity in no way hastened her uprising. Nearly three hours of time and happening passed before she appeared on the terrace to greet her father in his chair with the *Tatler* on his knee.

Beth, dancing with vitality and excitement, had waylaid Jimsy Bell as he approached the dining-room to fetch the paraphernalia of the master's breakfast in bed.

"Oh, Jimsy! What a beautiful present! Thank you, thank you, very, very much!"

"I'm glad you like it, Miss Beth."

"It's the loveliest present I've ever had. Daddy said we could go out to the island to-day for a picnic, and we can take it with us. Then we could go into the wood one day. There's all sorts of different flowers in there. I'm going," she announced, "to start a museum."

"That's a good idea."

Innocent pleasure informed them both. Beth could not leave her book; she flopped on the lawn and, her head propped on her hands and her long legs stretched out behind her, lost herself in the small world of pastel-shaded pictures. It was Jimsy's morning at the silver, but he had left out the master's chair, rugs, table and illustrated papers. Billy was happy for once to be alone in the day nursery, his clumsy hands and slow mind fully engaged with the toys of a more mechanical nature out of parcels that Beth had merely opened and put aside.

It was then that Festus Ferrier had appeared alone, pausing

at the top of the steps to appreciate the loveliness of still another fine summer morning. The sweep of his gaze took in the prone figure of his young daughter, and he called to her, crying out his wish for many happy returns of the day. The child was on her feet in a flash and running towards him. The pounce of her embrace nearly knocked him down.

"Thank you ever so much, Daddy!" she panted. "Yes, lots of lovely presents. Look at this one I got from Jimsy Bell. It's a smashing book—all about flowers."

"Flowers," repeated the father as another man might mention flying saucers, but he smiled and took it from her. "Looks very nice. Very decent of Bell to think of it."

"He knows all about these things. He's been teaching me. I'm going to start a museum. You know: all the flowers dried and stuck to cardboard and their names underneath. They've got Latin names, too."

"Have they, now?" he asked emptily. "Hardly in my line, Bettypet. Now run away like a good girl with your book. I must read my papers."

Beth retired to a far corner of the lawn under an old red hawthorn where she thought she might be reasonably safe from Billy, and Ketron came along towards her father, a lovely figure of a marriageable girl in a cotton dress in lime green. When they had exchanged those limp greetings that Ketron was apt to bring to all her dealings with others she said:

"I suppose that kid has been pestering you about her presents?"

"Beth, you mean? Hardly pestering." And Ketron perceived that he was in one of the milder, remote moods that had come on him after the shock. "She seems to be a bit excited about a book Bell gave her. Something about flowers. Not quite my cup of tea."

"But a present from Bell!"

"How do you mean, dear? Don't quite follow. Getting a bit thick in the old head, I suppose."

"Daddy! Beth accepting a present from one of the servants!

It's not done really." And then she dropped into the man's bemused mind the calculated gout of acid and watched him struggle to emerge from the state such as Mrs. Munn would have described as yonderly. "These two are just a bit too thick already if you ask me."

"No," he hesitated. "Hadn't occurred to me. Out in the boat together and all that sort of thing. No, Ketron; you're right. It's not done. I say you're right; *it's not done*. I'll have a word with these young devils."

He was agitated now, but he could bring admiration to the sight of his older daughter as she swung away down the drive, a clutch of letters for the post in her net-gloved hand. Smart girl, ought to make a good match. If only that other young kid . . . His retarded processes came round like the tentacles of a squid to the problem Ketron had so skilfully made Beth out to be. He cried her name across the lawn.

"Yes, Daddy." And she was on her feet at once.

"Come here."

She was standing before him, stiff and straight as a guardsman, even to the tidy stiffness of her thumbs down the outer seams of her grey shorts. He might have seen that he was dealing with quality, with human material of rare if vulnerable decency, but it was always his dreadful fate to hurt in his lifelong, pathetic quest for the assurance of power.

"About that book Bell gave you," he started weakly enough.

"Yes, Daddy." And the lips began to quiver.

"It's all very well, of course, my dear. But you don't seem to see that the daughter of a house like this just doesn't accept gifts from the servants. It's not done. Do you hear what I say, Beth? *It's not done*."

She started to sob, and this was no child's weeping for the discovery of error. It came out of wells deeper than such as Festus Ferrier could ever fathom. In his presence she was defenceless, desperate and, worst of all, beyond hope of being understood.

"That will do now, Beth," he took her on his own level. "I'm simply asking you to remember this. It's not done. And just to get the idea into your head, you can wash out the picnic to the island this afternoon. I allow you to keep the book, of course. . . . Now, run away. And remember—*it's not done.*"

Her sobbing turned to a series of dry, spasmodic convulsions, and even Festus Ferrier was bemusedly alarmed by the intensity of her feeling, but still the child could recover something of her own dignity and speak in a cold, small voice.

"I'm sorry, Daddy. I thought it very kind of Jimsy. But "—and this came on a gust of passion—"I don't want the book now."

She laid it on the table by his side, then turned and fled towards the house and the privacy of her own room. Her father's eyes followed her stormy passage, and he wondered a little if he had handled the thing quite correctly. But he was her father, wasn't he, responsible for discipline? Females were always damn fools about trifles. And he was himself, wasn't he, a sick man who should get a little consideration now and again?

He was still pondering the implications of the problem when Jimsy Bell came out to help him indoors for lunch.

"Ah, yes, Bell! The very man I want to see. That book you gave Miss Beth . . ."

He paused, and Jimsy said "Yes, sir."

"It was very good of you, very thoughtful. But tell me: how much did you pay for it?"

"I can't quite remember, sir." The little fellow stared at his master. "Something like eight and six, I think."

"Very well."

Festus Ferrier clawed and fumbled in the recesses of his right-hand trouser pocket and brought out a handful of silver.

"A half-crown and three florins—eight and six. There you are, Bell. You understand, don't you? I really can't have my daughter taking presents from any of the servants. Very nice of you and all that, Bell, but it's not done. You understand: *it's not done.* And there's to be no picnic this afternoon, by the way."

"No, sir." And the little fellow added on the note of

personal dignity that was to Festus Ferrier at once incomprehensible and irritating: "I don't think we should have the picnic after all."

He placed the stubby pile of cupro-nickel coins on the book that Beth had already surrendered and became the obedient servant once again.

"I'll collect the things if you're ready to move now, sir."

3

The Royal Firth Yacht Clubhouse was an agreeable feature of the front at Brendan. One of a terrace of tall houses built in an Italianate style for wealthy Victorian gentlemen, it stood out from its neighbours, all boarding houses now, in the brilliance of cream paint and window-sashes of emerald green. The gay, near-Mediterranean note was pleasantly heightened by the droop of the Blue Ensign on the gaff of a raking white flagpole, and two miniature cannon flanking the doorway nicely completed the general impression of a place set apart for the worship of a cult.

As he passed one afternoon between the dainty carronades and into the cool twilight of the Clubhouse hall Jimsy Bell had upon him a weight of concern much heavier than anybody observing his attractively comic figure would ever have guessed him capable of carrying. He had come to a decision that was for him deadly serious, whose conduct of his life must always be serious in terms of both expediency and temperament.

Of course, the story of the birthday gift had come round to the kitchen, virtuously carried from Miss Ketron's room by Lorna, and it aroused such a sharpness of social feeling as would have surprised, perhaps frightened, Festus Ferrier could he have been got to understand it.

"The dirty b . . .!" cried Mrs. Munn coarsely. "The dirty b . . .! Throwin' a wee present back in the laddie's face and takin' it from that innocent wee lass—the best of the lot of them!"

"It's a cryin' shame, so it is!" declared Lorna, believing in her own sincerity.

"It's a ruddy insult to the lot of us," said Jock Jamieson, spitting venom out of the side of his mouth. "This is wage slavery with nobs on. The man's a capitalist, but that's within the System. A man can be a capitalist "—he always emphasised the second syllable of this, one of his favourite words—"and still be a man and a gentleman forbye. Look at his brother Finlay. Thon's a tough nut if ever there was one, but he's still a man. As for that squirt upstairs," Jock concluded with magnificent contempt, "he's juist a blawn-up jeely fish."

Their easy sympathy was of little help to Jimsy. Indeed, he sat, miserable of countenance, brooding on the complexities of the personal problem their forthrightness ignored, and when the ceremony of washing-up was over he walked across the lawn and down the steps to where Jock was working at his fire. There they sat on up-ended boxes, their faces taking the glow of the furnace in the failing light of a stormy evening.

"I think I'll give him my notice," Jimsy had openly confessed his distress.

"No wonder," said Jock, his mood reflective. "Never mind politics. A man's got his own dignity. Never mind the rise he gave you the other day; you're giving him back the work of three men and a nurse forbye. I'd walk out on him *pronto* if I were you, even if it means the Buroo money for a while."

"But I can't, Jock," Jimsy protested unhappily.

"How can ye no'?"

"Because I've nowhere to go," explained Jimsy with an empty little laugh. "I've no parents, no home, no relatives in the world that I know of. If I want my bed and my meat, I've got to have a job."

"Is that a fac', son? That's not so hot, is it?"

Jock's thin face seemed wistfully gentle as he stared into the glimmering anthracite. He pronounced a reconsidered judgment at length.

"Well, you'll get another job easy enough. Ye see, son, a wee chap like you has great chances in your own line. It's no' as if you was a dwarf," Jock explained with disconcerting candour, pronouncing the word to rhyme with ' scarf.' " Ye're wee, right enough, but ye're neat built, and ye're as smart as a bag o' monkeys. I'll bet you a bob you could walk into Brendan to-morrow and pick up a dandy job at the first hotel you stopped at. And that's no' countin' the tips."

So now Jimsy passed into the Royal Firth Clubhouse in search of a job. He was far from confident in himself, but he had recalled the jocular suggestion of one of his new water-front acquaintances—the great, much envied Steamboat Duff, now house steward to the Royal Firth, once chief steward in the steam yacht of a millionaire in the days when the summer waters of the Firth would shelter hundreds and thousands of pounds worth of floating beauty, the transient flowers of a blind economy.

"Come in," he shouted from his office under the main stairway in response to Jimsy's knock. "What the hell do you want at this time of day? Oh, it's you, Jimsy? Lookin' for that job?"

"I was thinking of it."

Steamboat Duff was running to fat, and a pasty face perspired under the wreckage of a crop of sandy hair. He pulled at the glass of strengthening Guinness he was enjoying out of hours, belched and asked:

"Fed up with His Lordship at Ardyne? Ye're no' the first, and ye'll no' be the last—if he lives. When can ye start?"

"What's the sort of job, Mr. Duff?"

"Lounge waiter. Gees alive! " he swore oddly. "I'll have the Fortnight on me before ye could say knife, then the English and Irish boats till well into the back-end. Standard wages, nice room, good chuck and "—Mr. Duff winked fatly—" oodles of perks. It's seasonal, mind ye, but I'll guarantee ye a winter job in the Victoria. When can ye start?"

"Give me a day or two, sir. I'll let you know."

"Never heed lettin' me know. Walk in when ye're ready, and I'll have ye in uniform and a napkin over your arm before you could say Bob's yer Uncle."

The world seemed brighter to Jimsy, his problems easier, as he came out into the sunlight of an afternoon shaping to turn to a lovely evening. A band was playing *The Pirates of Penzance* under a canopy of Victorian ironwork on the front, and the trippers drifted up and down the esplanade, their world purged of care for a while. The snugness of the crowded anchorage had its own word to say to him, and he thought it would be fine to work here in independent impersonality, away from the shabby intimacies of the unhappy household at Ardyne. As Jock drove him home after they had collected the messages their conversation was brief.

"Did ye find a job?"

"If I want it."

"Take it."

Yes: to be free from the sluttish contamination of such as Lorna and the feeble langour of Miss Ketron; above all, to be finished with Festus Ferrier, the cad in power, so stupid in the exercise of that power as to be a monstrosity and yet contemptible. To have the satisfaction of teaching Festus Ferrier that he was weak. . . .

As it chanced, as the brake approached the gates of the big house, they saw the man taking his late afternoon walk on the shore road. He moved slowly, his legs indecisive, his right hand within the loop of his elder daughter's elbow; and you were suddenly sorry for him again as a fellow creature afflicted. He raised and waved his stick to halt the vehicle.

"Been having your day off, eh?" he asked as Jimsy lowered the side-window. "Just something I wanted to say, Bell. Seems a long time since Master Billy had his last rowing lesson. It's a nice evening now. You could give him a turn or two round the bay before dinner."

"Very well, sir."

Jock Jamieson let the clutch in with a slam and swung the car through the gates and up the drive.

"And you're a right mug, s'elp me God!" he observed bitterly.

"I'd rather be in a boat on the bay than messing about the kitchen with Lorna," Jimsy defended himself.

"Mebbe you're right there, son," Jock allowed, a wry smile on his twisted lips.

It was pleasant to be on the water again, with time to think and make his own approaches towards a decision; and the pretty little boy, away from the critical eye and superior skill of his sister, was in the mood this fair evening to make a proper pass at the business of oarsmanship.

"Now, take your time from me, Master Billy," Jimsy patiently instructed the child. "Keep the corner of your eye on the blade of my oar and don't look at your own. Right back now; wrists straight and tight. *In*—back—*out*! "

They went up and down the length of the bay three or four times before Jimsy allowed his pupil to rest and offered him fair words of encouragement, and as they lay on their oars he saw that Beth had come down to the jetty. She appeared not to be interested in their doings. Her performance was indeed an elaborate exercise in apparent indifference. Her back was to the bay and the boat, and every now and again she would walk a step towards the shore and then kneel as if to pick a remarkable specimen of marine growth.

Jimsy Bell had been a lonely boy in his day, and with the warm tenderness of pity he recognised every sign of her condition—the awareness of private loneliness, the unwillingness to ask for recognition, the hideously false integument of pride: always the yearning to escape the terrors that afflict the solitary. He moved Billy into the sternsheets and pointed the boat's nose towards the shore.

"Do you wish to come out, Miss Beth?" he called.

"Not specially," the girl replied in what she trusted would be recognised as a tone of calculated coolness. "But you could row me out to the island and leave me till Billy has finished his practising."

They were both silent as Jimsy took the boat across the bay once more. It was his morose reflection that her fool of a father had pulled down a screen of constraint between them, as it were of plastic material, transparent but distorting. They were both more than a year older since her birthday; they had been expelled from the paradise of childhood and been made aware of each other as maturing girl and mature young man, as the young lady of the house and a servant about the place.

As they neared the island landing place Billy made it awkwardly clear that he had had enough rowing lessons for the day and wished to go ashore with Beth to play; and as he was clearly prepared to scream if he did not get his way, they must needs all land together.

"What are you two going to do?" asked Beth, as if she had an appointment of her own, and Billy surprisingly provided a solution of the dilemma in which the other two so unhappily found themselves.

"I vote we start building a house," the boy suggested.

"Good idea, Master Billy," Jimsy approved the notion. "We could make that museum you were talking about, Miss Beth."

He had her beaten there. Even if his too-eager suggestion had raised the ghost of the little book about wild flowers, it was not in Beth Ferrier to stand aside from the play of imagination. She led the way across the islet to where the seaward shore rose in terraces of a reddish rock between the heaving masses of wrack and the tussocks of the shallow inland soil.

"There's a rare flat rock for a display of things," said Jimsy, placing his sandshoed foot on a weathered slab of greenstone and beginning to forget himself. "We could build the walls round it."

"I'm going to build the garage," announced Billy, adding helpfully, "that's for the lorries that bring in the mummies and things."

"You go ahead, then," he was encouraged. "But leave room for us to get the proper walls up first."

You lost yourself. Choosing flat stones from an indentation in the rocky foreshore and staggering up to the site. Choosing the exact place in which a small boulder of unusual shape could be placed without bringing the edifice down in ruins about the foundations. Watching young Beth break away from the building operations to gather wild flowers and lay them out on the slab of rock; checking her identifications with "Yes, butterburr, hairbell, vetch. . . . No, that's some sort of campion. . . . I wonder if there's any blue geranium."

Even Billy protested when Jimsy said at length they must go home; they were late already. On their short way across the islet to the boat, however, Beth fell silent again; and as he rowed the brother and sister towards the jetty Jimsy perceived with anguish what really lay between this dark girl and himself.

It was that each lived in separate compartments of private loneliness, each surrounded by unfriendly circumstance. As he pulled the boat out to the mooring buoy while the children ran up towards the big house and supper he reflected unhappily that his wish to leave the service of Mr. Festus Ferrier would be in a sort a betrayal of loyalties, real if undeclared.

4

In later years Jimsy Bell could think of the happenings of the next three weeks as scenes in a farcical comedy. He came to recalling Festus Ferrier as a comic character essentially, raised above the norm by his almost splendid stupidity, by the grandeur of his outmoded assumptions. What he could never forget or forgive were the darknesses the man's unreason brought upon the lives of so many other people.

The penultimate act of the pantomime started not long after Jimsy had followed the children up to the house on their return from the island. Lorna was lurking about to tell him that the master wished to see him in the morning-room as soon as possible.

"Miss Ketron's boy-friend's coming to stay," she confided in her bothy whisper.

When Jimsy had knocked and entered, Festus Ferrier looked up from *Picture Post* and started off in his jerky way.

"Oh, yes, Bell. By the way——"

When the master started one of his announcements with "by the way " the servant knew that it was precisely not so, and that a proposition, carefully thought out but not advanced with complete confidence, was about to be put to him.

"Fact is, we're expecting a guest next week. He'll be here for the Fortnight. Captain Brian Horsley-Moray. Regular soldier, of course, not one of the National Service lot. Seems he can't bring his own batman on a private visit, so I'll want you to do valet for him. I expect you know the drill."

All absurd, like something out of a satirical farce, but as Jimsy was to see it later on, it was the moment of decision, the moment when the scales tipped precisely as between the weights of two sets of emotions, prejudices and precautions.

"I'm sorry, sir," he said. "I was going to give you notice in any case."

"What!"

This was a yelp, and Jimsy feared for the human being who had been his patient. Already the eyebrows were beginning to work.

"It's not that I'm unhappy here, sir," he hurried to lie, "but I don't think I like private service after all. I've done my best, but if I've got to act valet to this gentleman as well— well, I'd rather give you a week's notice now."

"But you can't! "

It was like baiting a cornered stirk, and the little man knew for a moment the dark satisfaction of revenge, realising in the same instant that his was but a shabby triumph over a nonentity.

"I've arranged to take up my new job this day week, sir."

Then he saw Festus Ferrier in the condition of defeat. The familiar stigmata of shock had come over the man in the deep chair. His fingers drummed on its arms. Even so, he was still capable of a reach back towards mastery.

"I think you're being a bit foolish, Bell, rash if you don't mind a word of advice from an older man. Never knew you had any complaint; would never have occurred to me. Dammit, why didn't you speak to me before? However ... Where were we? Oh, yes! ..." And the physical person of Festus Ferrier confessed its weariness in a yawn. "Got to think about this; both of us, Bell. You think, I think." And Jimsy wondered if he had been drinking. "Tell you what. Come and see me here about nine to-night. Think. Don't want to rush things."

Of course, it was all back in the kitchen within the hour, the bald tale duly decorated by Lorna. Here was Miss Ketron's boy-friend coming, a real sodger at that, and them likely to get engaged, and here was that cheeky wee imp, Bell, asking the master for his books. Oh, you could have heard the cursing and swearing a mile away up the hill! Lorna would not be surprised, so she wouldn't, if the way Bell was carrying on would not bring upon the master another of his turns, and that would be very near manslaughter, would it no'?

At the rough supper table of the working folk later on Jimsy was again hard put to it to keep his temper. It was very well for Mrs. Munn, shovelling food into her mouth with the broad of a knife, to be vociferously on his side, urging him to lift his books and give that twister a lesson. Lorna advanced the thought that a servant, willing and a' that and never mind the National Health, shouldny be asked to do mair than what's right. Jock Jamieson, sucking the shards of stew from between yellow teeth, took it all with gravity, saying:

"Youse two women are juist wastin' time, shootin' off your mouths about sumpthin' you don't understand. This is an industrial dispute, see?"

Jimsy was grateful for this support, but Jock was as far from an understanding of the dilemma as the stupid women. An industrial dispute, when a man's mind and soul were a welter in which wages and working hours were the least of his concerns; to know what it was to be an oddity and to be beset by adult problems. They were incapable, these colleagues of his, of knowing what it was to have to carry so much pride and ambition and loyalty about the world within the frame of a midget.

He went to his session with the master without plan or

purpose. The pleasant small room was lighted only by a short reading-lamp on the table by Fergus Ferrier's chair, and the downward gleam gave life to the bubbles in a large whisky and soda by the man's side. Jimsy was defensively more interested in the fact that, for his further protection, Miss Ketron had been called in by her father to sit in a low chair in the shadow on the other side of the fireplace.

"Ah, yes, Bell! Come in. That little thing we were talking about before dinner. By the way "—the fatal phrase again!— "my daughter ought to hear anything we may discuss. She'll be pretty much in charge for the next week or two."

"Quite all right, sir." And Jimsy gave the lady one of his neat little bows.

"I didn't want to butt in, Bell," the young lady said her piece, "but we'll be very busy for the next week or two, and it would be very, very awkward if you were to leave us now. We were really wondering . . ."

"Yes, Bell," the master of the house took up the story, "the idea is that we should offer you a fair bargain. You've been a very willing worker, and we don't want to part on bad terms, do we? The idea is that we'll relieve you entirely of work in the kitchen and at the table. You do nothing but valet our guest and look after me now and again. After all, you're the chap who knows all about those drugs and things. We're bringing in extra help, of course "—and here Mr. Ferrier waved a patrician hand—"and you won't be asked to do anything about the house you won't want to do. I think you can trust my daughter to play fair so far as that's concerned, eh? So, Bell, if you'll guarantee to stay the month with us, I promise a bonus of ten pounds at the end of it. That fair? "

"Perfectly fair, sir."

"You'll stay, then? " asked Ketron, confessing her anxiety.

"Yes, but just for the month, Miss Ketron. I'd really like to go back to the catering side, and I want to get fixed up before the end of the season."

"Quite all right, Bell," said Festus Ferrier largely. "Chap's got to look after himself, hasn't he? So long as you stay the month, we're all happy. Good night, Bell!"

"Good night, Miss Ketron! Good night, sir!"

His instinct was to stroll down to the conservatory and report to Jock Jamieson, but what was there to report? Just that the Ferriers, on the defensive and their parts carefully rehearsed, had offered him all any page-boy could demand in a dream; just that the page-boy, for want of direction within his bemused self, did not know what he really wanted and had taken an easy way out of a dilemma beyond his own powers of definition.

He slipped out of the house by a back way and, through a grove of rhododendrons, into the wood that had been planted to shelter Ardyne from the sou'-westerlies. It was an uninteresting plantation of oak mainly, with an odd hazel and tangles of brambles here and there, but it was strangely lighted at this hour by the fires of a sullen sunset over the outer islands. He was alone in it save for the odd red squirrel comically scampering up one of the grey trunks on the side from the sun, for the odd flutter of the scud of a rabbit making for its burrow under the roots of an upturned tree. Little enough here to charm or divert Jimsy Bell, orphan.

Where the wood ended short of the drystone dyke that enclosed it from rushy marginal land on its western side he found a young ash grown to the height of some nine feet and wonderfully straight, and he cut it down. He was thinking that it would make a rough trolling-rod with which, and a penny fly on the end of a hank of line, Billy might learn to fish for mackerel and saithe off the island. Or was it really for Beth? he asked himself as he made his way back towards the house in the gloaming. His mind shied from the question. He did not know at all where now he stood, and as to what he meant to make of himself, his mind could not frame an answer that would comfort his lonely soul.

5

As he saw it later on, the irony was that Jimsy took a great liking to Captain Brian Horsley-Moray. Sometimes he seemed to see in this other man a simple chap walking, willingly enough, into the net so carefully arranged by Festus Ferrier and his elder daughter.

The young soldier's reception was grandly planned. Nothing would do but that the *Ron* be polished to the nines for one of her infrequent trips outside the bay, and that Lachie Macdonald and Jimsy, both neatly uniformed, should take her round to Brendan and receive the young gentleman off the afternoon steamer.

The white vessel's sweep into and round Brendan Bay at top speed was widely remarked, even on a Saturday afternoon of public holiday when yachts of equal and even greater grandeur were gathering for the opening of the Fortnight. Lachie's management of the pretty craft into the steps behind the pier had its admiring audience, mainly of urchins fishing hopefully for the small fry that darted in and out among the great timber supports of the quay, and Jimsy had his work cut out for him to reject their copious offers of help and keep their dirty hands off Lachie's paintwork and brasses.

He was up on the pier and across the gangway, in defiance of the rule, as soon as the *Marchioness of Ailsa* was warped in to Number One berth and whipped from the hands of the guest the two grips of the zip-fastener sort that were the sum of his luggage. The Captain seemed a fair, smiling, friendly sort of young man. He smiled in an embarrassed way when formally saluted by Lachie MacDonald and guided by Jimsy into the solitary handsomeness of the owner's cabin; and the *Ron* had in fact not long cast off from the steps with some circumstance and was only starting to put on speed out of the bay before he came clambering forward into the navigation department, passed round his cigarette case, and asked Lachie if he could have what he called a bash at steering the craft.

"A fine, fresh, young gentleman," Lachie summed up the case later on, adding, in the delightful Highland way, "and very jocose."

He was easy to deal with domestically. Jimsy in particular found it a relief to be working for just a friendly young man who made few demands as compared with Festus Ferrier and appeared, indeed, to find the page-boy valet's attentions surprisingly eager and intimate. He was sufficiently interested to ask Jimsy what he thought of doing with himself, and insisted that, despite his height, he could get into one of the technical branches of the Army; or the R.A.F. would snap him up for aircrew.

A pleasant young man: not one of those soldiers who compile highly individual anthologies or write stylised travel books; just an honest, healthy character shaped by a good public school and Sandhurst for a given job. Even Jimsy could see his presence at Ardyne as a scene out of conventional social comedy. It would run its course as plotted by the Ferriers, and within a fortnight the engagement would be ominously announced in *The Times*, the *Daily Telegraph*, the *Glasgow Herald* and the *Scotsman* at so many guineas per inch of space.

Jock Jamieson, a sourer observer of the scene than Lachie MacDonald, could sum up the situation exactly enough.

"How's your chunk of cannon-fodder the day, Jimsy?" he would ask. "Have they no' got him pinned down yet? Jings, but His Nibs is fairly purrin' these days! It's juist a plant, of course; it's juist the capitalists gangin' up as usual. These Moray's were in the same racket—big folk in soft goods in Glasgow. Where they got the Horsley and the hyphen God knows; likely one of their dirty marriages of an old crow of a daughter to a bankrupt block with a title. It would make ye laugh. Still," Jock allowed with ostentatious charity, "he seems a decent enough, friendly kind of a fellow, even if he was only born to get a clip of Rooshian bullets in his guts."

Yes, he often thought later on, Jimsy's last few weeks at

Ardyne were the best, as if the presence of the young soldier showed up and by its light abated a small tyranny. It was good to have life and order in the house again, to see the *Ron* sail out most days with Miss Ketron and the Captain for one of the regattas: even on occasion with Festus Ferrier himself, an elaborately nautical figure in white-topped cap, blue reefer jacket, white flannel trousers with sword-like creases and buckskin shoes.

Perhaps the small page-boy liked most of all the arrival from the Smithy Croft down the road of Mrs. William Gordon and her daughter, Mrs. William Cordiner: a distinction that had to be observed with nicety.

Mrs. William Gordon had been house-tablemaid at Ardyne in the great days of old Fergus Ferrier, knew her place and her job and had trained her daughter to do likewise. They both wore bright wrappers in the morning, black dresses, starched aprons and caps in the afternoon; and only they and Jimsy were visible in the front rooms of the big house during the working day. Mrs. William Gordon had made it clear to the mistress from the first that she would work in her own way or not at all. For her poor old Mrs. Munn was a dirty old ticket, Lorna that bit of trash from the High Auchentiber bothy, and Jock Jamieson a blethering bolshie below a decent body's notice. To Jimsy she said:

"You're the only clean, professional-like body in the place. My goodness, I wonder what old Mrs. Ferrier would have said about that lot in the kitchen! She would have taken her stick to their backsides."

It passed, the phase of contentment, in a glory of warm golden days, the last settled spell of the short West Scottish summer: so brief that, even in late July, the afternoon sunlight would have a golden tinge in it. So few and well-ordered were his duties now, so little did even Festus Ferrier ask of him, to Jimsy it seemed in later years he spent hours of every day with the children in the boat in the bay or on the island, building the house he had suggested in a moment of malaise.

He would sit on a rock and watch how Beth, the woman,

her fingers fine and nimble, would arrange small stones to make what she called her oven; he saw how Billy, male if a weakling, had brought out the toy cars to people his jerry-built garage with the turning wheels of imagination. It was often with a wistful detachment that he studied those children at play in the sun by the seashore, for his view of Beth must always be clouded now by the opaque screen her father had so brutally drawn down between them. But then she would call to him to ask if he had not somewhere found a new sort of flower for the museum and he would set off among the clumps of bracken, eyes on the ground, to see if the lush growth of summer had not somewhere brought to bud a small, unexpected trifle of bloom, perhaps just a pale white or blue starlet at the base of a lichened rock.

Then they were all children on the seashore, happy in the Indian summer of their rapture, lost in a fleeting enchantment that would still be the dear dream of maturity.

The engagement was announced, Festus Ferrier's delight symbolised in a bottle of one of his less exalted ports sent down for the staff to drink the young couple's health at the kitchen table; and when it had circulated, making Lorna more foolish in manners than ever and Jock Jamieson more destructive in social comment, Mrs. William Gordon announced that there was to be a swell dinner for the gentry on the following evening, that of the Royal Firth regatta day. There would be six extra guests, old friends of both families, and she, Mrs. William Gordon, expected everybody on the staff to put their best foot forward or she would know the reason why.

"You can count me out of that nonsense!" Jock Jamieson announced.

"I would never count you in," Mrs. William Gordon briskly disposed of an irrelevance. "You haven't even the manners to take your bonnet off when there are ladies at the table. But you'll have your best pot plants ready to-morrow morning just the same."

It dawned the loveliest day of the long spell. The breeze blowing up the Firth under high-sailing clouds of laundered whiteness was sufficient for good racing, the sunshine kindly to the body. It was a grand thing, thought Jimsy, to see the *Ron* swing out of the bay in the early forenoon with even Mrs. Ferrier among its passengers, and he was only sorry that he did not sail in her, following the yachts from mark-boat to buoy in angular reaches over and about the Firth: under the gleaming pillars of lighthouses and into the mysterious mouths of the lochs.

His forenoon task, however, was to help Mrs. William Gordon and her daughter to lay the great table in the dining-room and to arrange the pot plants unwillingly brought up from the conservatory by Jock Jamieson. Mrs. William Gordon praised him for demonstrating a decorative fold of napkins which, she admitted freely, she had never seen before; the invention of it must have been after her time, she said.

By contrast the afternoon seemed to start in nullity. The breeze fell, the warmth of the forenoon turned to heat. Jimsy thought of resting, then of washing and ironing his best white jacket for the festivities; and then from his attic window he watched the children playing aimlessly with a ball on the lawn below and saw them as pathetic creatures, forgotten in the glow of Ketron's hour. Soon enough, indolent on the oars, he was rowing them over the glassy lagoon towards the island.

He was himself in no mood for children's games. Serious in professional matters, the proper conduct of the dinner was much on his mind; and something drugged in the atmosphere of the afternoon was disturbing, even portentous. He saw from his seat on a rock while the young people played in their rapt way that two classes of white-winged racing yachts lay be-calmed short of the mark-boat below the Riccar Light: pretty little slips bereft of purpose and slopping about in the tide out of Everton Bay. His weatherly eye saw a blue-grey film creep over the eastern sky against the drift of the surface wind, and at least he thought to perceive a brassy quality in the sunlight still over the islands. He knew that the fine spell was to end in thunder within hours. He guessed that the racing would be abandoned, and that the party in the *Ron* would be home early.

A stumpy little steamship went panting past close inshore, and Jimsy stood up and waved, and his signals were returned by a series of toots from the squeaky whistle on the tiny funnel set far aft.

"What does that mean, Jimsy?" Beth looked up from her play.

"A friend of mine giving you the royal salute," Jimsy laughed. "No: that's the old puffer *Thane of Cawdor*. She'll be going down to the Brickworks Quay to load."

A load of bricks for the new hydro-electric works at Kinlochaskill; at least three days of leisurely sailing northwards among the islands, putting into a quiet Highland harbour every night, hearing the song of the Gaelic again! It would be grand to be going that way.

Jimsy's reverie was broken into by the drum and wash of a faster ship's approach, and he looked northwards to see the *Ron* turn about a mile off shore to enter the bay. She must have come down the coast from Brendan way, and he had the feeling of having been caught playing truant.

"Miss Beth! Master Billy! Come along. Here's the *Ron* back again. We'd better get ashore."

The children hesitated to answer the call, and Billy was in fact in tears by the water's edge. Having tired of his imaginary garage he had gone down to the rocks there, with the ash Jimsy had fashioned into a rough rod for him and with a hook unbaited, to be a great fisherman about to pull a fat saithe or a pink rock cod out of the greeny depths beyond the line of yellow weed. His hook had caught in the tangle, however, and now he wept and would not abandon his precious possession.

"Give me that rod," and Jimsy was abrupt. "Get into the boat at once; look, the *Ron's* at her moorings already. There'll be a row if we're late."

He held the rod in his left hand and tugged viciously at the line, leaving the hook in the weed. Running across the islet he saw that the house-party was already near the slip in the dinghy. His own boat was just half-way across the bay when he heard Festus Ferrier's hail, arrogant through the thundery hush of the late afternoon.

"Ahoy there, Bell! What the devil do you think you're up to? Come ashore at once."

Jimsy checked his pace for just a moment to take in the elements of the scene, and the first thing he saw was the confession of concern and shame on the brown face of Beth in the sternsheets. Over his shoulder a split-second later he saw Mrs. Ferrier make her way from the jetty up to the house, no doubt bored with it all.

"Come ashore at once, you damned fools!" Festus Ferrier was almost dancing now, and Jimsy dug the oars into the glassy water.

What happened thereafter was just a blur of crisis and alarm. From the look on Beth's scared face and her cry of alarm, from the movements of the boat alone, Jimsy guessed swiftly that Billy, bent on showing off to his elders what a wonderful sea angler he was, had stood up on the narrow thwart in the bow and was waving the fatal length of ash about his head. There was a lurch, then a shriek, then a splash. Billy was in the water, the bubbles rising from where he had gone under.

It was nothing for Jimsy to tear off his jacket and slip overside. A couple of strokes and he got the boy on his first bounce upwards; two back, and he was punting Billy over the side of the boat while Beth tugged fiercely at the spindly arms. Calmly, as he had been taught to act in emergencies at sea, Jimsy swam round to come into the boat again over the stern, and he could hear through all his concern the crescendo of bawling from his master on the slip. There were hardly a score of strokes between him and the jetty, from which Miss Ketron and Captain Brian Horsley-Moray were now hurrying away in plain embarrassment.

The cruel and greedy hawk of Festus Ferrier's anger pounced first on his frightened children.

"Get up to the house and to hell out of here!" he yelped at them. "I'll deal with you later. And you . . ."

Master and man were alone together.

"I'm sorry this has happened, sir," Jimsy said.

"Sorry! You damn' nearly drown my son before my own eyes, and you're sorry! You make a ruddy fool of me in front of my guest, and you're sorry! I want the boat to let my guest have a bathe, and I suppose you're still ruddy well sorry! And then my daughter tells me you have the effrontery to play at damn' fool Houses out there with her sister! Sorry . . ."

Jimsy spoke through an involuntary shudder. "I've told Master Billy again and again that he mustn't climb up on the thwarts, and there was never any real danger. And I could hardly know that the Captain wanted a bathe, could I, sir?"

"Don't stand there asking me insolent questions, you under-sized little swine! Get up to the house and change, and then come down and see me in the morning-room at once. You'll be sorry all right before I'm finished with you."

In dry clothes once more, Jimsy went downstairs to the encounter almost with relish. He was fortified by a purer anger than any passion Festus Ferrier could bring against him. Having knocked and entered the morning-room, he left the next move to his enemy.

"You, Bell? Yes. You know what this means, of course?"

"Yes." And Jimsy omitted the honorific 'sir.' "I am leaving."

"You mean you're fired. Better make it first thing to-morrow morning. Jamieson can take you into Brendan. You'll get your books and wages from Miss Ketron."

His passion evaporating, he spoke in jerks and Jimsy perceived the familiar signs of the uneasiness as the façade invariably started to crack in the face of calm opposition.

"I am afraid you do not understand, Mr. Ferrier," he said in his Highland way, now dangerously sweet. "I am leaving of my own wish; I am not being dismissed."

"You have the blasted nerve . . ." This was the passion coming back on a gust.

"I have my own pride. You lose your temper over things that are no fault of mine, and then you insult me because of my size. You can keep your wages; I will send for my books. And I am going now."

Festus Ferrier stared at this phenomenon among servants. His facial muscles started to work.

"But, Bell! Let's be reasonable. The dinner party to-night . . ."

"It's not for the likes of you to tell anybody to be reasonable," Jimsy flashed back at him. "The dinner party has nothing to do with me now. I am leaving at once of my own free will."

"But you can't, Bell! I say, you can't. . . . You can't. . . . My girl, my guest. . . . Can't."

It was like the running down of a worn record on an old phonograph, and Jimsy saw the physical collapse come on the man. As once before, Festus Ferrier sank back into his chair; the left hand gestured feebly towards the open mouth and the twisted lips. Jimsy was suddenly terrified, as if he had struck his former master down. He burst in upon Miss Ketron and her betrothed in the drawing-room and raised the alarm.

He left them to do what they could and hurried upstairs to his room in the attic.   He pulled his empty suitcase from under the bed. He was out of it now. The Ferrier women and the young soldier could look after their own invalid, and a thumping down below told him of action taken in emergency. He was out of it now with a clear conscience, he kept assuring himself; they would blame him, of course, but he was out of it now.

The scutter of gravel as the doctor's car swung up the drive between the gates disturbed his defiant conviction of innocence. If Festus Ferrier were to die, he thought in his innocent alarm, they would want him as a witness. He started to pack hurriedly, and then, the gnaw of conscience still active, he slipped out of the room and along the corridor to listen at the top of the stairs for the ringing of a bell, the doctor's voice, the sound of his own name.

Not a whisper reached his ears, and he ventured down to the shadowy landing of the second floor; and there stood Beth in a shadowed corner, as if she had been waiting for him.

"What has happened, Jimsy?" she whispered.

"Your father has been taken very ill again, I'm afraid, Miss Beth."

"I know. But what about you?"

"I've got to go."

"When?"

"Now."

"Oh, I'm sorry, Jimsy; I'm terribly sorry!"

She confessed her concern in a little gulp, and even in the poor light he admired again the uplifted dark head and the straightness of the arms by her sides with which Elizabeth Ferguson Ferrier faced her many tribulations.

"Please don't worry about me, Miss Beth," Jimsy begged her.

"But where are you going?"

"I don't know."

"But Billy and I . . . We'll have no lovely games now."

"Oh, yes, you will! And please, Miss Beth, I'll have to run down and see if they want me."

"Good-bye, Jimsy," she said in a small voice.

"Good-bye, Miss Beth."

It was a poor way for friends to part; and they did not want him, these other people. He found his way down to the deserted billiard room and waited there behind the slightly open door, but all he heard was the doctor parting from Captain Horsley-Moray in the hall, saying something about being back again and bringing a nurse. Then Miss Ketron was on the phone at length, explaining, apologising to guests no longer welcome.

Jimsy got back to his room by the service stairs. He knew now where he stood. He was not wanted any more by the people in Ardyne; all except Beth had ceased to think of him. He did not grudge them that in their latest distress, nor was he sorry for himself unduly, but he had to realise that he was just wee Jimsy Bell the orphan again, baffled by still another encounter with life. Nothing for it now but to finish the packing and clear out.

He was soon ready for the road, and he stood for a while wondering if he should wear his raincoat or his heavy overcoat with his funny little soft felt hat. The overcoat would be hot on his shoulders this thundery evening, but it would also be heavy over his arm. He did not consciously work out the better compromise; the thing was to be out and away like a thief in the night.

He was looking round his little room for the last time when he saw that a small parcel had been left on the top of the chest of drawers. It was crudely enough made up with much-knotted string in a sheet of lined paper from an old exercise book, and it was addressed in sprawling block letters simply to JIMSY. Beth —but he was now in such a hurry to be away that he slipped it into his coat pocket.

Down the flights of stairs, the case weighing heavily; a dash into the cover of the rhododendrons; so into the wood of oaks, and down by the drystone dyke to the track leading southwards by the sea.

It was a full mile to the Brickworks Quay. The atmosphere was heavy with wet heat. The black slugs were out on the verges of the path between walls of unkempt bramble. It was a blessing to hear the slap of tidal wavelets on a stone beach and come out into the relative airiness of the pierhead, with only a weighhouse in red brick at its inner end to mark its status.

The master of the *Thane of Cawdor* sat on the engine-room casing of his craft, his three-decker moustache bent over an accordion from which he was manipulating a version of "The Road to the Isles." He stared and stopped at Jimsy's approach, such an unexpected figure out of the island hinterland.

"Is it yourself, Seumas?" he hailed the arrival. "Would you be looking for a passage to Ballibeg? Just so. Jock Jamieson told me you wouldn't be doing long with thon one at

Ardyne. A hard man by all accounts and headstrong, head-strong. But here you are, son, and welcome."

Calum Blue looked up at the sky and then round about him.

"There will be wan hell of a storm of thunder before mid-night," he observed, "but you and me and the *Thane* will be off for the high Hielans on the morning tide. Step on board, Jimsy, and we'll have a mug of tea."

CHAPTER FOUR

Voyage Into Exile

THE *Thane of Cawdor* made her way laboriously northwards, the exhaust panting up the little funnel aft as if
her small engines were in the last stages of cardiac stress.
The craft was indeed down to the marks with her load of bricks,
and a traveller less experienced in seafaring matters than Jimsy
Bell would have been much alarmed by the sparse footage
of freeboard between the Hebridean waters and the long
hatch on which he liked to lie during spells of fitful western
sunlight.

Punching the strong tides of the Firth of Lorne, the *Thane
of Cawdor* was doing well at three knots; at six or even seven
on the flood, with a flying jib up to help her on and check her
inclination to yaw, she was fairly flying in the proud estimation
of her master, Calum Blue. Jimsy could always be distracted
on such occasions from his own worries by delight in the sight
of the skipper leaning out of the wheelhouse window, his black
pipe hard against his cheek under the triple moustaches, and
surveying the swooping gulls and perhaps a couple of Fleet-
wood trawlers heading south with a most distinct air of
superior indifference.

"I wouldn't swop with the captain of the *Queen Mary* himself," was one of Calum's standard assertions over his second
or third glass in any one of the inns that were for him as seamarks on his voyages.

It was one of the pleasures of sailing with this Highland
skipper of the old school that, once through the Canal and into
the western seas, the timetables of owners in distant Glasgow
ceased to matter, the wheels of commerce perceptibly to slow

down. Calum had a genius for so plotting the day's run that he could come to anchor or tie up for the night in a harbour where there was certainty of hospitality and good fellowship ashore. Jimsy could chuckle to remember a *ceilidh* in a croft house near Kilchoan in which after song and *puirst-a-bheul* and dancing, it was nearly dawn before Calum himself came to end an hour-long tale in the Gaelic about a Fairy Piper and the King's Daughter.

It was a world fantastically and beautifully different from that of Ardyne: as different from the service of the Ferriers' table as the hash and boiled herrings, potatoes and strong tea he cooked and served on enamelled ware from the galley of the *Thane of Cawdor*, and he had much, if not complete, comfort in its timelessness. This was an easy life of uncritical companionship, of labour taken at its proper value, the human values transcendant. It passed in a realm of loveliness, the rain-shot sunlight of the West falling on dappled mainland peaks and bringing up the fierce tan of those hundreds of islands that make it seem as if, once upon a time, a giant waded those green waters and gleefully scattered over them the stones from his pouch.

He tried to forget the past, to ignore the future, but the feelings of failure and frustration never completely left him.

"Man, Jimsy, but you're terrible donsy whiles!" Calum Blue upbraided him. "Take your holiday. There was never," he added cryptically, "much good come out of the Lowlands."

"I'm having a grand holiday, Calum," Jimsy protested, "but I've still got to find a job at the end of it."

"Och, that!" protested his friend, taking a hand off the wheel to make a gesture that indicated the largeness of the world and the wealth of opportunity it contained. "A smart wee chap like you!"

Jimsy accepted the reproof within himself, but he would worry all the more to know why he was so worried. He had learned that a passion for order was part of his make-up; he knew only too clearly that one of his deepest needs was to forget that God had made him so small. But that was not all,

and what the rest was he could not fathom as yet. Nor would
there leave him his thoughts of a slip of a dark young girl,
sobbing on a landing at Ardyne, though why he could mean
anything to her in the realities of adult life, or she to him—
that was a question beyond him. It would not, however, leave
him.

The *Thane of Cawdor* was well through the Canal before he
could decently look into the parcel done up so pathetically in
exercise paper. They were tied up at Bellanoch that first
evening, awaiting a place in the ocean basin, and Calum Blue
and his crew had taken to their bunks. He had the wheelhouse
to himself as he opened the package, and when he saw what it
contained he was glad to be alone with tears very near his
eyes and upon his spirit the agony of something like home-
sickness.

The child had folded within tissue paper three ten-shilling
notes and nine brass threepenny bits, no doubt what was left
of her birthday presents and her savings. A note in her un-
formed hand read: *Dear Jimsy, I wish I had more to send you,
but I hope this will help, and I hope you will not be silly and proud
about it. It was all I could think of. Love from Beth.* Within the
note she had put some pale sprigs of myosotis.

Love; and forget-me-not. Of course, that "Love from
Beth" was only the conventional phrase of a girl-child, and
the forget-me-nots were but a symbol of their harmless
community of interest in wild flowers. Even so, the sense of
her thoughtfulness came over him like a warm wave; they
had had their own secret. He thought carefully of how he
would find an opportunity in the crowded little ship of locking
the parcel away at the bottom of his case. All his life he would
owe young Beth thirty-two shillings and three pence, and so
much of affection and gratitude as well.

It made him ask himself where he thought he was going
now, to what obscure target his panic flight from Ardyne was
leading him. His spirits were low when, on the afternoon of
the fourth day, the blunt nose of the *Thane of Cawdor* was
turned off course and, her master disdaining the help of

Admiralty Chart No. 2496, felt his way up the short length of Loch Ballibeg, almost smelling his way between the poles that marked the winding channel, crosses on those to port, circles on those to starboard. A heavy shower with a sting in it was blowing in from between the Small Isles and Skye.

"There you are then, Jimsy," said Calum Blue, having stopped his engines and backed a trifle to check the *Thane of Cawdor* before a community consisting mainly of one large whitewashed hotel building and a low row of cottages along a stony foreshore. "Donald will row you ashore. Man, I wouldn't mind casting anchor for the night and putting in an hour or two with old Magnus Cameron. You'll know him, Jimsy? A fine man and jovial, jovial. But there's a wedding up-bye at Morar to-morrow, and the girl's father will be looking to me to tell a story at the *ceilidh* to-night."

"Not another word out of your mouth, son," he checked Jimsy's speech of thanks. "A pleasure for us all. If you was ever looking for the trip South, you going to a new situation or the likes of that, just you pass the word to the agent at Mallaig, and we'll be in to pick you up as soon as you could say knife. *Beannachd leat*, blessings upon you!"

After the warmth of the crowded life on board the *Thane of Cawdor* the hamlet of Ballibeg seemed an abandoned outpost of a former civilisation. To set foot on the mainland again was in itself an act of return to servitude, and he really thought with the unreason of sentimentality that the best life for him was with the uninhibited, undemanding free traders of the western seas. Not a soul did he meet on the long pull over the Morrach, the best part of two miles against the rain, and him burdened with his case and coats. The mist hung like a flabby curtain of cotton wool dropped to the very roots of the hills; the wayside ditches gurgled with running water, and only a few Highland cows and their calves, picking a living among peaty hags and groves of bog myrtle, watched his passage through their fringes, and with indifference.

Over the crest of the hill, however, he saw that it was lightening in the West, with gashes of blue in the clouds about

the peaks of Rum, and there was a glimmering on the slate
roofs of the houses in what had for years been all his world—
a colony of twelve-acre crofts running from near the main
road down to the verges of a wide bay: each cottage the spit
of its neighbour in the almost penitential design imposed by
Government. It looked bleak and remote in the grudging light
of late afternoon, but Jimsy recalled with warmth the day
when he knew every soul in each of the dozen croft-houses,
when he walked to school and back with twenty other boys and
girls, and played with them on the silver sands and in and out
of boats among the off-shore reefs; then with the interesting,
urban children of the summer tenants. . . .

That was long ago, however. The personal destiny over
which he had had no control had directed him to service in the
big hotels and houses of the Lowlands. His tenure of a corner
of this West Highland bailiwick had been on sufferance. As he
turned down the puddled track that led to the holding known
officially as 7, Morrach Crofts, he suddenly realised with a cold
feeling in his stomach that he might, reasonably enough, be
turned away. He was a man without an abiding place; his
trust now was in the Gael and his ways of doing.

He dropped his wet things in the tiny porch of the square,
harled house, and it was but a step then into the kitchen where,
mumbling to herself in the Gaelic, sat an aged woman with a
black mutch about her head. She heard his step, but the eyes
she raised towards the door were blind.

"Is it you, Granny?" he addressed her softly in the Gaelic.
"This is Jimsy here."

"Seumas, Seumas! *O mo chridhe!* Come to my side till I
touch you."

He stepped to the fire and bent his head near the hawk-
featured, ivory-hued face of the old woman. She put up a hand
and ran it down his features from brow to chin, her fingers
light.

"Pretty boy! Pretty boy!" she murmured in the English,
of which she had few other words; then in the Gaelic again:
"You will be hungry. You will be tired."

"Not so much, Granny. Wait you, and I'll make you a fine cup of tea and cook what there is in the house. Is my Uncle Murdo about?"

"Och, he will be in the barn, that one, blowing on his chanter when he might be milking the cow!" said the old woman of her son-in-law.

Murdo Mackenzie had been his foster-father. For his infinitely dearer foster-mother, born Caristiona MacLeod, he did not ask. She was away in the asylum at Inverness, driven demented by the loss of two sons in the minesweepers off North Africa in the late middle years of a life of hard work and monotony. Now her husband, lost in his own confused world, played the chanter in the barn while there was work to do about the croft, however little. As he passed round the gable of the house Jimsy could hear the reedy strain that seemed to express a most dolorous resignation.

His foster-father came to the doorway when it was darkened by Jimsy's shadow. He was a burly man in fisherman's blue jersey and trousers, and the heavy moustache under the shapeless tweed cap was nearly white over an auburn base.

"It's yourself, Jimsy," he said without emotion. "We had your postcard from Crinan. Yes, yes. You'll be with us for a while?"

"Just a holiday, Uncle Murdo," Jimsy fenced lightly, banking on the deliberate incuriosity of the sensitive Gael. "And how are things about the croft?"

"Middling, just middling. There was no summer letting this year, and how that was I do not know."

But Jimsy knew. To vacate the house for the people from the city, to advertise, to answer letters—these were exercises beyond Murdo Mackenzie now. The latter went on:

"It was a poor spring we had here, wet, wet; and the young beasts made a slow start. But you'll be here for the harvest, Seumas, and if you have a minute to spare now you could be taking the dog and bringing in the cow. Yes, yes. It is a hard life."

Jimsy might have smiled to himself, but he was too much

worried for that. His Uncle Murdo's evasive lethargy clashed
with his own harnessed impulses towards action, and he was
in that condition a little bit afraid of life. Oh, he knew fine
there were folk in the Lowlands to talk of Highland laziness,
Highland defeatism, but he, Jimsy Bell, who had been reared
in this place, knew it was more than that. It was the complete
acceptance of defeat, and a defeat inevitable in the given
physical circumstances, with an ancient and stubborn pride
vexing the outlines of the problem.

Just the same, he enjoyed bringing in the cow, a black and
white Ayrshire called Morag, and he delighted to see the young
dog, with the splendid Sassunach name of Prince, expressing
joy in a mazy arabesque of swoops at high speed about the
pasture, with many glad and harmless barkings at the three
young beasts and many pretended snaps at the indifferent heels
of the female animal. It was like a return to childhood, almost
to the womb, to lean his head against the beast's warm flanks
and pull at the udders and hear the milk hiss into the pail,
smelling richly of clover.

He even enjoyed himself making a meal for his elders,
though he could reflect sourly that it was mostly of scraps of
Canadian bacon fried with bread brought by rail from Glasgow.
He would himself have gone down to the tidal estuary of the
dark stream that flowed out of the Moss and, with his feet
feeling in the mud, lifted out with his toes three fat, fresh
flounders, but Uncle Murdo could not even bestir himself to
go down to the rocks at the mouth of the burn and take a
couple of large saithe with a penny fly.

Then, when he had washed up, the kitchen must be cleared
while Granny somehow loosened her garments and hoisted
herself into the bed by the fire; and Jimsy went out with his
foster-father to the door. The latter allowed that it had the
makings of a fine evening and that he would, maybe, take a
bit of a walk over the Morrach; and Jimsy knew that he would
be shaping for the bar of the big, white hotel by the shore at
Ballibeg. Himself, he said that he would take a walk down to

the sands, and his whistle brought Prince to dance and bark about him in a frenzy of delight.

It was but five minutes' walk down the length of the small-holding to the sea, and Jimsy saw the three young beasts in poor enough shape for the autumn sales at Fort William, as Murdo Mackenzie had morosely confessed; saw how broken gates had been replaced by the ends of old iron beds, loosely tied to the posts with hairy lengths of stacking rope; and saw that while the couple of acres of oats grew green and stout enough, the best field of all, the sandy one behind the dunes above high-water mark, still carried on its surface a thick coating of sea wrack but had never been ploughed—as if the foster-father had dramatically renounced as utterly impossible the making of a living out of twelve acres in such a climate.

Calling Prince from his idiotic chase of seagulls over the silver sands, Jimsy turned back towards the small, harled house, its roof of slates dark against a fantastic light, almost heliotrope, that the setting sun was conjuring from the face of naked rock above and beyond the Moss. He suddenly thought how strange it would be to bring young Beth here and say: "This is where I was nurtured, this the background about which you were so curious. Is it in the least like Ardyne?"... And yet, his eyes on the dark flow of the stream out of the Moss, it came into his mind, brooding more deeply than usual, that there was really not so much between the great seaside villa on the Firth and the shabby croft by the western seas. They both belonged to social worlds and economies outmoded—the world symbolised by the empty, rusting cans along high-water mark all round the bay.

He found his bed early, even as the uncurtained window of the upstairs room was taking the light of sunset reflected from that cliff-face beyond the Moss, and he lay long awake, blaming himself for having returned in panic folly to a blind alley. He saw himself going like Uncle Murdo, down into joyless surrender, useless, unproductive; and he jibbed, as a horse against the bit, against the prospect. There must be a door out of his prison, but where it lay and where he might find the key he could not think; and he was still awake when, in the half-darkness, the barking of Prince from the barn marked the return of Murdo Mackenzie from over the hill.

2

Bereft of most of his powers, including those of bluster and command, Festus Ferrier lay in the principal guest bedroom of Ardyne. The housemaid's pantry outside was now a dispensary in which much glassware stood on an enamelled tray under a spotless napkin, while less elegant coverings hid from sight the grimmer apparatus of the sickroom. The dressing-room had become the sleeping place of his constant attendant, Nurse Nairn.

This was a fresh, stocky, red-haired girl from Easter Ross, almost alarmingly clean in her person. As such, she had from the moment of her coming disturbed the near-slattern condition into which the domestic affairs of the place had fallen. For all save one of the three females native to the house she was the Other Woman and one vested with intolerable powers to command and complain.

Within Etty Nairn's experience of private nursing the hostility of the resident womenfolk must be taken as a professional hazard, and she was blessedly free of the accidie of introspection. Even as she thoughtfully prepared to sterilise a syringe, thinking of the injection she must make at noon into the person of her patient, she was being discussed among other things by his wife and elder daughter while the Lammas rains slashed against the window-panes of the morning-room in which they sat.

"Is Uncle Finlay coming by the afternoon or the evening boat?" Ketron asked lazily.

"Afternoon," her stepmother replied. "I suppose we'll have to give him dinner. But thank goodness he's staying at the Brendan Arms!"

"Yes. It would be terrible if Daddy got to know he was in the house. But I don't suppose that woman would let him near him."

"She won't let anybody near him!" Elaine Ferrier confessed her jealousy of another female's intimacy with her own. "Any more trouble this morning?"

"Oh, just the usual! A row with Mrs. Munn about her own breakfast. Then she was positively blazing with Lorna—something about Daddy's tray being untidy. I must say Lorna's trays are apt to be untidy."

"I know, but she needn't upset the whole house. You'd think she owned the place."

"Yes, and that young ass Beth hangs about her all day."

"Yes, I must speak to her," said Mrs. Ferrier, as it were scribbling a note in faint pencil on the fluffy tablets of her memory.

Beth had just a moment or two before arrived buoyantly in the pantry turned dispensary. Nurse Nairn had become her heroine. The child had fallen in love at first sight with the lovely headdress in starched linen, with the spotless apron and cuffs over the bright-blue wrapper, with Nurse's red hair—above all, with the winged badge of office above it. But it was the handsome symbol of so much more: of a young woman who seemed almost to smell clean as the very first condition of one who knows and respects her job. Etty Nairn was for Beth only the second acquaintance of her life with ravishing special knowledges beyond the range of her own people. She was another like Jimsy Bell, who knew about wild flowers and fish and boats, and could turn cartwheels.

The young woman and the young girl chattered happily while Nurse, mildly abstracted, checked over her bottles and pillboxes and Beth considered the fascinating paraphernalia of healing, her fingers itching to open boxes and count tablets and relate the numbers to the treatment of the patient next door, of whose condition in his majestic aloofness she knew so much more than the two grown women who canvassed his and her and Nurse's habits in the room below.

"Beth!" cried Nurse suddenly, scolding. "You wee faggot! My best hypodermic! What do I keep telling you? A nurse never fingers and fiddles about with her instruments. Wait till you get into a training hospital and get a room to dust. Yes, just dust. One speck left on the leg of a table, and you'll hear from the Sister Tutor. Get it to do all over again. Pass me that bottle of surgical spirit."

"Sorry, Nurse! I forgot." They were good friends. "I say, would you like to come and have a row round the bay this afternoon, if it clears?"

"Nothing I'd like better, dear, if Miss Ketron can give me an hour off."

"Oh, Gollikens, no! She can't. Uncle Finlay's coming for tea and dinner. Isn't that rotten?"

"Do you not like your Uncle Finlay?"

"I don't know," the child replied. "I suppose I've seen him, but I can't remember. It's all about Daddy, of course."

"Don't know your uncle!" Etty Nairn exclaimed and abruptly left it at that, remembering that there were many more shadows in the background of this pretty, eager young girl than she had been able to guess at as yet.

It was nearly thirty years, reflected Finlay Ferrier as the brake bore him down the shore road, since he had set foot in Ardyne, and then only to bury his old mother: Festus at the head of the coffin, himself at the foot and not a mite of sympathy between them even in that hour of farewells and emotion recollected. Festus had made his usual mess of things in India and had settled down with a rich wife to be Head of the Family, and he, young Finlay, must go back to the foundries, fighting to keep them alive and get an Honours B.Sc. at the same time. It was a dashed queer thought that the next trip might be to put poor old Festus away beside his mother, where, when you came to think of it, he had always belonged.

Finlay was in no mood now to enjoy the visit; it was another day of valuable working time lost. Trust Festus to marry two idiots of women in succession and then fail to teach them the first damn' thing about managing their own affairs.

That silly letter of Elaine's: could he come and give them his help and advice, things were so difficult? Why not go to their confounded lawyers? But Finlay Ferrier was at once a decent man and a man who hated muddle, and here he was, inwardly cursing, but rather looking forward to getting the sharp knife of his managerial sort of mind into the heart of a problem.

His approach to Ardyne was patiently waited for and closely observed by a young girl who had taken up her position on the low sea wall opposite the gates. As Jock Jamieson slowed down and swung out towards her to turn, Beth Ferrier, careful not to wave and attract his attention, had a good, feminine look at this uncle of hers in the front seat beside the driver. It slightly startled her to see that he did not look in the least like Daddy. He was taller, stouter, fairer; until she could meet him he must remain a mystery; and with feline patience and cunning, praying that Billy would not come and spoil everything, she dedicated the rest of the afternoon to the single purpose of bringing an encounter about.

She was too shrewd to follow Uncle Finlay into the house. There would be an awful row with Mummy and Ketron if she started showing off, as they would say; "always got to be in the picture, I suppose," was Ketron's standing jibe. So now the girl took a devious way through the shrubbery that divided the garden from the lawn and climbed into the ample fork of an old red beech that had been a favourite hiding-place for years, favoured by her for its command of almost every approach to the house. She had prudently stocked her eyrie with a slab of chocolate and *Emil and the Detectives.*

Neither woman of the house was in the hall to greet Finlay Ferrier, but he was pleased to see a red-headed young woman in nurse's uniform approach him with a fresh smile.

"Mr. Finlay Ferrier? Mrs. Ferrier and Miss Ketron will be down in a moment. Will you step into the morning-room?"

"Thank you, Nurse. It was my own home once upon a time, you know. And how's your patient?"

"Just as usual in cases like that, I'm afraid."

"No prospects?"

"I think you should ask Dr. Robertson about that," said Nurse Nairn primly. "But he does say to us all it may be five weeks, five months, five years."

"Well, *you* won't have to wait five years, Nurse," declared Finlay Ferrier gallantly.

He was delighted to see her blush. This was his sort of girl, he said to himself—clean, straight and none the worse if she had a bit of a temper. The entry of his sister-in-law and his niece pointed a contrast. They were so darned lost and languid, to his way of thinking. The compliments over, he took them in his best boardroom manner. He hardly realised it, but he was the typical 20th century slave of time. The night in a rotten hotel in Brendan, the early morning steamer to-morrow, a dash by car from the mainland pier to the airport, and a conference at the Ministry of Supply at two o'clock. . . .

"Now, Elaine. Let's try to make a list of all the problems, and then we'll think out the best ways of solving them."

"I'm not sure they're exactly *problems*, Finlay."

Then why the devil did you bring me down here? he wanted to ask indignantly. Just for a nice cosy chat? Don't try to bluff me.

"Lots of problems, if you ask me," he countered in his business man's way, the product of much dealing with fallible man in the mass. "And the first is, to be perfectly frank, poor old Festus's expectation of life. That's what you mean, isn't it?"

"But they won't say! Doctor and Nurse both tell you the same thing. ' Five weeks, five months, five years.' What help is that?"

This was Ketron, almost peevish, and her stepmother added with a heave of emotion "It's all so disheartening."

With a hardening of his spirit Finlay perceived something of the truth about these two women. For them his brother Festus was already dead; their concern was to count the weeks, months or years that might pass before the last cinder of life flickered to extinction within his useless frame.

"What can they say?" he asked. "I can only tell you that

it's a prudent rule to budget for the extreme case. Take it at five years, then. The running of the house just to begin with."

"But Brian has been posted to Aden!"

This was Ketron again, almost on a scream, and this was it—Ketron's fashionable marriage, five bridesmaids, an archway of swords and a picture in the *Tatler*.

"Whatever happens," announced Finlay Ferrier heavily, "you can fly or take a ship to Aden and marry your boy out there. Scores of girls do it every year."

"But I wouldn't know how to manage. And poor Mummy!"

"You'll manage all right. But I'd like to get this housekeeping business straightened out first of all. I don't suppose your servants are up to much, are they?"

The fork of the oldest and friendliest red beech presses hard on even the plump bottom of childhood, and after an hour in her seclusion Beth was glad to pocket her sweets and her book and slither to the ground. Her eye warily open for any sign of Billy's appearance, she made an elaborate circuit about the evergreens on the perimeter of the lawn and went to earth again on a carpet of twigs and rabbit droppings under a clump of rhododendrons so huge that, within her private world, it held the position of the fabled banyan tree. The front door of the house was still under her observation; and surely these grown-ups had talked a lot and drunk enough tea.

The speculation was soundly based. Even as she framed it her Uncle Finlay crushed out an unwanted cigarette and rose behind the tea table, saying in his chairman's way

"Well, I think that's about the lot, Elaine. I still think there should be a man in the house, though I suppose that little nurse is competent enough. It's a pity you lost that young chap—what was his name? Now I'd like to have a walk round and perhaps see the young children."

"Oh, they'll be kicking about the garden somewhere," said Ketron.

She did not like Uncle Finlay, and he thought poorly of her and her dripping discourtesy. He was very happy to come out alone to the top of the steps and fill his pipe and look across the familiar lawn. He saw that it was only roughly scythed nowadays, and he reflected that the old man would have a fit if he could see it. The old man, of course, knew nothing about the shortage of labour and the new scales of taxation. No: houses like Ardyne were finished, and the fact should be admitted, but what hope was there of getting a couple of dizzy females like Elaine and Ketron to understand? Getting mixed up in their affairs was going to be a confounded nuisance.

He had reached the southern end of the terrace when he saw a slim, young, dark girl come from behind a large clump of rhododendrons, apparently unaware of his near presence. She seemed to be absorbed in the book in her hands.

"Hoi!" he called to her in his forthright way, and she approached him warily. He thought she looked a nice, bright kid in her grey shorts and yellow jumper over the sweet curves of her near-maturity. Her virginal loneliness touched him, who was childless.

"Are you Uncle Finlay?" she asked demurely.

"Yes, and you must be Beth. Nice to meet you, Beth. What are you doing now?"

"I was just going to take the boat for a row round the bay. Would you like to come for a row round the bay, Uncle Finlay? Look, it's clearing up beautifully!"

"Nothing I'd like better, my dear! Man, it's years since . . ."

The special advantage of persuading Uncle Finlay into the boat was that there would be no interference by Billy. Ever since he had toppled into cold, salt water Billy had suffered from nightmares and could hardly bring himself to cross the shore road. Beth brought the boat in on the running line and held the bow while Finlay Ferrier, awkwardly enough, clambered overside and sank with a bump into the sternsheets. The girl turned the craft with a deft pull on one oar and a check on the other.

"You can certainly handle a boat, Beth," her uncle allowed handsomely. "Who taught you?"

"Jimsy Bell."

"That was the lad who was a servant here for a bit?"

"Yes. He knew all about boats and wild flowers and things. If Billy hadn't been a silly ass and tumbled into the water . . ."

"He left in a bit of a hurry, I'm told," said Finlay Ferrier with what he believed to be subtlety. "I wonder where he went to?"

"I don't know."

He was shrewd enough to perceive that her sullen profession of ignorance was the mark of a personal frustration. When you had been dealing with typists and tracers for thirty years on end, you learned to know something about those funny little points on which females were so oddly sensitive. He let her row on. She turned the boat to skirt the inner shore of the island.

"We used to play out here," said Beth, the line of her thought obvious. "You'd never guess how many varieties of wild flowers Jimsy spotted on that wee island. We started to build a house, and a museum."

"A bit early, surely," the uncle jested heavily. "Which reminds me, Beth. We'll have to start thinking about what we're going to do about you."

"I'm going to be a nurse," the girl announced a firm decision.

"Yes. A good idea. Or you could make it a doctor," Finlay Ferrier pondered with interest the first bit of sense he had heard out of the mouth of any Ferrier female in two hours. "But you're going to boarding school first, my girl."

"Oh, blow! I thought so. That's about all Mummy and Ketron can think about. Get the kid off to boarding school. Did _you_ know, Uncle Finlay, that a girl can start as a cadet nurse at sixteen nowadays? She can be a proper S.R.N. when she's twenty-one."

"Fair enough, Beth. Yes, fair enough. But you'll be a better nurse with a School Certificate or something of that sort behind you."

"I knew it!" said the young girl, apparently addressing her right-hand oar with resignation.

"No, I mean it, dear. I'd like to help. I'd like you to know," he almost stammered, "that if you're ever a bit bothered about things, or feel you're not getting on . . . I'd like you to know that I'll always be about somewhere. I wish you'd start by coming to stay with your Aunt Helen and me for a week or two."

A good kid, with guts and purpose. He felt an almost parental pride in the fact that the old fighting spirit of the Ferriers was coming out in this girl.

"I'd love that, Uncle Finlay. If they'll let me away . . ."

"I'll see that they let you away. Don't worry about that."

There was this about Finlay Ferrier, thought Jock Jamieson as he drove him back to Brendan late that evening: he didn't mind sitting beside the driver and having a bit of a yarn to pass the time; not like His Nibs, who tucked himself as far away from his workers as he could.

"Jimsy Bell!" he repeated in answer to a suspiciously leading question. "The best worker they've had in that house for donkey's years, and they'll never get the likes of him again."

"Cleared out pretty suddenly, didn't he?"

"Do you wonder, Mr. Ferrier?" Jock carefully avoided the use of the debasing 'sir.' "I don't know what they told you inside, but I was working at the foot of the garden and saw the whole thing. The wee boy, he falls out the boat; Jimsy goes in after him; then your brother fair losses his head, with Miss Ketron and the young sodger there, and pitches into the laddie something fearful. I'm sorry for any man that's ill, but he brought the shock on himself: no doubt about that."

"Yes," Finlay Ferrier allowed slowly, adding casually: "Any idea where the young fellow went to?"

"Not a sausage."

The thin lips closed, but the managing director of Ferrier Foundries had had much experience of dealings with the Scottish shop steward and had a sneaking respect for the defensive, if sometimes truculent, attitudes of the type. He waited until Jock started to slow down for the thirty-mile limit before saying casually:

"I could have put him in the way of a good job." And Jock negotiated his way among a clutch of cars thoughtlessly parked outside a sea-front hotel before proceeding as cautiously as the vehicle under his control.

"He was a queer wee chap—Jimsy Bell I mean. Never talked about himself. Told me once he had neither father nor mother, but he could talk the Gaelic like hey-ma-nanny, and I kind o' got a kind o' notion that he was mebbe one o' these boarded-out children: you know, the kind Glasgow Corporation sends out by the dozen to be brought up by poor folk in the Highlands."

"It wouldn't be difficult to check up on that."

"No. And if you're dead keen to find the boy, there's a man called Calum Blue, skipper of a wee puffer called the *Thane of Cawdor*. . . . But here's you at your hotel, mister."

Jock did not refuse the ten-shilling note the capitalist slipped into his hand.

3

The large whitewashed building which was the chief architectural feature of the hamlet of Ballibeg was what it seemed to be, a West Highland hotel. It bore no splendid name nor carried the arms of a chieftain, though its proprietor never ceased to wish that it did. It was just the Ballibeg Hotel or, in the native phrase of such as Murdo Mackenzie, the Inns, its surprising size in such a place a monument to the splendour of the coaching days and of more recent times when rich industrial gentlemen liked to feel they could pass their fishing holidays in what, with the stag's head above the entrance, might very well pass for a landed proprietor's shooting lodge.

Murdo Mackenzie would certainly not have recognised the familiar Inns in the appeal that, from 1946 onwards but with diminishing frequency, appeared in the more expensive London newspapers and countrified weeklies, thus:

WHERE 'LAUGHTER PUTS THE LEAP UPON THE LAME.'
Enjoy Highland hospitality on country house standards
at Ballibeg Hotel, Inverness-shire, on the Road to the
Isles. Sea and brown trout fishing. Rough shooting can
be arranged. Peat fires. Highland cuisine. Terms from
Resident Host
                    Major Athelstan Persse, D.S.O., R.M. (retd.)

Now on a wet afternoon of September some six years after
he had issued his first hopeful advertisement, Major Athelstan
Persse snored abominably in the only armchair in a small
room, at the inner end of the entrance lobby, labelled OFFICE—
PRIVATE. On a swivel-chair at a roll-top desk within the same
crowded chamber, two cushions raising his body to writing
level, sat a young man of small stature and surprisingly good
looks: smooth black hair above a well-moulded nose and
cheeks as soft and smooth as a girl's.

Jimsy Bell, profiting by his studies in the science of book-
keeping for caterers, was in the act of trying to clean up the
accounts of this lodging on the road to the isles. He had
learned that in the business of hotel management the first
concern must always be the actual condition of stock in hand
as against the quantities and values in the books; and now he
was puzzled to know why there should be so many disparities
in the records of the Ballibeg Hotel, especially in the Bar
accounts. Perhaps his own arithmetic was not so good, Jimsy
allowed, but he was moved to speak over his shoulder to the
man who slumbered in the armchair behind.

"I simply can't get it right, Major. It looks to me that we're
hundreds of pounds out."

Waking up with a start, Major Athelstan Persse made a
sort of interrogative noise like a bear disturbed after a glut of
honey. It sounded like a guttural *Worsht?* behind a snore, and
then it was immediately followed by the lucid, gentlemanly
assurance:

"Just carry on by yourself, Bell. You know all about that

sort of thing. What we really want to do is have another smack at those basking sharks. Big money in sharks."

He returned to slumber, his heavy breathing rhythmically puffing out of the heavy jowls of a face in the process of being coarsened by whisky drinking. It had been a fine face not so long ago, and Jimsy studied it for a moment with a look in which contempt and pity were strangely mingled. It was still another symbol of his own failure.

He saw in Athelstan Persse the victim of a common illusion and as much the victim of West Highland conditions as Murdo Mackenzie. How many gallant officers of H.M. Forces, mostly romantic Englishmen, had not dreamed of setting up the superior guest-house, run by a gentleman for gentlefolk, hypothecating their small fortunes and their gratuities and their futures in bank overdrafts, in the vision, so ravishing as seen from within the perimeter at Anzio, of an existence at once courtly and profitable, decorated with salmon rods and gun dogs, and a bit of shooting with the local laird as befitted their rank and station? How many had not thought of the Highlands as the land of heart's desire, far from the Underground and the new taxation, only to find it wet, costly in the mere detail of transport charges, peopled by a silent folk without any great love for the feudal assumptions?

Jimsy had heard much of Major Persse in particular from the people of the district, the defeated enjoying the spectacle of the incomer's defeat. He had started by being haughty and military, they complained, and the young men and girls from the croft houses would not stay with him—"as if he was Lochiel himself." He had started by turning away the hikers and casuals of the new generation. Then the railway station on the old West Highland line was closed, and the drivers of the buses would not halt, just to be bossed and overcharged by a Sassunach soldier.

The local lairds were London bankers and Midlands industrialists who occupied their lodges for six weeks in the year and were not impressed by ex-officers in trade nor even by the Companionship of the Distinguished Service Order. And then the poor soul must fall into another illusion and desperately sink the last of his credit in the hunting of the basking shark.

And now the major snored while Jimsy nibbled the end of his pencil and still could not strike an even approximately healthy balance in the books. He shook his head. The job was one for a chartered accountant, and that, he supposed morosely, might expose a bankruptcy if not trouble in the Courts with the Excise. He called himself a fool for having taken this job, and what was it when you tried to work it out—receptionist, cashier, assistant manager or plain handyman?

He left the major sleeping in bliss induced and went out into the hall with its old-fashioned hatstand and a motoring map of Scotland dating from 1921 and yellowing. As he stood, turning over the thick pages of the visitors' book without interest, there broke into his understanding, coming apparently from a room upstairs, a most dolorous plucking of strings, hesitantly enunciating a melody in a minor key. A foreign visitor would have rightly assumed that an unskilled person was toying with a primitive instrument. To Jimsy it meant merely that Oona, the major's wife, was off again in one of her Celtic rhapsodies, her long, unkempt hair drooping over the clarsach, the plangent but unsubtle harp of Gaelic minstrelsy.

He disappeared with purposeful speed into the smoke-room, its air heavy with the stenches of leather and yesterday's tobacco. Professionally he ran a finger across the glass top of one of the tables and saw what he had expected, that neither of the girls had got round to the place with a duster, but he relieved his feelings a little by throwing up one of the windows.

From this chamber he crossed a passage to the dining-room, bright within high windows overlooking the head of the loch but fusty in its turn with the stenches of fatty food turned cold and sour. Here, however, Bridget Cameron had at least laid the tables for dinner—three places at the window tables in all in this expanse: two for the Burdens, the rapt, uncritical honeymoon couple from South Shields, one for M. Etienne

Delcours who, black-bearded and black-cloaked, scoured the countryside during the day for material for a *discours* on the adventures of Charles Edward Stuart and spent the evenings writing interminable notes in purple ink and eccentric script on paper of shoddy texture.

Jimsy noted with vague approval that Bridget had even set a third table for four possible casuals, but it was more an act of pious aspiration than one of faith. He picked up the dinner menu he had himself typed after lunch and considered it unhappily.

Scotch Broth
Potage a la Reine
Fried Fillet of Sole
Roast Leg of Lamb & Mint Sauce
New Potatoes and Peas
Glace Vanille
Biscuits and Cheese
Coffee—1/- extra

"Highland cuisine," he quoted to himself in a sardonic mutter, knowing all about the canned soups and peas, the imported mutton, the blocks of ice in a refrigerated container from London and the mass-produced cheese from Canada. Again he relieved his impatience a little by throwing up two more windows and seeing with pleasure that the early autumn afternoon was failing, but hearing with less delight the twanging of the harp upstairs and now the voice of Oona, a clotted contralto, holding forth in one of the oldest of all songs

Tha mi sgith 's mi leam fhin,
Buain a rainich, buain a rainich . . .

Her Gaelic, based on some strange phonetic version, hurt his ears; and why indeed should Oona Persse, whose natural intonations were those of the old Anglo-India and

Roedean, walk deliberately into the twilight and feel unhappy, pulling bracken?

Deploring the sourness that fermented within his own person, Jimsy went out of doors by the back, only to be distressed again by the untidiness of the premises out there. The courtyard of any hotel is apt to be less attractive than its cocktail bar in chromium and three-ply wood, but that of the Ballibeg Hotel seemed to the young man quite intolerably slattern in its huddle of empty oil drums, beer barrels, crates, cartons and broken crockery. The refuse bins had not been emptied for long enough, and his country-wise eyes discerned that a large colony of rats was living well on the droppings about them. It was only a daub in the corner of the picture that Major Persse's old Vauxhall, its paintwork much flaked with rusty patches, now reclined like a scolded spaniel on two flat back tyres.

He was surprised to hear somebody moving within the public bar, a low-browed chamber fashioned out of an old harness-room, but from the clatter and bump of bottles and crates he realised that Charlie Cram had started early to prepare for the Saturday evening trade—Cheerful Charlie Cram, as he liked to describe himself, now singing in contrast to Oona's more impassioned piece, something from the Harry Lauder canon.

> *I cuddled her, hur-ur-ur-ur!*
> *She cuddled me, e-ee-ee!*
> *For I met a bonny lassie on the Portobello Pier . . .*

Passing into the bar by the back door Jimsy was greeted heartily.

"Hallo, son! How's tricks? Help the blind, you look as if you'd swallowed a can of paraffin!"

"So would you," Jimsy laughed, "if you could only see your own bar accounts."

"Nuthin' on me, boy! Nuthin' on me! You've got the chits signed proper for what you dole out, and there's the cash register for the sales. You're pinnin' no hanky-panky on me, brother."

Cheerful Charlie Cram was a plumper, heartier edition of Jock Jamieson. His loud ebullience, his tricks of glottal speech and, above all, his truculent self-defensiveness confessed his origins and competitive upbringing along the Glasgow waterfront.

"I'm not trying to pin anything on you, Charlie," explained Jimsy. "But tell me. When the boss or his wife draw liquor from the bar, I don't suppose you're paid in cash. So what record do you keep?"

"Chits," said Charlie crisply and pointed to a tumbler on the gantry almost packed with flimsy sheets of paper. "That's one thing you learn in the Boats."

"Could I have them? Just to check with the books."

"Nut in your natural, nut in your natural, son!" declared Charlie melodramatically. "These keep me right, and there they're stickin'. When I get out of this dump a fortnight from now I'll hand them to you and get your receipt proper, and that's me out. It'll be up to you to see the stocktaker at the end of the month, and then—O boy! O boy! How much," he asked more sympathetically, "how much are they out?"

"At least three hundred."

"Well, if he sends for a bottle of whisky twice a day, and she needs a bottle of gin to keep the old canary singin', it disny take long to run up three hundred these days. San fairy ann by me, just the same, china. A fortnight come Monday, and there'll be a fair riot in every pub inside a mile of Anderston Cross."

Charlie rubbed his hands in great glee, and Jimsy slipped off the high stool on which he had been sitting.

"And after that, Charlie?"

"The Boats. Back to the good old Glory Hole. Mind ye, it's hard to get in wi' the Cunard or the P. & O. That's the high-doh stuff, but if ye make it, O boy! Smoke-room steward or even four tables in the dining-room. Good pay, good conditions, good tips. See a bit of the world. A nice wee smugglin' racket on the side. A girl in every port, aye "—he winked lewdly—"a dizzen if ye want them. What a smert, educated wee chap like you's doin' in a dump like this . . ."

Jimsy wondered almost naïvely what was lacking in him that he must fail in all those enterprises that, for such as Jock Jamieson, Steamboat Duff and Charlie Cram, seemed easy avenues of gainful employment. He was still pondering the personal problem when, moving round the front of the hotel and observing that the gravel before the porch would be none the worse of a raking, he was brought to a halt by the opening of a first-floor window above his head and the sound of a rich female voice hailing him mellifluously.

"Jimsy Be-e-ll! Jimsy Be-e-ll!"

He looked up to see the clown's face of Mrs. Persse framed in the fall of her copious, straight hair, and he was alarmed lest, in her fuddled condition, she should lean out too far and overbalance.

"Yes, Ma'am," he said in a business-like way.

"Come upstairs and sing to me, and I will play for you—for *you*, *Seumas og!*—on my clarsach."

"I don't think I've got time, Mrs. Persse," Jimsy temporised in his most careful English.

"What is time while we dream on the verges of the western seas!" crooned the infatuated woman. "I have upon me a longing to see the peaks of Mull. There is a song in the book."

It was best in his experience to humour this fantastic creature, and he climbed the stairs to what she called in impossible Gaelic the Room of Music, with the square bottle of gin on top of the fretwork-fronted piano and a cigarette still burning sourly amid the cinders of a brimming ashtray. Mrs. Persse's original good looks were now a shambles, the mouth moist and sensitive in the way of those who drink gin in quantity. She was clad in a sort of bardic robe of crotal brown, gathered in at an increasing waist by a quasi-Celtic cincture in a dull bronze metal.

"And now, *Seumas beg!*" she cried, seizing the clarsach from the floor and tucking its base between her considerable knees as her form collapsed on a three-legged stool, "now we make music together."

Her fumbling fingers plucked from the strings of her instrument a series of blurred chords, and Jimsy started to hum the melody they approximately suggested. He did not use the open throat in the light, true tenor voice that so perfectly matched his physical neatness. It was enough to give the foolish, generous woman the illusion of co-operation.

"Ah, *Seumas beg!*" she cried when the dismal recital was at an end, clutching at his legs. "Some night you will climb to my window and make love to me in the Gaelic, crooning in my ear, and it waiting for the whisper of your desire."

"I don't know what the major would say about that," said Jimsy briskly.

"Ah, my poor Athelstan!" she sighed. "He does not know the sob and surge of the Celtic passions, the longing for the land beyond the sunset."

This stated, she toppled over from the stool on to the floor.

Jimsy was never disturbed by Oona's approaches as he had been by Lorna's animal assaults. This was common form with the besotted lady: alcoholic, sentimental, pathetic, and intolerably shabby.

He was glad to get away from the hotel once he had seen the service of dinner started. The evening was fine as he stepped it out over the hill towards the croft at Morrach, and the bay was calm under the sunset, its surface coloured with the golds and olive greens of the near-gloaming. He noted that the tide was far out but starting to turn in long, slow licks up the white sands. The very moment for the laying of some baited lines for the flukies. It would be a cleansing joy to be out in the boat in the freshness of the gathering night, a forgetting, however brief, of the grubby blind alley into which he had stumbled.

4

He was up and about at six next morning, the day dawning
with the golden charm of Indian summer. He opened the barn
to collect a herring basket and rapidly silenced the noisy
ecstasies of Prince; and then, making for the shore, he stopped
in amazement to see that a white motor yacht, the painted
ship on the painted ocean of the poet's fancy, had come in
overnight to anchor behind the southern horn of the bay.

It was the *Ron*. She was of a type, but he would have known
her by subtle little characteristics among fifty yachts at an
anchorage in the Firth. He was suddenly alarmed to see this
ghost of the old life creep back into his private world, nor
could he believe that this was coincidence. His own Traigh
Mor before Morrach was not an anchorage recognised in
the Sailing Directions. Then he had it; coincidence after all.
An inexperienced amateur had got the boat on short
charter.

Even so, he kept his eye on it for signs of life as he lifted
his lines. It was a rare catch this morning: more than a dozen
flat fish up to a couple of pounds each, rarely sweet for the
breakfast pan. The gentlemen in the *Ron* might buy a few
off him. His lines wound in, he let the boat drift and still
watched the yacht, far from sure that she was of innocent
portent.

At length a figure climbed out through a forward hatch
and stood in the bows of the white craft, surveying the morning. It was Lachie Macdonald, and the old life was closing in
again. Jimsy lifted an oar and started to scull quietly towards
the *Ron*.

"It's yourself, Jimsy," he was greeted in a whisper.

"Just so."

"It was thought you would be here."

"Who thought? Who's on board?"

"The master's brother, Mr. Finlay, and a friend. Just a bit

trip up the coast and among the islands, them fishing here and there. I think he's looking for a word with you, just the same."

"I don't want to see him."

"Your affair, Seumas, your affair entirely," observed Lachie largely. "That's a grand lot of flounders you have taken. Would you be selling me three or four of the big ones for the breakfast?"

Jimsy eased his boat in under the flare of the yacht's bow and knotted the painter loosely about the anchor cable. He took the best of his fish from the basket, passed a loop of string through their gills and threw the bundle on to the deck at Lachie's feet.

"There's four beauties," he said, "and that will be a shilling to you, Lachlan."

"Dirt cheap," allowed his friend, "and fine fish, fine."

While they haggled in this agreeable way a large man in a navy-blue bathing-costume of yesterday's fashion had appeared on deck from the owner's cabin. He was of ample build, sandy of complexion, and so running to middle-aged plumpness that a bulge was suspended above his surprisingly slender legs. He came forward, shrewd eyes on Jimsy's person.

"You're Bell, aren't you?" he said abruptly.

"Yes, sir."

"My name's Ferrier, Finlay Ferrier, your old boss's brother at Ardyne. I want to have a word with you, my lad. Just a minute."

This unusually direct person thereupon raised his arms in an elegant gesture, drew in a mighty breath and dived overside. With much shaking of the head and blowing of the nose with the help of his fingers he came up behind Jimsy's boat and easily treaded water while his left hand clung to the transom.

"Wondering how I found you here?" he hailed Jimsy again. "That was easy. I want to talk a bit of business with you. Where and when can I see you?"

"I work in the hotel at Ballibeg," replied Jimsy warily.

"Good. I'm going down there to arrange a bit of fishing. See you after lunch, perhaps?"

"I am very happy in my work, sir."

"We'll go into all that," Finlay Ferrier dismissed the falsehood. "Bo-o-of! It's devilish cold water you keep up here."

He pushed off, causing Jimsy's boat to rock, and swam to the ladder slung over the yacht's quarter. Five hours later he resumed the conversation with his faintly alarming directness.

"And what the deuce are you doing in this dump, Bell?"

"It's always a job."

"My foot! I'd have a strike on my hands if we served a lunch like that in our canteens. The woman's as mad as a hatter, and the man's just a soak. Tried to borrow ten thousand for some damnfool scheme for catching sharks. Off *me*! If he'd talk about building tractors for the land round here. . . . No, Bell; there's no future in it."

They were together in front of the Ballibeg Hotel on a garden seat that, once painted white, was pitifully flaked and rusted by weather off the sea loch it commanded. Scraggy hens scraped at the gravel round about them. It was a blessing, thought Jimsy, that Oona had not yet taken up the clarsach for the afternoon. He was still wary of Finlay Ferrier's approaches.

"I'll perhaps go South again at the end of the season," he said.

"Would you go back to Ardyne, then?" the big man asked quickly.

"No, sir," replied Jimsy, equally prompt.

"Thinking of my brother, I suppose?"

"Yes, sir, frankly. I couldn't go into his service again."

"You wouldn't be asked to. My poor brother will never trouble you or anybody else again. Now listen, Bell. You're a skilled domestic worker. I'm a large employer of labour. I want to book you for a special kind of job, and I'm offering you a deal on the best conditions. Now, listen . . ."

5

Elaine Ferrier had sent for Beth to attend her in the morning-room, and now she awaited her daughter's coming uneasily, her fingers drumming on the arms of her chair, her shallow mind seeking to rehearse those points Ketron had told her she must drive home to the child's understanding.

Beth duly appeared, a little ruffled and breathless, having run from a game at the hut in the wood, and for a moment her mother was in love with an only daughter, a pretty child in a short print frock.

"You wanted me, Mummy?"

"Yes, dear. There are one or two things I've got to tell you. First of all, Bell is coming back to us."

"Jimsy coming back! Oh, goody!"

"It's not goody at all!" protested her mother, now as peevish as one little girl quarrelling with another. "That's just what's been wrong with you all the time. I've often been very angry with you, and look," she added irrelevantly, "look what's happened to your poor Daddy."

"I'm sorry, Mummy."

Unconsciously the girl assumed the posture with which she was wont to face the world's unreason: chin up, shoulders back, arms tight by her sides. It could infuriate her mother; it looked so cheeky—and it spoke of a secret strength she envied.

"What you've got to understand from now on is that Bell is coming back to us as a senior manservant, and that you are a young lady going to boarding school. There's to be no more silly games; none of this nonsense about boats and houses and things. I hope we always treat our servants courteously," added Mrs. Ferrier with a pious smirk, "but Bell is going to be our houseman now, and you will keep him at his distance. You understand?"

"Yes, Mummy."

"Well, you can run away and play. But remember what I've told you."

For just a few seconds she wished that she could have taken the child close to her and put the hard counsel with persuasive, affectionate reason, but it was too late now on two separate planes of time. Beth had disappeared from the room, and her chance of making a sweetheart of the only daughter of her body had passed long ago.

6

But here they were, Beth Ferrier and Jimsy Bell, in a taxi making its way between traffic lights up the curving slope of Regent Street. Their general direction was Regent's Park, but they were more interested to recognise the slender spire of All Souls and the haughty mass of Broadcasting House ahead, and Beth kept exclaiming at the names above the great shops that told so much of the social and commercial story of Great Britain and were familiar even to a country child from Scotland.

"I wonder if we'll have time to walk down Regent Street after we've seen the Zoo?" she asked wistfully.

"Why not? Your Uncle Finlay doesn't expect us at the hotel till six, and I suppose the Zoo closes early at this time of the year."

"But I want to see everything!" the girl protested.

"It would take a year to see everything in this city," Jimsy opined.

"I mean everything in the Zoo."

They gabbled thus like excited children, but Jimsy was the neat little gentleman in a good blue serge suit and grey felt hat, Beth quite the senior boarding-school girl in the severe costume in fawn covert coating of her order, white blouse and coloured tie, flat blue felt hat with the ribbon and crest about it. The day was grey but mild for December. They had just lunched at the Corner House and had thought it wonderful in its bustle and chromium and colour, and the afternoon was their own, for both of them their very first amid the fabled glories of London.

"Oh, there's Liberty's!" Beth kept up her running commentary. "Golly! What a funny old house that is behind it! Looks like Shakespeare's birthplace or something. And look, Jimsy! There's Dickins & Jones. Have we passed Robinson & Cleaver's? Mummy used to bring me hankies, and I always thought of hatchets. . . . Isn't Uncle Finlay a pet?"

It was all Finlay Ferrier's doing, a characteristic bit of masterful management by the chairman of Ferrier Foundries Ltd.

Festus had faded out of life on a November morning; all right, not unexpected; bury him decently and close Ardyne for the time being till we see what's what. Elaine Ferrier thought she might go to her unmarried sister in Hove, taking Billy with her since Beth was at school in Berkshire. Fair enough for the time being, if Finlay Ferrier was not altogether happy about the schooling of Billy. Ketron's young man was waiting for her in Aden; right, book a passage to that fiery port in S.S. *Canberra* of the British & Australian Line. Elaine, who so much disliked the sea, felt that she could not either leave Billy or take him with her half-way round the world. Very well: Bell would go with her as her courier-steward; it wouldn't be difficult to fix it up with Charlie Catto of the B. & A.

The thing was to get moving in a more purposeful way than the women of the Ferrier clan had been accustomed to. They were not long back from burying Festus Ferrier in the old kirkyard of St. Marnock's before Finlay was at Jimsy Bell with his scheme.

"You would travel as a cabin steward, of course, but I've fixed it that you look after Miss Ketron specially and see that she doesn't fall into the Suez Canal or anything damn' silly like that. If you fancy sticking to the sea, by all means do so. A steward's job in one of those passenger ships is worth having in your own line. If you don't, come back and see me. I'm thinking of reorganising the canteen service in our companies. What about it, my lad?"

"I'd like to see a bit of the world, sir," replied Jimsy, glowing.

"Yes, and you're a dashed lucky young man. But good for you, Bell. I'll know in a day or two when you sail. Got to get your passport and all that, of course . . ."

The weeks had tumbled past, head over heels, and here was the penultimate crisis—the *Canberra* to sail from Tilbury at noon to-morrow; Elaine and Ketron to arrive from Hove in the evening; Beth already in London on special leave from school. Only Billy would not be of the party. Nobody ever counted Billy very seriously.

"Look here now, Bell," Finlay Ferrier had instructed Jimsy in the hotel lounge that morning, grasping the worn briefcase and black felt hat of the business man while the porter whistled for a taxi. "You meet Miss Beth at Paddington off the ten-forty. Take her to the buffet and let her have as many cakes and glasses of milk as she can stand. Then you get down to the B. & A. office in Cockspur Street and make quite sure that the luggage has been checked out. Then you and my niece do what you damn' well please till six. Here's five quid. That should keep you going."

As Jimsy carefully counted and put the notes in his hip-pocket, Finlay Ferrier laughed.

"Lord, I wish I was going with you two. I'm in London at least once a fortnight, and I've never seen the Changing of the Guard yet! Go and play yourselves, then. There's lots to see."

"Yes, sir. I've had a good look at the guide-book," said Jimsy in his northern way.

"I'll bet you have!" the big, fair man laughed again. "Well, don't be frightened to bang your saxpence. Take a taxi if you're stuck. See you later."

That was why Beth, her companion agreeing with her, thought Uncle Finlay a pet. If these young people in the cab, now bowling up Portland Place, could have defined it, it was that Uncle Finlay trusted you. He never worried about things that are Not Done or remembering your place; he seemed not in the least to assume that two young people let loose in London with five pounds and eight hours to spend, one of the master, the other of the servant grouping, were necessarily in a fair way towards an illicit association.

It was one of the first things Beth had said, dipping her face into a chocolate éclair in one of the buffets at Paddington, the time being still short of eleven in the forenoon.

"It's all so different since Daddy died. . . . Was that very terrible, Jimsy?"

"No," he replied thoughtfully. "We knew in the afternoon it was bound to happen within a few hours. The doctor came in the evening—and went away again. Only Nurse Nairn and I waited up. He didn't know anything; he went out like a candle—you know, Miss Beth: the quiet flame and then the flicker."

"I cried for hours when they sent for me and told me what was in the telegram."

"It must have been a great sorrow for you," Jimsy said in the Highland manner.

"It was nothing of the sort, Jimsy Bell!" Beth corrected him. "I was just beastly sorry for myself—poor little Beth all alone. Oh, don't be snappy! Billy and I never mattered much somehow, and when it was all over, the only people who thought about me were Uncle Finlay and Aunt Helen. She's a dear. Do you know? They came down to Newbury and took me away for a week-end. They were so kind, so anxious—about me! All I got from Mummy was a letter I could hardly read, a lot of weepy stuff about Ketron's marriage and what was she going to do with herself and Billy now. . . . No, I don't think I'll have an ice yet. I'm saving myself up for lunch and tea."

So the Zoo received them, as it has received and distracted millions of the human oddments that pour through London sooner or later, and they brought to their first sight of the animals and birds the candour of children, even if the social behaviour of such as the baboons on their kopje embarrassed them in the special relationship of their ages. They moved readily from the departments of the apes to see the giraffes and be convinced that the necks of these creatures were as long as stated in the picture books.

"The things you're going to see, Jimsy Bell!" Beth exclaimed.

"Not giraffes in the Far East," he laughed, "only in Africa."

"Well, elephants and monkeys and tigers and things. Don't let's talk about it. I'm nearly sick with envy already."

They ended their pilgrimage in the Aquarium, and that muted, strangely-lit chamber seemed to have the most power to still them with the senses of wonder and surmise. As they were going out, Beth slipped her hand into Jimsy's. It was to him the most natural act of companionship in the world, but the warm touch of the lithe, thin fingers within his was disturbing. It brought too near both the strange quality of their relationship and the imminence of their parting. He awkwardly resumed his place as courier and hurried her to the tearoom opposite the Mappin Terraces, penguins in a pond agreeably intervening.

They ate copiously of the bread and butter, cress and slabs of Dundee cake with which the Royal Zoological Society regales its guests in the lower income groups. Over the tea-cups Jimsy produced a yellow packet of cigarettes, and Beth, after a good look round, accepted one and puffed at it between the stiff fingers of young females unused to this form of libertinism. The lights went on suddenly, and she stubbed it out, staring through the windows at the greyness of the winter afternoon.

"And you sail to-morrow," she said bleakly.

"At noon. I join the ship at Tilbury to-night. You'll be interested to see a big liner like the *Canberra*."

"I won't see a thing. I'll be weeping buckets."

"Goodness, it's not for ever," he teased her. "At least, I expect to be back in the U.K. by June."

"Yes, but it's a big good-bye just the same. I mean, it's

good-bye to Ardyne and all that," she mused unhappily. "Will you write to me, Jimsy?"

"I owe you one pound, twelve and threepence," he sought to evade the point of crisis.

"You can pay me back when you make your fortune," she retorted rather sourly. "I want you to promise to write me when you can. No matter what happens, you must send me a Christmas card every year. Promise."

"Of course, I promise. But I can't see why you should worry."

"You never know," she said morosely, adding: "You ought to know as well as I what it is to be terribly lonely."

And that was their last of London proper. The shops of Regent Street, their windows brightly lit and gorged with Christmas wares, hardly halted Beth in the mood that had come upon her. He delivered her up to Finlay Ferrier in the lounge of their hotel, courteously thanked him for his kindness and carefully handed him back the change of five pounds; nor did Finlay Ferrier tell him to keep it.

The next was Tilbury on a December forenoon, the mass of the *Canberra* hanging over the landing stage like the side of a great house, an easterly wind whipping the rising stream and a washy sun lighting the haze over London River and the spires of Gravesend.

The Blue Peter flew from the foremast above the ship's signal pennants and all the bunting was slung fore and aft above the monstrous funnel, yellow with the two red bands of the B. & A. Jimsy felt himself excited in merely belonging to the huge congregation housed within the shapely shell of steel. He was on duty now, cabin steward for B.120-126, with special attention to the lady, V.I.P., in No. 122. There was no place for him now with the Ferriers, now lunching in the glass-walled dining-room and at the Captain's table, where Miss Ketron was to sit. The throb of the generators might have been the drums of advance in war.

He busied himself going over Miss Ketron's stateroom, checking this and that as he had been taught—so many towels in the right order of convenience, cakes of soap, ashtrays and what not. Still another bouquet had arrived to clutter the dressing-table, and when he returned from his search for a container for it, there was Beth. As she had foretold, she was sobbing.

"Sorry, Jimsy! I'm just sick and sorry for myself. I suppose I look a sight."

"No, you don't. You just make me feel awkward and unhappy. . . . I wish you wouldn't cry, Miss Beth."

"I'll cry if I want to, Mr. Bell! " she flung back at him. "No, Jimsy, dear; I really want you to kiss me once. Goodbye!"

"Goodbye! "

It was an awkward enough peck on both sides, and Jimsy retreated, frightened lest he be discovered in this extravagance at the very outset of his seafaring career. He made for the pantry and started to polish glasses with the wild idea that Finlay Ferrier might wish to open a last bottle to toast Miss Ketron good luck on both her voyages. A bell rang peremptorily, and the loudspeakers took up the tale of warning, the hollow voices reverberating along the alleyways and echoing from one to another. The whole fabric of the ship started to throb. It shivered to a blast from the siren.

Twenty minutes later the Tilbury landing stage was moving backwards as the vessel seemed to move miraculously broadside into the stream. Beth and her mother were two shapes like small saucers, far below as Jimsy saw them from a corner of B Deck, their upturned faces mere decorations of a confused pattern. He could not even know exactly to whom the see-saw signals of the handkerchief in Beth's hand were addressed.

The pier and its temporary inhabitants receded. The flatness of the Essex bank of the Thames asserted itself in a mediocrity almost majestic as such. The pilot rang for more speed. The *Canberra* gathered way towards Dungeness and the many hundreds of miles beyond.

CHAPTER FIVE

Outward Bound

As HE reflected often enough in his later years, himself
by then a veteran traveller, Jimsy Bell's first voyage in
the *Canberra* was critical within his private experience.

He had been born a funny wee chap in body, just saved
from being ludicrous in the sight of his fellow-creatures by
good looks and a great eagerness of spirit. As such he
had prospered within reason, if with a little suffering on the
way, as a domestic worker within a small, understandable
world.

To be pitch-forked into the multi-dimensional system of a
great liner at sea was much like being dropped into the un-
explored jungles of the Brazils; it was to have to observe the
expansion and contraction of accepted vistas of experience, to
be prodded by the spear-points of unexpected circumstance, and
to have to endure the exposure to all manner of abrasions of
the weak links in the armour of pride with which he had
girded himself in his vulnerable state.

The ship herself was one thing, 28,000 tons of her. The
Thane of Cawdor and the *Ron* could have been laid side by side
on the Games Deck under the yellow funnel, and they would
have been just so much odd lumber in a corner up there. The
majesty of the ship on her way out of the Channel enchanted
Jimsy Bell; taking his ease on the crew's deck space on the
poop of an evening, he rejoiced in the churn of the screws
underneath the counter and in the diapason of their drumming.
He felt romantic about the Bay of Biscay, and he hoped that
the sou'-westerly storms would be piling the seas up on the
rocks of Finisterre.

The vessel's progress out of the Channel was decorous on the whole. It was squally and cold, the gusts from the Atlantic hitting at the fabric viciously, but with no more effect than the hiss of a farmyard cat at an intrusive cow. The *Canberra* proceeded. Even when course was altered southwards towards the Bay, the swell out of the Western Ocean would have been a catastrophic storm on the familiar Firth at home, and its cohorts threw fangs of white venom at the rocks of the Burlings, but the stabilising fins reduced the movement of the vessel to a point Jimsy felt to be disappointing.

The *Canberra* proceeded. As old Uncle Apples, his room-mate in the cabin in the Glory Hole aft and two decks down from the poop—as Old Uncle Apples put it frequently: "There ain't no real ships them days. Just engineering jobs. An 'ome from 'ome for the first-class passengers. Mustn't be troubled; wrap 'em up in cotton-wool. Kid them on there ain't no sea at all, excep' when it's as calm as a chamber pot. Cor! They should 'ave seen what I seen. Way back when Mr. Asquith was Premeer. . . ."

That was Jimsy Bell's second gate of understanding. The ship was not any sort of vessel, sinking deeper into night towards a land unknown, as he remembered the lyric that had strangely touched him during his early explorations among the poets. Her life was in parts. You could think of the watch-keeping officers and the quartermaster on the bridge, darkly absorbed in the business of the keeping of the vessel on her course and off the rocks, their eyes strained in the darkness over the sea. You could think of the engineers in their white over-alls, their eyes at close range on gauges and bearings, watch after watch through the long night, while the dance band played and the radio was relayed along the range of the public rooms on A Deck, the lounge stewards sweating as they hurried to meet the clamorous orders for drinks. So many drinks.

"Ruddy floatin' hotel," said Old Uncle Apples as he worked on a rug during one of their off-hours together. "Cocktails," he would add oracularly. "Young wimmen in next to nothin'.

Stand quiet in any one of the alleyways an' you'll 'ear Tarquin's ravishin' stride hall up and down the passenger accommodation."

The passenger was the thing. Never mind the strained eyes on the bridge, the sweaty eyes in the engine-room. The passenger was the thing in his or her capacity of contributor to the pay-load. So such as Jimsy had the passenger in general to consider, then Miss Ketron Ferrier in particular.

She was not to be seen by such as him for the first three days. Ketron belonged to the class of person for whom sea-sickness is a form of wishful thinking, almost expected of a female, almost ladylike. Thus she and her cabin were at first in the care of a stewardess, Mrs. Cundall, an experienced and unmerciful matron from Bridlington. Jimsy marvelled to hear her scold Festus Ferrier's daughter in tones and terms of undisguised contempt.

"It's up on deck in the fresh air you should be, instead of laying here, bein' sorry for yourself. Sickness is nowt but the sign of a guilty conscience."

This sort of thing alarmed the young steward. He could easily imagine Miss Ketron's shocked horror at being spoken to candidly, especially by a servant. He thought, and rightly, that Mrs. Cundall's technique was mistaken in the special case of Ketron Ferrier, and he was much concerned to decide if his status as courier granted him the right to protest. He did screw himself to speak to the formidable stewardess, opening mildly with an inquiry as to his lady's state of health, and he might as well have saved his breath.

"Ee, but that's just a sham. She's as lo-ovely as the day, your young leddy, but there's nowt *to* her, lad. Nowt. Just wait till the weather warms about Gib, and then you can keep your eye skinned for her leddyship's little games. And it won't be seasickness neether."

Jimsy found Mrs. Cundall's prophecy cryptic, and discovered that it was in part inaccurate. The Middle Sea was in one of its many unpleasant moods, and in place of the sparkling blue of romantic tradition there was nothing but a welter of green-grey and turbulent seas within a ring of driving mists. Gibraltar itself was but a large dark rock, apparently diminished in size by whirling rain-clouds, and Jimsy concluded shrewdly that it had perhaps been photographed too much. He particularly regretted the concrete watershed, like the dam of a municipal reservoir, built when siege seemed imminent during the anxious 'forties.

Even so, the *Canberra* remained a ship at sea. There was still the lick of salt on the lips of all who ventured on the open decks; the wind whipped viciously at awnings, boat-covers and ends of rope. The vessel would have seemed to a stranger to be carrying a mere handful of passengers for all that were to be seen in the open—some two score vigorous men who solemnly did the rounds of A Deck every morning for the liver's sake, and a handful of hardy females in slacks and scarves and heavy coats, faithfully trundling their penned infants in fancy little wheeled chairs, their weather-pinched faces quite beyond the help of make-up.

Thus the scene was bleak so far, except within the warm lounges, and Mrs. Cundall's prophecy did not come true until the *Canberra* was in the longitude of Malta, passing the islands haughtily on a southerly course and in the darkness. Then at dawn off Lybia it was suddenly hot, the sea sparkling; the flying fish scuttered like birds away from the ship's passage, and the occasional dolphin leapt with what seemed joy under the burnt peaks of Africa. At the same time, with the unanimity of a rise of minute insects above a trout stream, the *Canberra's* female passengers swarmed the decks in garments so few and flimsy that Jimsy Bell forgot his position and frankly stared.

It was a spectacle outwith his experience in the craggy North, and he was honestly scandalised. It was not really so much on the moral account, but he was a romantic at heart, and what he found offensive was the obvious element of competitive exhibitionism in almost all the women under thirty, married or single, and not a few in a still more dangerous decade. He was terrified to discover that in this efflorescence of near-nudism under the sun Ketron was among the foremost in daring.

Jimsy wondered how a Scots girl, no matter what her position and means, could have rehearsed her part in these displays, but he was not well read in the periodical literature supplied on glossy paper for the enlightenment of all who aspire to be women of fashion, obliquely paying the cosmetic manufacturers for their pabulum. Miss Ketron certainly contrived to be startling on singularly sparse resources.

Her chief garment was a pair of silken shorts, cream with a bold blue stripe down the seams, and it was impossible to ignore the fact that the ultimate protection of her modesty was a skimp contrivance indeed. Her breasts were held by another device that looked for all the world like an outsize pair of spectacles knitted in white wool and held in position by a narrow ribbon across her beautiful back. About her head was a brilliant scarlet scarf; the little feet at the ends of her lovely legs were protected by white socks within high-heeled golden shoes.

Bathing, yes; but sunbathing only? Jimsy could discern the basic pathos of the bid for prominence, but he was revolted by the vulgarity of the confession. Above all, he found his conscience troubling him, for was he not in a fashion his sister's keeper? The portentous personality of Finlay Ferrier shadowed much of his thinking during those early days of the voyage, and he was sure that Miss Ketron's uncle would have had something to say about her appearance.

It was on the evening of that first hot day that he began to be still more worried about his nominal charge and on another account. He had made down her bed and run her bath at the appointed hour, merely glancing at the fripperies Mrs. Cundall had laid out for the evening, and Miss Ketron was late. Then he heard her before he saw her. She came down the main staircase, laughing shrilly in response to the baritone rumblings of a man. They came up the alleyway as Jimsy sought to flatten himself obediently against the panelling, Ketron now sweetly and fitly clad in a cotton dress. Her hand rested within the crook of the man's arm, and she giggled. They parted at the door of the man's stateroom, Number 126, the man saying darkly:

"And we'll dance after dinner, enchantress."

"If I can stand," laughed Beth's half-sister again.

He saw her bump into the panelling opposite the door of her own stateroom, which shut with a bang. He sidled up, wondering if his help was needed, and he heard her being sick into the washbasin. He could have been sick himself for the pitiful vulgarity of it. But he waited and waited, lurking in the doorway of the ironing-room, now silent for a space, and it was something that she went steadily enough towards the lift and the dining-room only five minutes after the gong had gone.

The gentleman in stateroom Number 126 was a Mr. Pallister, and Jimsy did not like him for himself. It was around among the experienced stewards that he was a director of rubber companies with headquarters at Penang and an old hand in the technique of Far Eastern voyaging: a tough egg, they called him and not without admiration for his various social skills. Jimsy had classified him as a battered 38 or so, handsome in a dark Celtic way, with what seemed the scars of many potations on his face, and he was apt to be ill-tempered and unreasonable in the morning. It was the odd circumstance that the little steward, nurtured in the Highland tradition, had discerned at once and with certainty that Mr. Pallister was far from being the gentleman he believed himself to be: a belief in defence of which he would, at the very hint of a doubt, produce a scowl, a jutting chin and a heavy fist.

Miss Ketron making a bit of a fool of herself with a lad of her own age would have been one thing. The collapse of a child flattered and fed with alcohol by a practised breaker of hearts was a sad thing to watch. Poor little fool, thought Jimsy Bell miserably. Beth would never, never so cheaply cast away her personal dignity.

The pattern, so conventional, so wholly accepted, was un-familiar to him who had been a page-boy in the simple enough world of Ardyne. He painfully recalled that the women of that household normally drank nothing but a ritual sherry or mixed vermouth before lunch on Sundays. It was no business of his to be on the promenade decks, but that evening he slipped up by small companionways and for a minute peered into the chamber in which the First Class were now—instead of horse-racing, table tennis, the tombola and the interminable sweep-stakes—dancing.

It was hard to see from the half-lit A Deck into the brightness of the room, but at length he spotted his quarry, two of them at a small table against the windows on the starboard side. They were not of a noisy, harmless party. They were two close together: the girl laughing foolishly, the man eating her body with his eyes, smiling, his dark half-closed eyes admiring so carefully that the act had an almost architectural grace. There were drinks on the table between them.

He should have been in his bed two hours before, but Jimsy waited in his hiding-place until they came down together. They were not fantastically late, and now Miss Ketron could walk with some decision. But she listened to flattering badinage, tapped the dark face playfully with slim fingers and suffered her own to be kissed with the grace that cloaked so much animal strength.

Old Ted Apples looked up from the intricate pattern of the rug he reckoned would keep him employed in his off hours to Sydney and back again to London.

"Been pushin' back the pints in the Dog and Duck?" he asked sardonically.

"No, I've been watching my passenger making a fool of herself." He quickly explained his problem to the old man and declaimed against the circumstances that rendered him powerless. "But is there nothing I can do about it?"

"Nuthin' but keep your trap shut," said Ted morosely, squinting through his spectacles as he placed a length of lavender wool in the hook. "First thing a stooard 'as to learn in the bread-and-butter line. Wot 'e sees along the alleyways is between them and their Maker. And you ain't seen nuthin' yet. Wait till the return voyage w'en the tea planters and such is goin' back 'ome with their pockets full of money. Scandals! 'Igh livin'! Tarquin's ravishin' stride! . . . That's why I took up the rug-makin'. Keeps me from turnin' Bolshie."

"It's a rotten way of earning a living," Jimsy grumbled as he started to undress.

But already he had begun to know himself imprisoned within the ring of an impregnable professional cynicism. Gossip as much as you pleased, laugh at the passengers within the sealed lodge of the Glory Hole; but talk outside the guild, carry stories, snoop and report—no! That was professional suicide. The line was precisely to smooth the path of indulgence since thence came the Big Money, the Fat Tips.

It was on the second of the warm days that Ketron decided she must follow the fashion of the Younger Set and have supplies of liquor in her room.

"You know the sort of thing to order, Bell?" she assumed airily. "Whisky, gin, vermouth—all that sort of thing. Oh, and rum! I've rather fallen for rum. It's awfully good with lime. And glasses, of course. Don't forget glasses."

There was nothing he could do in the way of protest; it was his physical fate to be incapable of offering adult advice to anybody. The worst of it was that he despised Miss Ketron. She was like her father, without subtlety; one who could see life only in terms of black and white. Something of the mantle of professional hypocrisy descended upon his own shoulders as he placed the order with Paddy Friel in charge of the dispense bar.

"So your young lady's determined to go her mile," laughed the Irishman ironically. "That's a grand wad of blotting-paper for ye! Drink, is it? Get you behind the bar in the Verandah Café any morning and see what she can sink. It's not straight drinkin' like anny man. It's mixin', mixin', till it's a God's wonder she's not sick into the swimmin' pool—the first a Tom Collins, the next a rum and lime. Then it'll be an Old Fashioned. . . . Ah, well! She'll know what's happened before Mr. Pallister is finished with her. I've watched him at his games before this and, believe you me, the same man's a mighty old hand with the gyurls that lose their heads with the booze. But there's your chit, son. Get her to sign it when she's sober and turn it back to me as soon's you can."

As the ship headed towards Damietta and the entrance to the Canal there were in the mind of Jimsy Bell many thoughts, confused and conflicting, of a remote and obsolescent croft near Ballibeg, of Finlay Ferrier and the obligation he had put on a man young and inexperienced, and of a straight young girl called Beth, who could never be imagined falling into vulgarity and the surrender of personal dignity. These places and persons seemed very far away.

2

Elaine Ferrier had never liked her brother-in-law. It was not merely that he had prospered where poor Festus had failed, nor even that the latter had suffered public defeat in the matter of The Case. His widow had few illusions as to the wisdom of Festus's judgment in most concerns. It was simply, as she had often phrased it to Ketron, that there was something about Finlay she could not like, and Ketron had often admitted sharing her stepmother's view of her uncle.

"He's far too bossy and sure of himself," she would agree with Mummy. "I suppose he's good at business, but he hasn't an atom of charm."

Elaine Ferrier spared herself the task of analysing her mistrust. She had long ago found self-analysis to be an uncomfortable business. Perhaps she was afraid of meeting in her subconscious mind the intolerable fact that, from their first encounter, Finlay had notably failed to surrender to the charm she believed herself to possess in considerable abundance, and that he had in fact seemed sometimes to be laughing at it. Had not his bossy manner too often indicated that he lumped her with Festus, if with amusement, as just another fool. He was coarse; that was the truth about Finlay. You could hardly believe he was Festus's brother. Of course, the first Ferrier had started as a common moulder.

And if he was not Top Drawer somehow, there was that woman he had married—Helen Carmichael she had been, the only daughter of a poor little parish minister somewhere in the North. She had had to go out to work, the good little darling, thought Elaine of her sister-in-law cynically—and had done so well, or so Finlay declared, that she rose to become head cashier in one of the foundries. And the next the other Ferriers knew was that Finlay had determined to marry her, which he promptly did in an Edinburgh registry office. No friends, no reception: nothing but two lines in the *Glasgow Herald* and the *Scotsman*. Festus was livid, she remembered; it was such a horrible slap in the face.

The closer analysis of Elaine Ferrier's mind hereabouts might have revealed another set of subtleties. Might it not be that Aunt Helen, the frank *bourgeoise* with her feet on the ground, was kind, competent, talented in house management, gifted with humour and popular among the young of the family? Elaine declared to herself that she was simply sick of hearing Beth say "Aunt Helen's such a dear!" Nice, motherly creature indeed! She had not been able to produce a child of her own, and she had had plenty of time, even starting at thirty.

There rankled deeply the memory of how when she herself, Elaine Ferrier, was in confusion and distress after Festus's death, these two had dashed down to Newbury and snatched Beth away for a week-end, butting in where they had no business. Very well, she thought as she poked the fire of her sitting-room in Cherry Gables, Hove 3—very well, if they thought they were going to steal Beth for the last half of the Christmas holidays, they could think again.

The innocent prize of these hostilities was at about much the same time engaged with her three room-mates at Thruston Grange in the happy business of packing. Every chair and bed was heaped with the sensible garments of young ladies at school, and the air of the chamber was loud with their competitive yelps about the Christmas excitements before them. It was agreed that Tubby Corcoran, about to fly to Gibraltar to rejoin her military parents, was chiefly to be envied for the prospect of dancing with naval officers and without much competition: naval officers being, as an article of young female faith, all lovely boys. But it was also admitted that Scotty Ferrier, with a Christmas card from Port Said (and from a boy-friend) already to her credit and an invitation to a house party in her uncle's big place in Scotland was not far behind in good fortune.

Jimsy had bought and posted the card in Simon Arzt's store, being himself greatly taken with the picture, which amusingly contrived to associate a fat gully-gully man and his chicks with the seasonable sentiments. Was he good looking? Did he dance well? The two stay-at-home girls sighed their wish that they had friends abroad.

"And when there's a dance in your uncle's house, Scotty, will the boys be wearing kilts and playing bagpipes and all that sort of thing?"

Flushing, Beth defended the social development of her native land, and the riot started up all over again. Amid the babel, for a moment detached, Elaine Ferrier's daughter wished she felt as happy as she sounded. The dream of the big dance in Scotland and of interesting young partners in kilts was so unsubstantial as yet. She was aware, without as yet being able to define their nature, of the conflicts that surrounded her.

Most clearly was she aware of something sadly amiss between her mother and herself. It was as if they had resumed a distant acquaintanceship only since Daddy's death. She could not remember Mummy caring much for her growing up; it was strange and painful that she had found her companionship with Ketron, who was not of her blood.

So it was frankly a bore to be met at Paddington by Mummy, all fussy and moody and jerky at once. The London day was a raw one of half-fog that would thicken by nightfall, but Mummy must make it a gala occasion, pressing her to eat up, you're probably starved at your school, in an uninteresting

Oxford Street restaurant, then whirling her off, as a special treat, to see the toys in Hamley's. There it was! For Mummy she was still just a kid, her ripening unnoticed. Hamley's, when you wanted to look for your first evening-frock!

Oh, Mummy must go round the shops! Characteristically, she had failed to plan her Christmas presents, and each emporium was a riot of battling females in the same condition. Mummy did buy some things for her little Beth, but they were of the useful, sensible order; and it was no use wandering into the dress departments and starting to look round. There was always Mummy at your heels, Mummy almost invisible behind festoons of parcels, crying "Come away at once, Beth, or we'll never catch that train. Don't forget we've got to get your cases out of the Left Luggage."

It was Mummy herself who nearly made them miss the late afternoon train, exclaiming as they came up from the Underground at Victoria that she would die if she did not have a cup of tea. But they caught the train, with Mummy shouting to the guard to hold it up and dropping parcels as she tried to run, and it was something to be speeding on the electric line towards Brighton, even if you could hardly move along the vestibules for women's knees, handbags, parcels, and the occasional toy tricycle, and could not get your cases on the rack because of more parcels. It was still better to be in the taxi, dashing uphill towards the neo-Tudor house in the lee of the Devil's Dyke so oddly named Cherry Gables.

It was best of all to be at last in your own room, even if it was Aunt Cicely's house really. Beth felt terribly tired, but she was most oppressed by the feeling that her meeting with Mummy had been another failure of its peculiar kind. They could not be open with each other somehow, and the girl mournfully concluded again that this was because they did not truly love and trust each other. It was sad enough to think that she had had to argue and fight to get a room of her own and to persuade Mummy it was high time that Billy learned to sleep by himself without blubbing through the night. Did Mummy really not remember what it was to be a girl increasingly conscious of her body as was the dolorous fate of all women?

And not a word about Aunt Helen's invitation. As she changed out of uniform after a bath into pretty, soft garments she had inherited from Ketron, she knew that this was to be the exquisitely crucial issue between herself and her mother within the next few days. It could remain unmentioned, and so it would if Mummy could manage it that way; and the child realised with alarm that the opening must be made by herself, her opening confessing what Mummy would assuredly construe as a disloyalty. As she dabbed on her cheeks a dusting of the powder forbidden by school regulations, Beth felt the weight of a new and not unpleasing burden of maturity and decided it must be for her to pick the moment.

Aunt Cicely, a striking figure in Red Cross uniform, had returned from a meeting. This was a woman with the looks of the family but older than Mummy, her greying hair cut short in a mannish way. She looked and spoke exactly like the sort of person who lives by meetings; if it was not the Red Cross, Cicely Ferguson was an exalted figure in the local hierarchy of the Girl Guides and a dauntless worker for the Conservative Party, even in a constituency in which singularly little was required of such vehement endeavour as she could bring to the Cause represented by Mr. Winston Churchill.

"I often wonder," Beth had once overheard Uncle Finlay observe to Aunt Helen, "whether that blasted woman is a spinster because she's a born boss or bossy because she's a spinster." But the girl rather liked Aunt Cicely, her decisivness, however abrupt and sometimes wounding, so greatly preferable to Mummy's ramblings.

It was as if Mummy had fled to her spinster sister's bosom, needing some form of masculine protection. And that lay close to the root of her own trouble. Cherry Gables could never be a home. It was spinsterish all through, from a selection of toy poodles in the chintzy chairs to coyly-worded plaques in poker-work by the fireplaces, but mainly in its atmosphere of being wholly occupied by two mature women in whom all passion was long ago spent, who had even forgotten its possession once upon a time.

"Well, young Beth!" she was heartily greeted and kissed. "It's nice to see you again. And what are we going to do with you during the next week or two?"

Here was the point, reached in the first lunge of that swash-buckling tongue, but the girl was shrewd to let it pass.

"I'm sure Beth needs a good rest," piped up Mummy inevitably. "We'll have Christmas dinner and our own quiet fun, of course, and I'm sure there are lots of nice families round about."

"I wish I was so sure!" said Aunt Cicely crisply, lighting a fresh cigarette from the butt of another. "Most people round here are apt to be a bit like myself, married or not; run to poodles and fast cars and cocktail cabinets; anything but nappies. But I tell you what. We could organise a jolly good kid's party out of the infants at Billy's school. . . . Where is that boy, by the way? Of course, they're having their Christmas party this afternoon."

Beth was happy to see her little brother when he came home at length. The colours of his seminary were purple and white, and the bright blazer he wore above grey flannel shorts conferred upon him a certain air of masculinity. He was still Mummy's boy, just the same, leaning against her knees and being shy with his big sister. He looked unhappy when Aunt Cicely spoke of the party in prospect, herself much looking forward to another job of organisation, and when she added "We'll work up a jolly good programme of games—'Kiss-in-the Ring' and all that sort of thing," he turned and hid his pretty face in his mother's lap.

"He's so sensitive, poor darling," observed Elaine Ferrier, having the unfortunate habit of discussing the unique person-ality of her son in his presence, as if he were a rare specimen in a showcase.

"Oh, don't be a sap, Billy!" snapped Beth with the old familiarity.

"Come along, Billy, buck up!" contributed Aunt Cicely,

speaking as if, again, he was not present. "He'll be all right when we get him away to a good tough prep school next year."

Perhaps Beth's mood was uncharitable, but she was tired of life at Cherry Gables before the party took place. Christmas dinner with only Mummy and Auntie and Billy was dreary enough, the pulling of crackers an anticlimactic farce, but when she saw the party assemble the girl's spirits drooped.

It was a children's party indeed. The oldest guest was a girl of thirteen, in itself a measure of poor Billy's backwardness and, with early youth's acute awareness of differences in age, Beth felt herself an auntie already. She was the big girl at the round games, pushing the infants through their paces, and on occasion she took to the lavatory little girls overwhelmed by the physiological consequences of excitement. She helped at the tea table and was the first to notice when Billy was about to be sick, the first to signal Mummy to lead him away.

She even discovered she had sunk so low that nannies had called to collect their charges and must be separately entertained to tea. The slang of Thurston Grange came to her aid. It was a cheesy show; in fact, on the lowest level of schoolgirl condemnation, it stank. Haunting the chambers of her mind was the wholly selfish thought that this was the 27th day of December. Aunt Helen's New Year party was to be on the 31st.

Beth knew that she was being a bit of a pig; she did not know quite so clearly that she was playing her allotted part in a drama of conflicts, familiar in its pattern but nevertheless novel and trying to those who must take part in it.

"Well, I think that was a very nice party," sighed Mummy while Aunt Cicely was seeing the last of the children from the door. "Now we can all settle down and have a nice quiet holiday."

"But you got a letter from Aunt Helen, didn't you? One of us ought to reply to it."

"Oh, that!" Mummy started to prevaricate in her most maddeningly evasive way. "I didn't pay any attention to it."

"But she wrote me too, Mummy, and I'm certainly going to reply one way or the other."

"Running away to Scotland at this time of the year," Mummy went on, peevishly pathetic. "Look what it costs in fares alone. Clothes . . ."

It was unreasonable, but it had to come out: "What about fares and clothes for Ketron? There was plenty of money for that."

"Don't you dare to talk to me like that, Beth Ferrier," retorted the mother, stung. "This is quite different. You're only saying that you'd rather be with your Aunt Helen than with Billy and me."

"I'm nothing of the sort. I'd only be away a week. Really, Mummy!"

"Oh, yes! You're very virtuous and reasonable. You always were a disobedient and ungrateful girl. Selfish; must have a good time, no matter who else suffers."

It was all very feminine; it was nearly sordid. Beth was in her old fighting attitude, the dark head tilted and the arms straight by her sides; Elaine Ferrier sniffed genteelly into a fine handkerchief. The elements of the situation were perfectly clear to Aunt Cicely when she came in from the front door.

"What's all this now, Elaine?" she demanded to know.

"I've been asked to Aunt Helen's for New Year," Beth was quick to seize her advantage, "and Mummy says I can't go."

"I said nothing of the sort."

"You haven't even replied to Aunt Helen's letter."

"Just a minute, you two. I must say I don't see why Beth shouldn't have a few days in Scotland. For heaven's sake, Elaine, stop sniffing. Nearly a month with us two old frumps —and Billy . . . death and destruction for a young girl."

"That's right. Encourage her to be selfish and have everything her own way. And there's an evening-frock and things . . ."

"My good woman, if Brighton and Hove can't produce a dress for the child, London can," insisted Aunt Cicely, another feat of organisation in pleasing prospect. "You'd better ring Helen to-night and say that Beth will travel by the morning train on Wednesday. Remind me to book a seat for her to-morrow."

It was wonderful to have Aunt Cicely on your side, capable of brushing demurrers aside like Uncle Finlay, but it was not a pleasant thing, thought Beth as she prepared for bed that night, to have your own mother against you, almost your despised and resentful enemy.

3

S.S. *Canberra* led the afternoon convoy into the Canal, riding high and handsome past the cream-washed front of the Canal Building and seeming to brush aside the small craft that scuttered up and down and across the long harbour of Port Said like so many waterbeetles on a pond at home.

The Canal received the great ship, and Jimsy Bell, eager across the rails of his allotted recreation space, was stirred to acute interest in every movement and vista unfolded, down to the rhythm of the slow wave and backward surge along the banks of confined waters tortured by displacement.

To starboard stretched the green and brown clumps of the Delta; to port were only miles and miles of the sandhills of the Sinai Desert. He saw the great American cars of Egyptian wealth and the functional jeeps of the Zone forces tear up and down the main road by the Canal bank, slowing only occasionally to pass a line of white donkeys ridden by hooded figures in dirty gowns or the occasional camel train. He perceived how the imaginative drive of Ferdinand de Lesseps had linked West and East in a slice as a butcher might cut out a shoulder of lamb.

The sun shone, the air was muggy, and there was dust flying about from under wheels and hooves ashore. Jimsy's lively sense of having travelled far was sharpened by the fact that, according to regulation, officers and crew had been clad in white since noon: the deck officers like figures from musical comedy in their shorts and epauletted blouses. This was a ship going East through the Tropics and across the Line at length.

Now the vessel wore a wholly gala air. The sun had taken it and its company prisoners. Along the upper decks came and went the parade of female passengers, more daring than ever in *déshabillé*, the shapeliness of their curves in strange contrast with the fishlike anonymity imposed on their faces by sunglasses. There was a vast and almost continuous splashing in the swimming pool, and men and women sucked greedily at long gay-looking drinks served in and from the Verandah Café above it: the former determinedly hairy-chested above their maroon trunks, the latter almost desperately determined to allure in their decorative breastplates and skimp shorts, only those goggles under wide, floppy hats concealing the mystery of their ultimate purposes.

The little cabin steward called Jimsy Bell, bred a Calvinist, could somehow not learn to take the spectacle and the atmosphere of a fashionable liner with detachment. He could not get away from the responsibility that Finlay Ferrier had imposed upon him; he could not surrender to the cynicism counselled by old Ted Apples. He was courier to Miss Ketron, Beth's half-sister. She was silly, and Mr. Pallister was pervasive in dark good looks. It was the most daunting thing of all that, within the considerable world of the big ship, there was nobody to whom he could turn for help, even for advice. The negations of discipline and convention had isolated him. Stewards see many things but keep their traps shut.

The bottles in stateroom No. 122 were emptied and replaced.

"She's runnin' up a fine, fat bill," observed Paddy Friel in the dispense when Jimsy went to him with a third order. "Pallister must be about ready to pounce on the gyurl, and her stewed like a pig from noon on."

There were parties along Jimsy's section of the alleyway at least twice a day, before dinner and after the dancing or the cinema show. In the Great Bitter Lake, while the ships lay at anchor to let the north-bound convoy pass and Jimsy waited to get to bed, there burst from stateroom No. 122 an explosion of laughter, then a crash of breaking glass, and then a hush broken by a man's voice, cursing. Mr. Pallister staggered out, a bloody towel about his left hand, and swayed aft towards the Doctor's quarters.

Her other guests having departed sheepishly enough, Miss Ketron clung to the edge of the door and drawled: "While you're there, Bell, you might clear up this ruddy mess and I'll try to have a bath. I said—*try*. Oh, God!" she yawned, "I'm puggled. I tell you, Bell: I'm stewed."

They were far away from Ardyne now, indeed, and here was Christmas almost upon them, to be celebrated in the middle of the Red Sea. Already the lounge stewards were busy decorating the public rooms as for a fiesta and laying the foundations for a monster tree in the middle of the dance hall, from which the Staff Captain, arrayed as Santa Claus, would distribute presents after the Children's Party on the great day. The vast spaces of the air-conditioned dining-room had been so treated with miles of coloured paper and tinsel that it had lost almost all its familiar resemblance to a public baths. Even the cabin stewards had been set to work, and such as Jimsy were issued with rolls of coloured paper, spangles, sprigs of holly and even mistletoe and told to do up the staterooms as their fancy suggested.

All this under the relentless sun of the East. The Red Sea, however, was not living up to the torrid legend on this trip at least. A strong, steady headwind blew from the South, and there were moments in the mornings and evenings when the white uniform of seafaring convention felt dangerously thin.

The vast desolation of the shores of this basin nevertheless enchanted Jimsy, and continually he saw it as the West Coast of his native land monstrously magnified in bulk and so burnt that it could nurture only fragments of civilisation, such as a huddle of white, dead-looking shacks and a dhow drawn up on the beach under tawny mountains. A friendly quartermaster pointed out to him the peak of Mount Sinai, one among many peaks that might have been the Red Cuillin of Skye on the giant scale, and he understood how primitive mankind must invest such a chaotic region with strange legends.

Still the dolphins and the flying fishes played, and an occasional whale spouted under the forbidding hills of Africa. One day from the crew's deck some of them saw a school of giant rays alongside, unbelievable brown creatures, their diamond-shaped backs the size of large tables, sinister freaks of mysterious depths. It was fantastic that the music of the band, playing smooth western airs for afternoon tea, should be pouring through the loudspeakers: stranger to think of the hotel within the ship decorated for a festival of which the origins were rooted in just such a country as they could see to the eastward.

The traditional heat came with Christmas Day; the head-wind had slackened, and the sea was glassy. At a carol service in the morning it seemed the strangest thing that they should be singing of Good King Wenceslaus and the snows of the Bohemian winter, smooth and crisp and even.

It was Jimsy Bell's first experience of the English passion for preserving the ritual of the feast. He laughed when a wit in the Glory Hole, taking his afternoon ease in only a cellular singlet and a towel, invented and embroidered a story to the effect that a Yule Log was to be lighted in the Verandah Café towards nightfall. He laughed again when old Jock Shaw, senior steward in the engineer's mess, declared that this Christmas business was a lot of damned Papist nonsense, and that all proper men should wait for Hogmanay which, he reckoned, would fall somewhere between Bombay and Colombo.

So the Western Christmas was carried into the East, whence the first idea had come. The lounge and dining-room stewards cursed their lot, even if the Library still held its hard core of Bridge addicts and a couple of brace of enraptured chess players. It was an easy day for the cabin stewards, so eager were their charges to be high on the upper decks in the sunshine and among the drinks or far below with the food and air-conditioning. Jimsy alone was free not long after seven in the evening. Miss Ketron had come down early for her bath and to change into her best, and he took her to be steady on her feet, but he was worried to hear in the gossip of the Glory Hole that she was to be hostess at a cocktail party Mr. Pallister had ordained for an hour before the climacteric of the gala dinner.

They had their own dinner in their own mess, the stewards off duty, and a sing-song after, even those cynics of the seafaring world melting as beer and nostalgia worked on the day of domestic associations. Jimsy's contribution of Scottish song fitted the sentimental mood of the gathering, and old Jock Shaw, flown with many bottles of export ale, told him with sobs that the melodies of home had nearly broken his ruddy heart. They would have had him sing again and again—he was now their Little Tich as he had once been Jock Jamieson's Wee Georgie Wood—and it was good to be a man accepted among men, but he slipped away from the company of his mates and went out on deck as the disgruntled men of the dining-room staff dribbled in to join the fun.

His old friend, the quartermaster, was out there, smoking his pipe. The ship surged on into the night. There were straining eyes up there on the bridge and steady hands on a little wheel. Far down below young men in white overalls, sweat-rags about their necks, stared at gauges and watched the drip of oil through dirty little windows in vertical pipes. With the spittled mouthpiece of his pipe the ageing quartermaster pointed out to Jimsy the first, dim emergence of the Southern Cross in the eastern skies and counselled him to look ahead to see how the conical peak of Abu Ail had a tended light on its summit: to the young steward a sight more moving than the mass of Gibraltar itself, making him wonder, as a child might at a fairy tale, how a couple of Maltese and a handful of Indians lived their lives in such exalted loneliness.

The mystery of the night held him long enough, even until his wise friend started off for the bridge and a two-hour trick at the wheel. Jimsy felt that he could happily stay up for hours, just hearing the clamorous hiss of the ship's wash and watching the glint of phosphorescence in it. That conscience of his troubled him, however; the passion for order was irksome. He made his way forward as eight bells sounded from before the bridge.

The alleyways seemed deserted as he climbed in his soft shoes through C and B to A Deck, and you could imagine a great party of decent folk happy as they danced and drank and flirted up above. He entered his own little cul-de-sac off the lobby, and it seemed as quiet as any other range of sleeping quarters. Outside Stateroom Number 122 he hesitated, almost tempted to knock, and then he became aware that at least two persons were within. He caught the deep, broken rumblings of a man's voice, and he heard Ketron Ferrier sobbing, sobbing; and why she should cry so sorely he could not, and probably never would, know.

And to-morrow afternoon her betrothed would come on board at Aden and claim her for his bride.

4

There had been snow over Scotland, and as she went to pull the curtains of her bedroom in Uncle Finlay's town house Beth Ferrier paused to relish its rich blueness as it lay on roofs and hung on the boughs of trees in the fading light of New Year's Eve. It was so beautifully right that there should be snow on such a night, and Beth could have hugged herself to think how it would seem to enhance the warmth and brightness of the hotel suite Uncle Finlay had booked for the party. It was heavenly in this very moment, in her own bedroom with a blazing coal fire, to have nearly two whole hours in which to bathe and dress.

It was to be her own party, too. Uncle Finlay had laid it down that it was for her as his guest, reported Aunt Helen with a chuckle, adding " That uncle of yours would spoil you utterly if I were not here to stop him."

Aunt Helen, thought Beth shrewdly, did her own share of the spoiling. Once the new dress from London, virginal white, had been laid out on the bed, inspected and admired, she had tilted her greying-fair head to the side, her mild blue eyes on the frock and announced " Now we must get you a nice evening-cloak to go with it. If there's anything I hate, it's to see a young girl wearing an ordinary coat over her pretty dress. We'll go into town to-morrow and see what they have."

"It's sweet of you, Aunt Helen," said Beth, suddenly daunted by one of the complexities of life, "but I don't think Mummy would like me to get a cloak."

"But if I want to give you one as my own present, child, surely . . ."

Then the delirium of finding the very, adorable thing in Dalby's at length. It was a beautifully cut affair in a soft oyster silk, with gathered epaulettes in cream velvet and a deep collar in pure white fur. Sweetly tolerant, honestly envious, both the saleswoman and Aunt Helen smiled to see the young girl swagger and sway about the fitting-room, using her slim hips to give the grace of the garment its full value. Then, when Aunt Helen had written a cheque and the saleswoman went to get the receipt, Beth must rush to the older woman and hug her.

"Beth, dear! " Helen Ferrier protested, reacting in the Scots way against overt emotion. "If you think it's lovely, then I'm happy. After all," she added with a long look into the girl's eyes, blue into brown, "you're something worth dressing."

Beth knew that look of Aunt Helen's. If she had commanded the words, she might have described it as wistfully covetous. She knew in her bones that Uncle Finlay and Aunt Helen wished to have her for themselves, to fill some empty place in their own lives, and in that indifference of youth that can hurt so terribly, she would have cheerfully left her mother's and made her home with them. But it was not simply that they could and would spoil her; they were both too strong and sensible for that. What they gave her were affection, interest and security, those supports she had needed so long.

And now the party, herself for the night the daughter of the house, even if she was to be nearly the youngest among the guests. It had been fun all day, the big house suddenly filled at noon with what Uncle Finlay called "the Edinburgh lot," a niece and nephew of Aunt Helen's and three friends.

There had been no time to sort out their identities beyond the satisfactory fact that they all fell within the grouping of boys and girls in the upper forms of good schools, the circumstance providing them at once with funds of common experience and slang. Otherwise they were just Ian and Anne and Gillian and Sandy and Andrew, all nice, all nice looking. Then, there was to be "the Glasgow lot," Uncle Finlay's phrase again, more than twice as strong and deliciously unknown factors, ten couples of young people all told, and the few grown-ups would play bridge while they danced, and Paul Robin himself was to lead the band.

It was all to be super, in a word, but when she had bathed and started before the fire to get into her flimsies, including her first pair of nylons, Beth could easily have been persuaded to confess that she was living in a fairy tale. The motif of magic was maintained in the great hired Rolls that came at length to take the young people into town while Uncle Finlay and Aunt Helen followed in their own less resplendent vehicle, picking up a couple of friends on the way. There was magic in the lighting of the rooms, in the hooded electric candles above the laden tables in the buffet, even in the feel of an experienced woman's hands gently lifting the evening-cloak from your shoulders; magic in the rising strains of the fiddles, in being approached for the first dance by Aunt Helen's nephew in a red kilt (as the lad had been bidden to ask her, to be sure) and in the first dizzy launching, as in the dangerous passion of a parachute jump, into rhythmic motion within the arms of a male.

They would dance all night, those young girls; it was their most natural form of sensual expression. Mothers and widows and spinsters, burdened and distressed, they might be in God's good time; to-night they were the brides of to-morrow. Uncle Finlay claimed Beth for the second dance, a waltz, and revealed himself as belonging to the Viennese school. His balding head gleaming, he swung his niece round in the good old one-two-three time, following the walls of the room and occasionally reversing to ease the pressure of blood in his head. This he frankly mopped with a fine white handkerchief when it was all over.

"That was champion, Beth! Thank you, my dear. And do you ever touch the ground with those pretty little feet of yours? You slip about like a feather."

Helen Ferrier sat for a moment alone, watching; affectionately amused to see Finlay take the dear girl round the room in the outmoded way; tolerant of modern youth in its suaver motions. With a remarkable degree of detachment she saw them as a fair cross-section of the prosperous industrial middle-classes, but she would have defended with her life the thesis that they were good specimens of boyhood and girlhood.

She liked their eagerness for the dance. It amused her to see that, while most of the younger boys wore the kilt, a few older ones were very neat and a trifle self-conscious in their first double-breasted dinner-jackets. She saw the conventions forgotten, and the racial wildness come out, when the drum rattled on the platform and the young plunged into an Eight-some. But she found that her eyes must always follow Beth. Yes—Beth: tall for her age, bright-eyed, dark and alive. It had been her own little stroke to insist on the child wearing her own rope of pearls; their milkiness broke the rather long neckline and somehow enriched the virginal aura the girl carried with her through the dance.

Gradually the older folk withdrew to the apartment set aside for them, and the dancers discovered the buffet. They were one and all in that singularly happy state of life when the healthy appetites of childhood have not been in the least cankered by the worm in the bud.

Meeting a number of young males for the first time in her life, Beth had discovered them to be much given to talking about themselves and their careers, each one especially concerned to decide how National Service should be taken; and she had never before realised what a hole there must be in the life of every boy of her sort and generation. At the same time, she could not have told how many ices, glasses of cup and cakes and biscuits she and her partners had consumed before, as

Uncle Finlay had insisted, the party was to reunite and sit down to supper at eleven in order to be ready to greet the New Year together.

The buffet had been cunningly arranged for this feast. The older people gathered about one central table, but tables for two had been discreetly laid against the walls, and at one of these Beth found herself seated with the least skilful of the dancers but the one who had most assiduously sought her partnership. He was a large kilted boy as dark as herself. He had been introduced to her simply as Gillie and that he remained while she was just Beth to him; and that he was in the Fifth Form and the first fifteen at Oliphant's were facts which, discreetly produced, had duly impressed her.

"Oh, golly! I'm tired and famished," cried Beth settling down in her place with glee. "I've lost count of the ices I've eaten, but I'm going to have a jolly good guzzle now."

"I bet I can eat you under the table," retorted her companion with his slow, dark grin.

"I expect you can," she allowed, gazing with innocent admiration at the shoulders of the boy. "Cold turkey and thingummies. Yum, yum! Let's start with that."

It was no more than a start, but Gillie won his bet. One heaped plate of turkey and cold ham was enough for the girl, who wanted to get back to the ices, but the boy could face a second, and mere ices were nothing to him. They felt duly thrilled by a glass or two of the discreet hock cup Uncle Finlay had ordered for the young people. They were impressed to be served with coffee out of proper percolators and offered cigarettes from expensive-looking boxes. Beth refused the smoke, remembering the London Zoo long, long ago, but she admired the skilled nonchalance with which her partner lit up.

Through the first puffs of smoke he found her eyes with his and posed the question now conventional within their age-group: "What are you going to do when you leave school?"

"Nursing."

"Fair enough. But why not medicine?"

"Everybody asks me that, but I haven't the brains. Nursing's a jolly interesting job and decently paid nowadays just the same. What are you going to do?"

"Aeronautical engineering," Gillie announced portentously.

"You mean Spitfires and all that sort of thing?"

"Spitfires are a bit out of date," he explained tolerantly. "More like jet propulsion and aerodynamic stresses at supersonic speed. Take the Comet, for instance . . ."

He proceeded with his subject and at length. She could hardly understand a word of what he said, but she listened devoutly, besotted like so many young women before her by the sheer passion of the male enthusiast for the job of his heart, not knowing that the time might come when, passion spent, the job could remain more alluring than the woman chosen on the impulse of the flesh.

He was still talking of aircraft when Uncle Finlay rapped on his table and rose to announce that they would now return to the dance floor for the ritual singing of *Auld Lang Syne*. He characteristically added in all seriousness that his watch couldn't be more than four seconds out one way or another, and that they were all, the band included, to take the signal from him.

So they carried their glasses into the long room with the polished floor, and they toasted the New Year on the last stroke of twelve, and they sang the old song with emotion, even if not everybody knew the words with certainty. The pressure on the fingers of her right hand let her know that Gillie was beaming the seasonable sentiments direct to her alone, and she gave his great left paw a responsive squeeze.

Uncle Finlay had so laid it down that the last dance was to be a good old-fashioned Waltz and Gallop, and when the band struck up "Charmaine," Beth and Gillie were the first to sweep into action, and when it broke into the cavalry trot not a couple in the room romped more furiously.

"Just look at little Beth," Uncle Finlay said to Aunt Helen as they proceeded more sedately through the throng of young people. "Did you ever see a girl dance so happily?"

"It's her first taste of calf-love, poor darling," returned

Aunt Helen tolerantly. "She's not in this world. Look at those eyes of hers."

An hour later, bone-weary and satiated, Beth dropped her clothes about her body before the coal fire, still burning bright. Ketron might be having a wonderful time in her big ship and at Aden, but never, never in the history of the human race had a girl had a more wonderful, wonderful night than she, Beth Ferrier. Dear Uncle Finlay! Nice Gillie! Tired as she was, it was long before she fell asleep.

CHAPTER SIX

Without Trace

THE PEAKS of Aden, grotesque in their outline, towered above the ship moored at one of the berths on the pipe-line off Steamer Point. In their very colour those relics confessed their death by fire in the birth-agony of the world. Even the bright afternoon sun could touch no colour from their ashen-grey screes. They existed in terms of shape only, the fantastic serrations emphasised by fringes of light reflected from rock and dust.

This, thought Jimsy Bell, was a queer place for a honeymoon and a start in married life, but he had no time to stand and wonder. All Miss Ketron's trunks and cases were packed, but he must check them again and again. Scores of casual dockside labourers, their heads strangely wrapped up in rags as if they feared a blizzard, had contrived to climb aboard, and he had been warned that all cabins in his care must be locked and watched. He had her papers ready in his pocket, but he would not part with them until she was safe on the landing pier and in the arms of her future husband.

He had watched her all day, and she had been good, according to his anxious rights. She had been in the stateroom most of the morning with Mrs. Cundall, packing. However his young mistress had stood in the dark and roving eye of Mr. Pallister, that was all over. She had rung for Jimsy after lunch, and he had found her nicely dressed in a cool cotton frock and a floppy white hat, looking quite the lady again and sounding in complete possession of herself.

"I think that's everything, Bell," she said, "and thanks for looking after me."

She pressed a packet of notes into his hand and, judging the amount by the thickness of it, he protested:

"But that's far too much, Miss Ketron."

"Don't be silly. I must have been a bit of a nuisance to you sometimes," and he could almost believe that she smiled a little, as if wisdom were starting to grow in her. "Is there any sign of the launch?"

"If you'll stay here and just look round to see that you've left absolutely nothing behind . . ."

The next thing was Captain Horsley-Moray stalking up the alleyway, a fine figure in khaki blouse and shorts, a cane-handled fly-whisk in his hand like a field marshal's baton.

"Hullo, Bell! Nice to see you again. What do you think of Aden after Ardyne? It's number one-two-two, isn't it?"

Jimsy went out on the open side of B Deck and considered the barges and bumboats now crowding about the precious white sides of the big ship, their native life fascinating. You wanted a day or two of thinking and reading to sort out Arab from Berber, worker from tout, chatter from orders. All queer. Queer that Miss Ketron and her conscience should now be in the arms of her soldier. Queer that it had all started on an island in the Firth so far away from this muddled, alien anchorage under preposterous hills. Still, it was a pity that the ship was to sail when duly oiled and no shore leave for the crew.

He darted inside at the call of his name. The launch was waiting now. He seized her grips from Miss Ketron and snatched her forgotten handbag from the dressing-table. One, two, three, four, five . . . he checked the heavier luggage from the gangway into the rocking boat. It sped across the harbour. They were on the pier, native porters loading the luggage on to an Army truck.

"Well, Bell. Thanks very much. Look after yourself."

The captain shook hands in his pleasant way, and another couple of notes slipped under Jimsy's fingers. Miss Ketron held out a straight arm.

"Good-bye, Bell! The best of luck. Give my love to everybody at home when you see them again."

And that was the end of that leg of his long journey. Back in the ship, he realised completely that he was now a man on his own. It was odd that Miss Ketron had been his last link with the old life, and he wondered if he would ever mingle with it again. At the least, Finlay Ferrier had offered him this career. The fact remained that he was utterly alone, not for the first time in his life; and as the big ship sped past the eccentric headlands that protect the port he looked back on Aden as the last milestone on his road away from what he had known as home.

Having looked to his staterooms, Jimsy Bell went aft to his quarters and, unlocking his big suitcase, started to line his nest with seven good Treasury notes.

2

He had been told in the way of routine that Miss Ketron's stateroom No. 122, would be occupied from Aden to Colombo by a Mr. Niccols Font.

It seemed to Jimsy a strange sort of name, but the buzz of the Glory Hole informed him that a team of American movie men, having been on location in the arid backblocks of the Protectorate, was now heading for the gentler landscape of Ceylon. Jimsy's colleagues, for whom Film spelt Culture, had all the phrases right. These interesting Americans were making a sort of story-travelogue; his friends could tell him enviously that his new passenger was the travelling script-writer: you know, the chap who wrote *Pearl of the Carribean*.

The arrival of the unit on board at Aden had been spectacular enough. It was late. Captain Cutforth on the bridge was thinking of his schedule, and the voice of the siren, like that of an angry bull-moose, filled the harbour and brought roaring echoes back from the walls of the crater, the vibration shaking the fabric of the ship from stem to stern.

At length a lighter had appeared in tow, laden with a most curious assortment of hooded cameras and other eccentric machines of film-making. Chanting stevedores had somehow hoisted this stuff on board while Captain Cutforth's finger pressed on the buzzer at frequent intervals. A small army of khaki-clad American citizens, preceded by a horde of natives carrying their grips, came up the ladder and poured through the starboard side. The natives scuttled back to the barge, all grossly overpaid, and Captain Cutforth had his engines going so promptly that the lighter was nearly knocked over in his lordly anxiety to be off towards Bombay.

Of the large party that had come on board only three were for the First Class, and the stewards on duty, Jimsy among them, stared as they made their way along B Deck towards the Ship's Office. They were all bearded in one way or another; all wore jungle shirts outside loose trousers of khaki drill and sandals on their feet, and they carried themselves with the self-conscious swagger of Western men who have been long out of touch with the amenities of their natural world. Among themselves the stewards whispered the amused conviction that the Yanks were going to upset the ordered conventions of the *Canberra's* social life in interesting ways.

A little buzz and the trembling of a red light on a board duly called Jimsy Bell to stateroom No. 122 to meet his new patron.

He lay on the bed, an expanse of hairy chest exposed by the removal of his thin khaki jacket. His stomach betrayed the onset of middle-aged corpulence. His beard was wispy. But his brown eyes, however tired after days in the desert, were alert, interested.

"Hullo, son! You looking after me?" he greeted Jimsy. "That's fine. Now, the first thing, bud, is that you fetch me a couple of bottles of Scotch and a bucket of iced water. I said two bottles. I'm a good old alcoholic, see? I'm the founder-President of Alcoholics Unashamed, if you wanna know. I live on the stuff, and I always need the support of that second bottle. The first might give out any time. Got me?"

"Yes, sir."

Jimsy Bell was not hoodwinked by the patter. He guessed quickly that this was the familiar case of the educated American who must, for the protection of his sensitive skin, parody the conventional slang of his country.

"I'll get your order right away, sir."

"Aw, drop the ' sir ' for Gee's sake! Run away, little man, and fetch that Scotch."

Jimsy had just left Mr. Font with his supplies of drink and the intention to sleep until dinner-time when the tremble of the buzzer told him that he was wanted in No. 126 by Mr. Pallister. Bidden to enter on his knock, he found Miss Ketron's friend scowling at him.

"Where's my travelling watch?" he growled.

It was an accusation. Jimsy stared at the dressing-table on which he had so often admired the lovely little masterpiece of Swiss craftsmanship in its folding case. The watch was not there, and he felt the stab of alarm.

"I don't know, sir. I'm sure it was there when I locked the cabins before Aden."

"And it damn' well wasn't here when I came down ten minutes ago. You unlocked the cabins, didn't you? You're responsible, aren't you?"

It was like a police interrogation. The horror of it for Jimsy was that he must be tongue-tied by the rule of his trade, forbidden to point out the various ways in which a valuable article might be stolen from a stateroom in a large passenger vessel at an eastern port. The Chief Steward would understand when the complaint came before him, but only he, Jimsy Bell, could know the subtlety of sadism that made Pallister ready to convict him without trial.

"I'm certainly responsible, sir," he agreed. "I'll go and report it now."

"No, you don't. I'll do my own reporting."

But Jimsy had the rules on his side for once. With some difficulty, for he was a remote and important factotum, he made his way into the cabin-office of the Assistant Chief Steward in charge of personnel.

Mr. Lurkin was a heavy, middle-aged man with jowls the colour of tallow. The very pattern of smooth deference to the passenger, he restored the balance in his own soul by the gruff truculence of his dealings with the serving men beneath him. Jimsy knew himself to be peculiarly unfortunate in having been disapproved by Mr. Lurkin from the beginning of the voyage. Mr. Lurkin liked to choose his staff from among his friends and the friends of friends. It gave him a most gratifying sense of power. He did not, he had made it clear, like what he called director's narks being wished on him.

"Hell!" he said when Jimsy had made his report. "Mr. Pallister of all people! This'll go back to London for sure. I suppose you're going to tell me you know nothing about it."

"I know nothing whatsoever about it, sir. You can search me and my kit if you wish, and Mr. Font in one-two-two can . . ."

"Shurrup! You all say the same. Telling me how to do my job. Search you! Ten thousand places in this ship where you could hide a watch. Get to blazes back to your work and I'll see you later."

Sick at heart and afraid, Jimsy went about his work in the staterooms mechanically. It was the sheer blankness of the suspicion and his helplessness in the face of it that appalled him. He was too weary in mind even to think of working out his own defence. The black mark was indelible. It most miserably seemed that he had somehow betrayed Finlay Ferrier's trust and failed himself. Miss Ketron; then this. His single positive decision was that he hated this artificial life of a passenger liner and would willingly walk off the ship at the first port of call, cutting himself off for ever from home, throwing himself into the whirlpool of an unknown sort of life in these foreign parts.

Mr. Font had not stirred from his bed. He was awake, and five fingers of whisky were gone from one of the bottles, but he showed no sign of stirring for what a well-trained man-servant accepted as the inevitable preparations for dinner.

"Shall I run your bath, sir?" Jimsy suggested. "And lay out your clothes?"

"Little man," chuckled Mr. Font in his deep, creamy voice, "you're just too pure Wodehouse English to be true."

"I'm a Scot, Mr. Font."

"Well spoken, son. You'll understand this from now on, then. My clothes, or most of them, are on me right now. The stuffed shirts in the restaurant will never see Nicky Font in immaculate evening-dress. As for baths, I'm a pragmatist, boy; I keep them to help wash away the hangover in the morning. By which token, I ain't one of your big breakfast hogs. Gallons of strong black coffee and a couple of dry crackers served right here is my line. For that matter, I guess I'll skip dinner this evening. I've been starved long enough of Scotch as good as this."

"I could easily bring you up something light, Mr. Font. Perhaps a little cold soup and an omelet."

"Now you're talking, boy, now you're talking. And I say, son. Don't get me wrong about this, but I'm a writer to trade, and I'm apt to get interested in folks. I'd like to talk to you just because I guess there's a story in you. I guess, son," he went on persuasively, "that life ain't too easy for you?"

"I suppose you mean my height," Jimsy said bitterly.

"I mean your height, Bell, yes," Nicky Font replied, picking his words and enunciating them with slow care. "I mean the problems it must build up for you. I'm interested profession-ally; I'm all on your side as a fellow-creature. And now you can bawl me out for a butterinski if you feel that way."

Jimsy hesitated and then said: "I don't think I do, Mr. Font. Most people think that dwarfism—what's the word?—is just funny, or something you shouldn't talk about."

"Nanaism is one technical term."

"But it isn't funny if you are one. You're right about the problems, sir, if you haven't been born stupid as well—the very small man, I mean."

"I'd be most sincerely interested to hear about them," said the true voice of the Princeton graduate, the affection of slang discarded for the moment. "It's one angle on life that the professional writer can't easily measure. Walter de la Mare had a pass at it in his own way, and it was exquisite, of course. . . . But skip all that." Mr. Font returned to the rough manner. "Fetch me up that light repast once the soup-and-fish have levered themselves away from the cocktails, and we'll have a bit of a yarn. And just once again, son, I'm on your side all the way."

"Yes," said Jimsy gloomily, "it's lonely being a bit of a freak. Excuse me, sir. That's one of my other passengers ringing."

Jimsy approached his interview almost with eagerness. In the loneliness of his dilemma he felt a strong need to talk, even of that subject which British reticence regarded as taboo. He had perceived in the eccentric American a true interest that was both detached and sympathetic. And what could it matter now to one whose life was in a mess to confide in a man who had come into it by accident and would be out of it within a few days: somebody who seemed to see him as something more than an automaton?

Nicky Font was still a-bed when Jimsy arrived with his tray. He motioned him to lay it on the commode and asked him to pass the insulated pitcher of ice water. He filled himself out more whisky.

"Still in the mood to talk, son?" Mr. Font asked gently. "I've been thinking and guessing a whole lot. But if you've begun to feel I'm just a rubberneck, say the word and we'll call it a day."

"I'll be glad to talk, Mr. Font. You're the only person who ever asked me to, and I need advice very badly."

"Advice! I'm an inexhaustible well of good advice so long as it don't apply to myself. Here, son. Sit down on that wicker chair and take a cigarette."

"If you don't mind, sir, I'll stand and not smoke."

"Is this the Jeeves act again?"

"No, but I'm in a bit of trouble, and it'll be the worse for me if I'm caught taking it easy in a passenger's stateroom."

"Trouble? Well, well, well! Care to talk about it, little man?"

"No, sir, if you don't mind. You'll hear soon enough. It doesn't take long for gossip to get round this ship. I'd only like you to know that I'm not guilty."

"I guess you're not," said Nicky Font, forking chunks of omelet into his mouth. "Say, son, what do your friends call you? . . . Good! Well, Jimsy, you're sure building up a big story about yourself. You've got me wondering. I could take you as you are and make a good mystery out of you. What about telling me how it all started?"

"That's just what I don't know, Mr. Font," Jimsy was eager to explain what he had so long suppressed. "I don't know who my father and mother were. I was brought up by the Welfare people in Glasgow. They boarded me out in the Highlands."

"Hoi, son! Stop there till we get the first sequence straight. What's all this about Welfare and boarding out?"

Jimsy earnestly explained the system, and Nicky Font guessed that John Bull seemed to care more for his lost children than Uncle Sam. He was curious about that croft in the West Highlands. Yes: Jimsy could speak the old Gaelic tongue; he had spoken more Gaelic than English in his childhood; and he could sing a Gaelic song and dance a Highland step or two for that matter. His friend lay back on the pillows and seemed to address the ceiling.

"Well, well, well! This is a natural, a'n't it? Bilingual at ten! Jimsy, your story is writing itself. Can you bear to face up to the second reel?"

"That's when it began to get difficult for me, Mr. Font," Jimsy went on, subconsciously surprised by the collapse of his habitual reticence. "When manhood started to come upon me, I realised that I was going to be a little fellow all my life, and that I was only being brought up on charity, I was hurt in my pride. I had done well enough at school, you understand. They sent me to the secondary school, and I took my certificate, and maybe they would have helped me to the university for that matter. I think, however," he added wistfully in his Highland way, "the pride in me was too strong."

Mr. Font asked for the pitcher of iced water.

"What would have been wrong with a university degree?" he asked quietly.

"Nothing. But taking the charity all these years! . . . They were kind about it in Glasgow, the Welfare folk. They put me to a school for catering for a couple of terms, and they found me my first job, and here I am."

"But lonely and unhappy?" murmured Nicky Font.

"Very lonely and unhappy, sir. Not just because of this trouble I'm in now. Because I'm Little Tich, born to be the funny little page-boy, and because—it's an awful-like thing to say—because I know I've a mind for better things."

"It's a realisable asset, you know, your size," observed his friend after a pause, "and just because, Jimsy—I'll be frank—you've got such darned good looks to go with it. You're not a dwarf, see? You're a darned fine-looking young fellow in miniature with a brain above slinging hash. Yes, son, you're dead right. It adds up to a problem, and you can't solve it for yourself. That so?"

"Yes. That's so."

Automatically he took the supper tray from the commode, piled the plates, arranged the knives and forks and put it on the dressing-table, ready to be taken away.

"What's the dream, then?" asked Nicky Font suddenly.

"To make money, to make myself independent. That's why I took to this. I was willing to be the comic wee man just long enough to get enough money to let me do what I want."

"Meaning? . . . This is where the plot thickens, young Jimsy."

"And I couldn't properly tell you, sir," Jimsy had to laugh at himself. "I've thought of a boarding-house or small hotel of my own. Or something in the medical line—I mean, massage or physiotherapy. One of the boys with me in the Highlands is doing very well as a chiropodist. But och me! I haven't even started making money in this job nor a sign of it. I won't say it's all bad luck. I doubt it's the pride in me."

Mr. Font's white fingers felt out blindly for his packet of Camels; Jimsy, the trained servant, was quick to whip out his box of matches, though he felt that the stateroom reeked sufficiently of toasted tobacco.

"Will I open the scuttle, sir? And that's the second table coming up from dinner. I ought to be getting back to my quarters."

"Okay, son. Guess I might arise after all and take the fresh air. Just remember, Jimsy: see that coffee's hot and strong in the morning."

"Yes, sir. And thank you very much for listening to me," said Jimsy, lifting the tray.

"Little man, I'm paid to listen when there's a good story around. Yours is a good story. Believe me," and he ended on a little lilt like the cadence of a song, "I'll be thinkin' of you."

3

Niccols Font seldom wakened either easily or happily, and it took him some time to realise on the morning after his long talk with Jimsy Bell that a stranger, having laid the coffee tray at his elbow, was now moving about his stateroom. It came upon him slowly that this was a tall, fair fellow instead of the small, dark one with whom he had hoped to resume an interesting conversation.

"Say, boy," he asked, blinking through blurred eyes above a tangled beard, "what the heck are you doing here? Where's the little fella, Bell?"

"Bell's off duty to-day, sir. I'll be looking after you from now on. Parkhouse is the name, sir."

"Isn't that just swell?" drawled Mr. Font, raising his body up to get at the strong, hot, black stimulant of coffee. "Bell's off duty, is he? Nothing about the little fella being in a spot of trouble?"

"I'm sure I don't know, sir. I've just got my instructions."

"Sure you don't know; sure you've just got your instructions. I'll hand it to you limey stooards," said Mr. Font, dipping the edge of a dry biscuit in his cup, "you were all born with your lips buttoned up. Some day, Parkhouse, I'm gonna write a thesis on how the renowned English reticence lost the great British Empire."

"That should be very interesting, sir," said Parkhouse. "Shall I run the bath now, sir?"

Jimsy himself had been called to Mr. Lurkin the night before and told that he was suspended for the time being. There would be work found for him somewhere in the Tourist until Mr. Pallister's charge had been proved or disproved.

"So I'm guilty before I'm tried!" Jimsy had spoken hotly.

"You're the Company's 'umble servant for the round trip," Mr. Lurkin had returned brutally. "Another word out your cheeky gub an' you'll be up before the Master and get logged."

There was no use saying anything. You just went back to your quarters and watched old Ted Apples working at his mat, told him your story and heard him repeat his fatalistic views on the lot of the passenger liner steward, serving a lot of swabs living above their incomes.

Days passed. Mr. Lurkin hardly troubled to find a real dirty job for him, as was within his dark power. Helping to pass dishes from the kitchens to the hatches in the Tourist dining-room. Nobody would have missed him much if he had skulked in the Glory Hole or sat down to read a week-old paper in a pantry.

The ship sailed into Bombay harbour, and Jimsy saw it from the poop. Its loveliness stirred him mightily with its haunting echoes of more familiar waterways of the North. Even if they were mostly tufted with palms, the shapes and disposition of the islands were the familiar Firth on the grand eastern scale, and he was enchanted to see the yachts racing between them as between marks in the mouths of lochs far away, the breezes brisk even under the high, hot sun. The splendid lift of the city on its hills, with the brown loom of the

Ghats behind, was entrancing; it took on majesty in the high buildings along the Apollo Bunder and in the ceremonial arch above the many-stepped landing pier, looking out to that special island in the Middle Ground built up of ballast jettisoned by generations of seamen and now crowned, like an old tooth, with fortifications.

S.S. *Canberra* was manœuvred slowly round the point and laid against Ballard Pier, and now Jimsy looked down for the first time on the incredible glitter of an Indian crowd, the pale, uplifted faces and white clothes of the few Europeans among them seeming without character in this riot of coloured saris, scarves, shawls, ornaments and turbans. He saw the gangways heaved up, the first scutter of officials into the bowels of the ship, and then the first dribble of the Bombay passengers landing. He saw his late colleagues, the cabin stewards concerned, starting to manhandle the luggage ashore, and he was sick to realise there was no place in that picturesque bustle for a small steward under suspicion, suspended and apparently forgotten.

Almost academically he considered from his eyrie high above the quay the possible ways of escape from his imprisonment, and he saw that it would not be difficult to get off the ship. Mix up with one of the working squads; dash down the gangway with an official-looking letter; everybody was too busy to observe the individual's movements. Or would his fate overtake him in the too easy recognition of his lack of inches?

It did not matter. Jimsy perceived that there was no way out of the dock area except through the block of buildings, solid and guarded like a fortress, in which the new India neurotically protected its integrity with a second zareba of customs, immigration and medical forms. Even if he had been one of the native monkeys, blissfully able to leap from a tree on the inner side of the iron fence to the boughs of one on the other, what hope for a British deserter with a charge against him in the world of pullulating cheap labour, of which the mob on the quay was only a moiety?

He was too intelligent to take his own day-dreamings

M

seriously. He knew that they were only the expressions of his feeling of frustration. That was the real problem, and there was no rational solution in sight.

Still hanging over the rail, having like any prisoner so little else to do, he saw Mr. Niccols Font and one of his friends of the film unit, a paunchy little man, walk ashore, enviably free to go sightseeing for the afternoon. They still clung to their affectation of untidy khaki clothes, and Jimsy wondered vaguely if it was not the symbol of irresponsibility after all. It was too easy to imagine in depression that he had amused Mr. Font in his cups for an hour or two and that, the mists clearing, the interest had departed. He could see nothing before him save the long round voyage, return to Britain in disgrace, and then the need to make a fresh start, however that might be compassed. He went below to his quarters and spent the afternoon, just reading and sleeping while old Apples, who had passed through his own fires, still worked silently at his mat.

The *Canberra* backed out from Ballard Pier at nine that evening when the city lights made the loops of a splendid necklace all along the front and hung in mazy clusters on the slopes. Jimsy Bell, escaping early from his parody of a stint in the Tourist, was out on the after-deck again, fascinated once more by the bustle of the dockside, now dramatised by the floodlights reflected from the sheer white sides of the great ship. The night wind was sharp, but he stood to watch the city slip backwards into the darkness of a sub-continent, to pick up the seamarks and the red balls of fire on the pilot tender, and at length to feel the slight lift of the hull's first curtseys to the Arabian Sea.

A finger tapped his shoulder from behind. He turned to identify Parkhouse, the lad who had relieved him in the First Class.

"You're wanted in A one-two-two, Tich," he said. "Mr. Font and a fat little guy. No, it's on the level, Tich. Instruction from Dirty Lurkin himself. Lucky little devil!"

Jimsy made his way forward and up.

"Come in!" shouted Mr. Font in answer to his tap on the

door, and it was a fresher Mr. Font than he had left a few evenings before. "Hiyya, Jimsy? Meet Munt Kopaks, the big chief of our unit. He looks tough, but he won't eat you. This is the young fella, Munt."

"Glad to meet you, son," observed Mr. Kopaks wheezily. "Find a seat."

He spoke under the handicap of a large agglomeration of fat about neck, chin and chest; his belly filled the angle between his short, columnar legs. The intonation of his American English had a Slavonic thickness. His eyes in the sallow face were wary, merciless. It most gravely interested Jimsy that, having greeted him, Mr. Kopaks thereafter seemed to regard him as a specimen and addressed himself exclusively to Nicky Font.

"I'll say he looks the part you've written into the script," he admitted to his colleague.

"Munt, I keep tellin' you—he wrote it in himself."

"Oh, yeah!"

Jimsy was then aware that he was under a wholly optical scrutiny by the Director of Transocean Films on location. The great, bright-eyed head dodged about, regarding his face from all angles. Mr. Kopaks went to the extent of standing up, bending down, and surveying Jimsy's person backwards from between his legs: a considerable physical feat.

"Call it a day," he confided to Nicky Font at length. "I'd like to get Hank to shoot a couple of hundred feet on that dial in all sorts of lighting, but it looks good enough to me."

This was a decision, Jimsy perceived. The short man, refusing Mr. Font's offer of a highball, punted himself to his feet and still addressed his colleague exclusively.

"You talk terms to the kid, Nicky. I got a poker school in the lounge. There's a guy called Pallister looks like losing a wad of good money."

He paused on his way to the door and laid a thick, gentle hand on Jimsy's head.

"See you in Ceylon, son," he said.

Nicky Font filled himself out the highball Mr. Kopaks had

declined and offered Jimsy a cigarette. The latter could see that
he was nervous.

"Light up and don't worry. We've got your nasty Mr.
Lurkin where he lives. And—well, hell, there it is, Jimsy! Just
before you give tongue: Munt Kopaks may look like an ape
with a dicky metabolism, but he's one of the finest directors
ever thrown up by the American movie industry. Fifty
thousand boys and girls in the States would give their souls
for what you got from him this evening. That's the set-up.
Think before you speak. I've got the night before me."

Jimsy took his time. He had filled himself out a glass of
iced water and sipped it while his mind turned over and over.

"But isn't it," he asked morosely at length, "isn't it just
the old trouble—letting my silly little body being used because
it's funny?"

"Yes, it is," agreed Font softly, "if you'll allow me to
substitute a gentler phrase for ' used.' Nobody's turning you
into a whore, if that's what's biting you. You can tell me to
go to hell and sanfairyann, even if I've spent two days writing
the part for you. But, son, that's only the one horn of your
dilemma."

"I'm very grateful, Mr. Font."

"Hell, grateful! It's me using you, son. Shrive me: if
we're going to swap claims to unique virtue, just have a look
at the other horn of your dilemma."

"I don't understand, Mr. Font."

"Your own words, Jimsy, your own words. You want
money as your way of escape. Okay. You'll make more money
on this one assignment than you could save in ten years in the
Glory Hole. And in dollars, son. Not pounds sterling."

Unconsciously or not, Mr. Font dramatised the scene by
switching off the roof-light and leaving the cabin lit only by
the discreet glow of the reading-lamp at the head of his bed.

"And you're not gonna be asked to be funny. You'll be
asked to be exactly yourself," Nicky went on, still speaking
softly. "I've written your own story into our settings, and
you're free to knock it sideways when you see the script. I'm

your debtor, son, not the other way round. You gave me the notion I had been groping for ever since Munt had his big idea of superimposing a story on a travelogue. You're the story. So think—then shoot."

Thinking was quite beyond Jimsy Bell in that moment; he could only feel. His first demurrer was only a mere confession of confusion.

"Mr. Kopaks said he'd see me in Ceylon. You know I can't get off the ship."

"Oh, yeah? . . . Jimsy boy, I don't know if you've ever been in Colombo Harbour, but any guy who couldn't skip his ship there is just plain dumb. Get yourself on to the landing-stage and leave the rest to Uncle Sam and Transocean Films. Immigration? Forget it; we've got an omnibus entry for the unit, and you've got your British passport. Or," Nicky Font drawled maliciously, "are you so terrible fond of Mr. Lurkin and the outfit here?"

"I hate the lot," Jimsy was vehement. "But I don't like to desert. It would look like running away from the charge."

"But you didn't swipe Pallister's watch. Your conscience is clear. You said it. Between you and me and the chamberpot, I don't think Mr. Lurkin is gonna shed bitter tears if one little stooard ain't around when he calls the roll."

"Yes," said Jimsy suddenly and after a pause.

"Meaning?"

"Yes, I'll do my best, sir."

"Attaboy! . . . And for cripe's sake, Jimsy, drop that 'sir'! You're half-way to being an American citizen already."

4

It was the easiest thing in the world to slip off the ship, a social entity so complex as to be indifferent to the movements of the individual. Dressed in mufti, Jimsy merged himself in a party of junior engineers bent hilariously on the evening ashore, and if his shortness of stature might have been reckoned to make him conspicuous in ordinary company, now it seemed to conceal him amid the noisy throng tumbling into a native ferryboat.

It did not trouble him that he had left his kit behind, and he looked up at the overweening white sides of the vessel as a man might look back on the walls of a prison that had held him long enough. Nothing of his love remained within it; a small affection for such as old Ted Apples and the veteran quartermaster were little as against his feeling of having escaped from the humiliation of bowing and scraping to the unworthy, of having to be servile to the Pallisters of this world, incapable of decent self-defence in their presence. And even the mighty S.S. *Canberra* was now just one of several great ships at anchor or moored inside the long mole that had made a great harbour out of an open roadstead; a score of the loveliest ships of the seafaring nations of the world: British, French, Dutch, Swedish, even one big, clumsy-looking freighter flying the Hammer and Sickle, an armed sentry at the top of the companion ladder.

As the native boat surged through a choppy sea towards the landing stage under the tall office and hotel buildings on the sea front Jimsy comforted himself with the feeling that he was now well lost in the seething life of an eastern port, but when he jumped ashore he did not follow the facetious engineers past the sentries on the stairways. He had begun to act already, and in the part in which Nicky Font had carefully rehearsed him.

He mingled with the native throng parading the pier within the barrier, and he kept his eye alert for any landing from the ship that might bring such as Mr. Lurkin ashore to spot him. His anxiety, however, was subdued by his interest in the strange charm of the foreign people about him: in their bright clothes, in those vivid saris, lemon and purple and gold, in the ebullient jewellery and ornaments worn by the women, in the dignity of their profiles and, above all, in the proud, equable poise of female heads trained like Victorian misses to carry weights without faltering.

He waited. One turn round the pier took him to where, in

the innermost corner of the harbour, the dhows of the Arabian seas were moored. He was far, far from the Western Isles, but Jimsy recognised these ships as the big and little brothers of the sort his kinsfolk knew how to manage in distant, colder waters. He considered the small coastal craft; he studied with almost professional concern the rigging plan of the Maldive schooners; he wondered at the high carrick-sterns of the big dhows that, as the old quartermaster had told him, would be making across the Indian Ocean, very much by guess or by God, towards Djibouti and other eastern ports of distant Africa.

One of these cast off while he waited, and Jimsy watched with excited admiration as, without the help of even a primitive engine, the apparently clumsy craft with creaking spars was jockeyed through the tangle of inert steam shipping towards the harbour mouth, as nimble in the crowded fairway as a terrier after a rabbit in a thicket. So absorbing was the sight, he jumped when a finger tapped his shoulders.

"Okay now, son," said Nicky Font in a crisp mutter between tight lips. "Follow me. Just smile to the immigration fella as we go through the barrier."

Jimsy did as he was bidden. A handsome young Sinhalese official glanced at the paper Nicky held out, gave one intelligent glance of rolling brown eyes at the small man's face, and smiled. He was on the soil of Ceylon. A large American car waited by the kerb outside.

"Get in," he was ordered, "and we'll get to hell out of this."

It was fantastic. It was one of Nicky Font's stories. Sitting beside the native driver, Jimsy was aware that Munt Kopaks sat behind him, the smoke of his cigar aggressive, but all that the director had to say in the course of a ten-mile journey was:

"Guess we'll have to find a camel somewhere."

"There's a zoo right here in Colombo, and I guess there'll be a camel around," said Nicky nervously. "Skip all that just now, Munt."

"Sure. I was only thinkin' out loud. Gee, I'm rarin' to get on location again. This island has certainly got something."

The car sped along the southern boulevards of the city, past great houses and gardens crammed with trees in incredibly bright flower, crimson, white and pale blue, and Jimsy made a private vow to learn their names. His eye was most closely held again, however, by the evening parade of the native folk, so charming in their poise and natural colour, so odd in their habit of holding above their pretty faces and gay garments a plain black umbrella that ludicrously recalled a northern city on a wet day. He could have laughed, if he had been in a mood less tense, to see how the barefooted cyclists pedalled with their heels, their feet splayed and their knees out so that their gowns should not be tangled in the works.

Soon enough they were out of the city on tracks that cut blindly through groves of palms monotonous in their dusty straightness, and then they were suddenly under a porch of a great hotel on a headland.

"Snap out of it, Jimsy," Nicky Font advised him. "This is our hideout while the unit assembles. Say, son, you'd better lie doggo in your room till the old ship sails again on her lawful occasions. Some of the boys may be out here on the bend, and we don't want you recognised just yet. I'm going right back to town; got to buy you some kit and square things with the American Consul. Quite happy, little man?"

"Perfectly happy, Mr. Font. I believe I could sleep for an hour or two."

"Go to it, brother. I'll send you up something to read from the news stand. If you want anything, ring for service. It's all on Transocean Films."

That was the marvel of it. He was no longer the funny little fellow who raced along hotel corridors at the bidding of impatient and impersonal autocrats; he had suddenly and magically become one of those who can pick up a receiver or press a bell and so have barefooted servitors in turbans awaiting his pleasure. His vanity was not touched by the fact, however. His immediate pleasure was in a fine bedroom with fans revolving against the high ceiling, with its own bathroom, with a verandah that commanded the view along miles of a sandy, palm-fringed bight towards Colombo: the Indian Ocean pounding and creaming up to the roots of the palms themselves.

This was the East in all its effulgence; absolutely nothing here to recall, however subtly, the atmosphere of home; nothing of resemblance between a Loch Fyne skiff and the catamarans, mere aggregations of planks and ropes, on which the native fishermen charged ashore on the crests of the waves to be thrown up on the sands like so many bits of flotsam. The very pound of the eastern ocean was sharper in his eyes and ears than the familiar swell that slowly filled the lochs out of the Atlantic.

It was an afternoon of strange remoteness, one of the strangest of his life, he reflected afterwards. He lay down on the bed, and the mere fact of enclosing oneself within mosquito nets was amusing enough to keep a man awake with the sense of present novelty. He seemed to have been hours alone when Nicky Font returned and threw a large parcel on top of a chest of drawers.

"Some duds for you, Jimsy. I just took a chance and rigged you out S.W. We'll get the rest to-morrow. Now for a bite of food in a quiet corner downstairs. Guess the boys from the ship won't come out this far now. Ever tasted a prawn curry?"

"No."

"Son, you haven't lived."

It was strangest of all to be eating now with two first-class passengers, but Jimsy found much to distract him in studying the eastern technique of service. It was efficient, he agreed, but it seemed odd that it took half a dozen smiling, barefooted bearers to serve one dish of curry with its piquant embroideries. Cheap labour; no Catering Wages Act here. . . . Into his professional concern broke the heavy voice of Munt Kopaks, so far a silent, absorbed but appreciative partaker of the feast.

"Say, son. Can you ride an elephant?"

"I'm afraid not, Mr. Kopaks."

"Aw, forget it, Munt! I've explained all that," drawled Nicky with weary patience. "There ain't no elephants where the kid came from in Scotland."

"No," agreed the director on reflection. "That was just me running over my sequences. Scrub it."

Jimsy was early upstairs and for a time watched the raucous and insolent Indian crows foraging and fighting for scraps of food about the now deserted tea-tables on the lawn below. Coolness was being blown in from the ocean by the steady wind out of the sou'-west. At length, watching for her appearance, he saw the *Canberra* pull out of Colombo harbour and make her slow turn to head southwards. She was a wonderful thing to see afloat in the gloaming, her own lights on the white sides giving her the grace of an apparition.

There was in all that big ship, however, not a single soul to care for Jimsy Bell, who had wilfully fallen out of the sort of life she represented. He had made his choice, even if under pressures; he regretted little now. But it was a queer thing to hear the thin piping of the geckos darting along the beams of his bedroom ceiling and to realise, that slipping overside from the *Canberra*, he might have been saying farewell to home for ever. There were certain kindnesses at home it would not be easy to forget.

5

In Scotland it rained mercilessly over the Easter week-end. The squalls drove in gusts up the Firth and smashed on the windows of the drawing-room at Ardyne so coarsely that it was difficult to carry on an equable conversation about the fire that had been built up, high and unseasonably, of logs from the clearings Uncle Finlay had ordained in the woodlands round about the big house.

He had taken the house on a long lease from his father's trustees, explaining himself vaguely as being anxious to keep the old place going for sentiment's sake. Perhaps his wife, Aunt Helen, would have said that he secretly dreamed of providing an inheritance for his nearly-adopted daughter, Beth. We've got plenty to live on, haven't we? I'd like to have a place where I can take it easy after a bit. . . . Helen Ferrier knew all the phrases. She did not herself like the house, thinking it remote, old fashioned and unworkable; give her a five-roomed bungalow on one floor every time; but if it pleased Finlay, she was quite happy that he should be so.

This was the house-warming, reopening the place for the first time since Festus Ferrier's death; this was to have been the Easter holiday for the small party of three, Beth having been lured from Hove after one of those sordid, catty squabbles with Mummy. Uncle Finlay was already talking of the great party of young people he planned for a fortnight in August, but to-night it seemed a ludicrous dream. They were a group marooned by the storm.

Uncle Finlay dozed by the fire, Aunt Helen knitted under the standard lamp. Restless, Beth had walked to the windows and stood watching how the half-gale up the Firth had lashed the waters into a state of grey insanity, lifting the tops in sheets off the waves it had itself created. She saw how these swept over the reef on which she and Jimsy Bell and Billy had once upon a time started to build a house.

"Uncle Finlay," she turned to hail the man at rest by the fire.

"What's that?" he cried, starting from his light slumbers. "Oh, it's you, Beth. What is it, dear?"

"I was just wondering if Jimsy Bell isn't home yet. Or is it a terribly slow voyage to Australia and back?"

Finlay Ferrier knocked out his pipe on the top bar of the fireplace.

"I was wondering when you were going to ask me that," he said.

"Why, what's wrong?"

"If you ask me, I don't think we're likely to see Master Bell again. It's been a bit awkward between me and my friends in the B. & A. But that's all in the day's work."

"You still don't tell us, Finlay," Aunt Helen intervened gently, "what happened to the boy."

"Well, it's all a bit mysterious," said Uncle Finlay, starting to refill his pipe and proceeding judiciously: "It seems a passenger lost a valuable watch, and Bell being the cabin steward—well, he was a suspect from the beginning, naturally."

"Jimsy Bell would never steal anything from anybody."

The protest was vehement, but Finlay Ferrier just smiled wryly at the bowl of his pipe.

"That may be, dear. But he deserted the ship at Colombo. That was a technical crime in itself, and you can't be surprised if the shipping people read something more into it."

"I just don't believe it."

"No," her uncle allowed "I thought there was a lot in the wee chap myself. But when you come to my age, Beth," he added with that claim to superior wisdom youth finds most nearly intolerable, however kindly it may be proffered, "when you come to my age, Beth, you'll never be surprised by human nature. That's simply not predictable. I think we'll just have to forget about Bell."

Beth turned back to the window, her eyes as full of tears as the darkling evening of rain. It was a shame. Jimsy was always being misunderstood and punished for things he did not do. Now, like one who tries to appreciate the fact of death within a near relationship, she found it terrifying and incredible that she would never see Jimsy Bell again.

CHAPTER SEVEN

Growing Up

"HERE SHE comes," announced Munt Kopaks. "Gee, isn't she a picture right now, just walking across the lot with them two native girls behind her?"

They sat on folding chairs, Munt and Nicky and Jimsy, beside a folding table that still carried the plates and bottles of their lunch. The unit had set up camp in a clearing among palms and strange trees under a nobbly hill near Kandy. The wild contours of the peaks and the fall of the screes, with vegetation hanging to them for dear life in contortions, kept reminding Jimsy Bell of West Scotland, but with an ever-weakening force of nostalgia. He was an important member of an American film unit at work in the heart of Ceylon. Now, with the sense of melodrama the slaves of Film can never shake off, Munt and Nicky were presenting to him the girl with whom he would be working henceforward in a curiously complex intimacy.

Feng Lee advanced towards the encampment, but it was truly more of a floating than an advance. Her two Sinhalese girl attendants in dark saris, one on each side and slightly behind her, were as the wavering acolytes attendant upon a *prima ballerina* in a mazy set-piece. All three, in the natural way of the Orient, had decorated their dark hair with scarlet flowers out of the forest from which they had emerged. They were as heroines in a fairy tale, the lost princess and her maids of honour: anything but the hired actresses of 20th century commerce approaching their alien, harsh masters.

Jimsy Bell at least surrendered to make-believe. He saw these three girls as simply lovely, crossing the clearing from

189

the edge of the palms; and none of the professional cynicism of his American friends could abate his personal concern at being about to meet the girl who, according to script, would be very near him often enough and ultimately in his arms.

She came up towards the table and halted some ten yards short of it, her attendants following her movements as if they had been rehearsing the scene for days on end. She bowed, as if to her mysterious gods, her fragile hands folded across her lap; and the two Sinhalese girls bowed in unison.

"Come right forward, kid!" cried Munt Kopaks, the rawness of power and international inexperience torturing the soul of Nicky Font. "Step right up, Feng, and meet your own fighting weight in l'il Jimsy Bell. Jimsy—meet Feng Lee."

The girl approached the table, her attendants remaining demurely in the background, but she halted a yard short of it and dropped another curtsey. With this she made a ceremonial gesture of submission, as it were, the palms of her small, frail hands slipping down the fronts of her thighs. Her eyes fell to the ground, and when she raised them at length they fluttered above a faint blush under the rice powder on her cheeks. For the rough shaking of hands of Western custom she substituted a smile, pale and utterly enigmatic.

"Ready to start work, Feng?" Munt Kopaks blundered on in his rough way among racial niceties.

"I am very happy to work," the girl returned in a small voice that tinkled like wind-bells on a rock-temple in the jungle.

"Good girl! We'll get cracking on some of your scenes to-morrow."

Her name was Chinese, but you would have said that several of the bloods of South-Eastern Asia had contributed to the making of her doll's body. She wore in fact the dress of the Burmese women—the little starched jacket over a thin white blouse and above the black tamain skirt that sheathed her exquisite hips and legs. She made her obeisance again and started to back away, showing how that difficult movement can be made a thing of grace; her little hands played like leaves in the air as she went. Nor did she turn until her acolytes had closed behind her, and then the three became figures in a tapestry as they moved away across the clearing into the mystery of the background of rustling bamboos, flowering trees and palms.

"Gee, ain't she a flower?" grunted the director.

"Munt, your metaphors are inadequate," Nicky protested. "The child is as the petal of a rare white blossom that floats on a slow stream under the full moon. Or you could say she is the dearest pearl in the treasury of an empress long dead. Or, to vary the figure . . ."

"Cut it, Nicky! Okay, okay, okay! She's anything you like in the fancy line, but she's just the cat's pyjamas for my picture and your story. Reminds me . . . H'ya gettin' on with the elephant, Jimsy?"

For day after day on end Jimsy had been thinking and living elephant, in the closest bonds with Ma Palai of the pearly eye and her oozie, San Po See. They were of Burma, both of them, and San Po See, now a wiseacre of seventeen, had grown up with his charge. The great grey elephant and the boy with the knotted hair, tied by a length of red silk, were wedded in mutual wisdom: nay, in a mystic understanding, and it had been Jimsy's allotted task to break into their private circle and be accepted in friendship and trust by the incredibly large and strong, the incredibly shrewd, beast of the teak forests.

San Po See and Jimsy had been friends from the end of their first day of work together. The jealous Burmese boy had perceived in the man from the West the instinctive understanding of animal sensibilities without which it is impossible to deal with the elephant, and he was delighted to have an obedient pupil. Jimsy was willing for hours on end to approach Ma Palai slowly from the front and stand and let himself be smelt and sized up by the great beast. He learned from San Po See how to pet her, even to make her do little tricks for him, and then reward her with bamboo shoots. It was only a matter of days before Ma Palai was delighted to put her strong trunk gently round Jimsy's body and, at a touch of San Po See's big toe on the muscles behind her ear, lift him up and swing him through the air to sit on her shoulders behind her own trusted oozie.

Now they were rehearsing in a separate clearing, and until Jimsy's body was sore, the shot Munt Kopaks insisted must be Jimsy's first appearance in the picture. To the soft whirr of hidden cameras, turning as they would in action, he was to cartwheel across the clearing into the clutch of Ma Palai's trunk, and so be picked up and lifted to her neck. Patience, patience; bit by bit by bit; tutoring the fine great beast to take the shock until it became a joke for her; feeding her with sugar cane; timing, timing.

"I think we can do it almost any time now, Munt," Jimsy answered the director's question. Then he asserted his position as a star performer. "But there are to be no megaphones or people bawling about the place. You'll have to leave it absolutely to Ma Palai and San Po See and me. We can work out a code of signals."

"Okay, okay! It's your show, Jimsy. I guess, Nicky," he turned to his script-writer, "we can start shootin' action right now. I've sure got a bellyful of scenery. And then across the wide Pacific to the dear old Golden Gates and the white lights. Jimsy boy, if you haven't seen San Fran you haven't started to live."

Within a couple of days the atmosphere of the camp suddenly changed as Munt Kopaks came out of his drawling interest in mere rehearsals to be for a hectic week the director of genius, surly and relentless. In these days Jimsy came to know the nature of the agonised tedium behind the flash of the finished product of the screen. He was wakened at six in the morning to snatch a cup of tea and eat a little fruit, then submit for an hour to the make-up experts, the sweat oozing through the cosmetics. He had to sit about the lot while the lighting cameramen peered through and at their lenses and instruments and impartially announced at intervals that shooting was impossible. The lenses of the cameras fogged in the damp heat; the dynamos ran to a stop with a blue sputtering in thundery air. Even when Munt Kopaks at length clapped his hands and called for a rehearsal, the same small piece of action had to be gone over and over and over again until every movement, gesture, word had been rendered down to the stark minimum the medium demands.

The sun was relentless, the heat a burden that could not be thrown off. Often enough the sun declining over the Indian Ocean was starting to gild the peaks above Kandy before Munt Kopaks would turn with a chuckle to the cameras and say " Roll 'em." It was bliss that jeeps came along to take the principals back to camp after a full twelve hours of delay and then but a few hectic seconds of the real work that would at length show on the screen for a moment and be gone.

Jimsy Bell and Feng Lee made friends during those long hours on the edge of the jungle. Before any scene that would require their presence together they sat side by side on folding seats, Jimsy eager to be friendly and talkative, the girl no more than receptive in her Indonesian remoteness. For him she never became a person with a mind of her own; she was just lovely, smiling, negative, desirable for the pretty flesh of her. One evening, after he had seemed to fall asleep over the shards of the supper table, he had stirred to hear Nicky and Munt discuss them beyond the flaps of the tent.

"I keep tellin' you, Munt," Nicky was protesting testily, "the doll ain't an actress. She's a natural, and I just wrote into the script what she would do naturally. Now, little Jimsy started as a natural, but he's beginning to act intelligently."

"Sure he is! Gee," the director added coarsely, "I'd like to mate these two! Guess we'd get something phenomenal."

"Guess you might get another Johnny Weissmuller," retorted Nicky with brutal impatience. "Get down on your knees and give thanks for two kids who can act most of the top-ranking stars of Hollywood off the map."

Jimsy was often to wonder in later years if he ever knew Feng Lee, or if there was anything to know save a perfect body and an eternally baffling simplicity. The business of acting with her irked him not at all. Even in the odd passages of simulated emotion he found himself the actor, detached in absorption under the eyes of the cameras; if her body was soft and warm and submissive, she was for the moment only another player of a part whom he might have loathed as a person. Within the camp she dwelt apart in a sort of *purdah* with her own native women, and he often thought that they were no more mature in mind than boarding-school misses as they ran hand in hand across the clearing to pick flowers for the adornment of their black hair or to bathe in a rock pool at the foot of the hills.

They made friends as a young boy and a young girl will. Often, when Munt Kopaks had released them after a wearing spell of rehearsal and the brief tension of shooting, Feng would take Jimsy's hand and lead him, at a laughing run to where, within the edge of the jungle, they could buy nuts and fruit or drink the fresh milk of yellow coconuts, haggling blithely with the pretty little girls who miraculously contrived to appear fresh and clean from the *bustis* of matting in which they lived in clotted intimacy with hordes of relations.

But one day on such an expedition they were caught in mid-afternoon by a thunderstorm. It swooped without any warning that even Jimsy's weatherly eye had seen. The sky above the trees had glowed with golden light, and then all was dark. It was as if the storm were a bomb deliberately dropped on the camp site and the echoing crags above it. Feng Lee's pale face was the colour of death in the flashes of lightning. The thunderclaps were as salvoes of shells malevolently aimed to burst above their heads. The rain came ripping along the treetops like shears through a coarse fabric. Great drops began to fall upon them where they stood in the rough track to the native hamlet. Feng Lee started to whimper.

He seized her hand and felt the trembling of her person. He tugged her into the shelter of a thick clump of bamboos and put his arm about her, sorry in the way of a brother that she should be so greatly terrified. He rolled up the *lungyi* he had been wearing for his part, and they sat down on it to wait, his arms still about her shoulders. Then her whimperings became a sobbing, and then a crying; and then Feng Lee threw her arms about Jimsy's neck and curled her slight body into his, her knees tucked up into his groin. She was thinly clad in Chinese costume of wide pyjama trousers and a long tunic in jade green, decorated with silver dragons.

Unhappily enough, his northern conscience troubled, Jimsy held her there till the storm passed. He felt like an uncle, patting her damp shoulder, but he knew that she would be his in the flesh at the lifting of a finger. Innocent, because without any more morals than a cat, that would be her natural mode of expression, while he was bound by pity and a tenderness for that very innocence and could not of his nature think of a love that was not based on at least a few qualities of the mind and heart.

He was glad when the storm had passed, leaving the evening skies clearer than ever in the light of a sun now falling to its eclipse in a green flash under the Indian Ocean. He was exasperated, as they rejoined the group about the cameras, by something like a quizzing, leering look on the face of Munt Kopaks. Even in their brief hour in the jungle together, he realised on a gust of irritation, Feng Lee had complicated the pattern of living for him.

2

The first half of the school winter was once more nearing its end, and the frets of maidenhood were again disturbing the fourscore immortal souls who had for nearly three months submitted meekly enough to the conventional order of a high-class boarding school for young ladies. Home had ceased to be the remote place to which one wrote each Sunday morning a dutiful letter, finding it difficult to report anything interesting save a creditable hockey result; it had resumed its warm importance as a place of belonging, with a daddy and mummy instead of the headmistress and the housemistress, with a brother to play and fight with, brothers' friends to dance with; lying in bed, not knowing beforehand exactly what the next meal would consist of, presents—the irresponsible warmth of it all.

In the room Beth Ferrier shared with three other maidens Tubby Corcoran admitted a disappointment.

"Daddy says it's far too expensive to fly me out to Gib., and I've got to go and stay with two frowsty old aunts at Lincoln. Not my own aunts," she stressed the hardship, "Daddy's aunts."

"But how bleak, Tubs!" commiserated Jacqueline Gorringe, the thin, clever one with the wispy hair and the specs. "What about you, Scotty?"

"Oh, just the usual. Hove first of all, and then my uncle's house in Scotland."

"Whence the letters from Oliphant's," observed Jacqueline humorously.

"Mind your own business, Jacky Gorringe!" retorted Beth hotly and blushing. "What about yourself, if it comes to that?"

"I, cads," announced Jacqueline, who was a student of radio and had engineered this situation, "am going to Germany. My Uncle Bill's on the staff at Bad-something-or-other. Think of the regimental parties, all sorts of ducky officers. Whoopee!"

It was agreed that this was the most brilliant prospect of all, and poor little Nancy Coghill, the baby of the room, could have wept to think that she was only going back to Preston and the eternal battle against four brothers and a stepmother.

"Anybody got any thrilling cards yet?" asked Tubby Corcoran.

"One from Aden, from my sister," said Beth.

"Oh, your sister!" commented Tubby, as if the fact were slightly discreditable.

"Last year you had a scrummy one from Egypt with chickens and things on it," said Jacqueline, the clever one. "Or has the boy-friend forgotten Scotty's dark eyes?"

"He has nothing of the sort!" Beth protested hotly. "You wait."

For Beth it was all so much more than the light give-and-take of four girls sharing a room. The ghost of Jimsy Bell would never desert those chambers of her mind that echoed with the nagging, secret arguments of her lonely soul. She could not have phrased it so, but he remained the necessary symbol of that sense of continuity in living she so often felt to have lost amid the bickerings between Mummy and Uncle Finlay, between the old-maidish dullness of Cherry Gables and the exuberant, but still not quite real, comforts of Uncle Finlay's homes in Scotland. It was awful to feel, sometimes, that you were most yourself in the alien world of a good boarding-school for young ladies.

"I shall wait with complete composure," said Jacqueline in her irritating way, squinting slightly behind her glasses. "I can always send you a New Year card from Germany."

The miracle was that it came, the card from Jimsy. She got it at break on the day before term ended and flew to the bedroom to enjoy it in secret. The thin Air Mail envelope had been readdressed from Uncle Finlay's house in Glasgow by Aunt Helen. The stamp—the stamp alone was exciting. It portrayed the severe visage of George Washington; it had been clearly postmarked as from Hollywood, Cal. But the writing of the address was gloriously, certainly that of Jimsy Bell.

Beth realised that she would tear and spoil the packet with her too-eager fingers, and she disciplined herself to take her long nail-file from the communal dressing-table and slit it open. Then, between an unsteady forefinger and thumb, she found herself staring at a photograph of Jimsy himself—Jimsy in fancy dress, with a turban on his head, Jimsy obviously made-up as an Oriental boy, Jimsy seated behind the ears of a benevolent-looking she-elephant with a small, intelligent eye, and against a background of palms.

As a photograph, it was beautiful, but it was as empty of information as a label. Beside the picture there was nothing but a neat note, reading

Yes, this is me and my friend, Ma Palai.
Best respects, Jimsy.

The bell rang outside the class-rooms downstairs, and in her flurry Beth tucked her strange missive inside one leg of her folded pyjamas. Her instinct was to keep it a secret at least until her own mind could accept the astonishing story the picture purported to tell. The exotic envelope, however, had been duly noted by the inquisitive eye of Jacqueline as it waited collection on the rack in the outer hall, and when school was over for almost the last day of term and the four girls were starting to pack in their overcrowded room, the card had to be produced.

"Here he is," said Beth, by now decided to be proud of him. "That's my friend."

The card was almost torn by quick, competitive fingers.

"Gosh!" crashed the chorus.

"Isn't he a duck?" Tubby Corcoran demanded to know. "California, here I come."

"He looks awfully small," hazarded little Nancy Coghill.

"If you were stuck up on the back of an elephant, Coggers, you'd look like a pimple," Jacqueline squashed her. "Scotty, you never told us he was a film star. I certainly never heard of a Jimsy anything in the big titles."

"I never said he was," returned Beth, flustered on the defensive. She plunged into invention recklessly. "This is his first picture. That shot was taken in India somewhere. Of course, they've gone back to Hollywood to finish the picture."

This was conclusive. In the small, pathetic competition of four young girls Beth had won first prize.

"Tell you what," said Jacqueline, still in charge of the picture. "We'll pin him up above the mantelpiece beside Gregory Peck."

"You'll do nothing of the sort. He's mine."

Beth was enraged. She snatched the photograph from her friend, not thereby improving its shape.

"Okay, Scotty," said Jacqueline with a shrewd, small smile. "But you could write and ask him to send a real smasher of a picture to cheer the gloom of four starved virgins."

"Oh, of course!" Beth lied gallantly. "That's easy."

She never did so. She could not bring herself to beg of Jimsy Bell, making herself a goggling schoolgirl in his eyes, nor could she bear to hazard a rebuff. He had sent her the exciting card, yes, but that was only the keeping of a promise to a kid. He had betrayed the trust of Uncle Finlay, and he would never come back again. It seemed in the issue that Jimsy Bell was her own secret, if almost a guilty one, and Beth could not bear that it should be complicated by a sharing and by an exposure to the cleverness of Jacqueline Gorringe. Better, in fact, to pretend that her film star was too great and remote and busy to be bothered with a pack of schoolgirls, even to pretend that she had quite forgotten him.

Time was on her side in this small private concern, time the remorseless leveller of values. Back from the holidays, each of four young girls who dressed, undressed, slept and chattered in the same not very large bedroom for day upon day and night after night on end had all the happenings of four blessed weeks of freedom to discuss. The dangerous one, Jacqueline, was so full of her triumphant sojourn in Occupied Germany that not many other topics could arise. The Hockey XI was still unbeaten, and could they keep it up until just before the distant Easter break? Over three of them loomed the terror of certificate exams, the nearer shadows of form mistresses even intruding on their dreams with the rasping shibboleth of *Work, work, work*!

Beth learned how easily to evade Jacqueline's occasional thrust or to turn it off with a fine pretence of secret communications across the Atlantic, and it was little Nancy Coghill who surprisingly revealed that the legend of Jimsy Bell, that had taken on a dreamlike quality by the time April came round with the daffodils, was an exciting reality after all.

The child had been given as a Christmas present a subscription to a film magazine of such effulgence that she had become one of the most sought-after inmates of Thurston Grange. It was a periodical which, enormously illustrated, conducted its readers inside the Hollywood film industry and a long way into the private lives of its more prominent personalities. If it was trivial for the most part, at least it had the solid value of chronicling the work in progress at the studios and their ultimate output. For that considerable section of the public for which Film is warp in the texture of living "The Picture of the Week " in *Movie Mirror* had the validity of a Papal bull.

It had been laid down by the headmistress that *Movie Mirror* was to be neither read nor even passed from one hand to another except during the few free hours of the schoolgirl's day, and the cylindrical bulk of the critical number had to lie on Nancy's bedside commode until, on a cool April evening about five, she returned from the first tennis practice of the season.

She could not wait to change; she tore the wrapper open and flopped on her bed, belly downwards and her head propped between her cupped hands, to drink her ration of celluloid life to the dregs. Her first flick of the glossy, curved pages opened the book at the centre spread and its leading feature, and there it was, seeming to hit upwards from the page at her goggling eyes—the familiar picture, much enlarged, of Scotty's friend behind the ears of Ma Palai, the wise she-elephant.

Agonised was the young girl's waiting until her older room-mates returned from match practice, and they thought at first that little Nancy had had a turn, so incoherent were her phrases and gestures.

"Calm yourself, Coggers! " advised Jacqueline, parodying their headmistress. "Now, in a word——"

"But look! " the child screamed, holding out the magazine and pointing to the picture. "Scotty's friend—the boy on the elephant—the Picture of the Week! "

The three others shrieked in unison and pounced for the sheet with the ferocity of wing forwards. It was torn from its owner's grasp, struggled for and at length, by common consent, laid out on a counterpane so that all might feast their eyes at once.

There it was, now embellished with the florid vocabulary of high-powered publicity, this travel saga. It was magnificent, true to life, educative, heart-stirring, romantic; the publicity man had nearly run through the thesaurus. Two famous names headed the list of the cast, but at the foot, in letters only slightly smaller ran the legend

FEATURING TRANSOCEAN'S LATEST DISCOVERIES IN
UNSPOILT FILM GENIUS

SEUMAS BELL AND FENG LEE

The turmoil of excitement subsiding a little, Jacqueline must drop her little gout of acid into the stream of delight.

"Seumas Bell—how do you pronounce it? You said his name was Jimsy, Scotty."

"So it is. Seumas is Gaelic for James, same as Hamish or Shamus. Shamus is nearest."

"And who's Feng Lee?"

"How do I know?" returned Beth, nettled. "I didn't produce the film."

"But she's the Chinese girl, Jacky!" little Nancy fortunately intervened to display the fruits of her longer study of the pictures. "Down at the foot there. Isn't she lovely?"

The dirty forefinger pointed to a print in which a young Chinese girl was shown kneeling, her folded hands to her face, before Jimsy on his elephant.

"Look out, Scotty!" advised Jacqueline, still mischievous. "Write and demand an explanation. In any case, you can write now and ask for a big copy of the Christmas card to pin up beside darling Gregory. And if you won't," she admitted Beth's triumph handsomely, "I will."

"And I suppose," mourned Tubby Corcoran, "it will be ages before we see it—I mean, the whole film."

3

It was an embarrassment so long as she remained at Thurston Grange, that picture, and often she lay at nights thinking with mortification of her weakness in displaying Jimsy's Christmas card to her room-mates. Brought up outwith the range of picture houses, Beth had not realised how much the art had become so much a part of the life, the dream-life at least, of so many of her fellow-creatures. Even Miss Sycamore, the headmistress, had condescended to mention the, to her, faintly amusing association.

This was after the last tennis match of the season, in which Beth and Tubby Corcoran, playing first couple for the Grange, had fought Cordiners' best pair on a glowing evening of June to a 3-0 victory and by five matches to four preserved for the school an unbeaten record for the season.

"Well played, Ferrier, jolly well played! " the Head had said in her throaty, slightly mannish voice that was a parody of the voice of every schoolmarm on stage, screen and air. "And I hear you actually have a film star in the family."

"I don't think he's actually a film star, Miss Sycamore," returned Beth as coldly as she dared. "He was a page-boy in my father's house."

"Quite, quite. But a not uninteresting coincidence. I hope the picture is suitable for young people. Perhaps we could make it a special privilege for the girls."

"I'm sure I don't know, Miss Sycamore," Beth insisted stoutly.

Allowing for her own folly, she resented the intrusion; and now she realised that the story of Jimsy Bell and herself was a secret and one she would henceforth keep to herself. Uncle Finlay could never understand how deliciously secret it was; he had washed his hands of Jimsy Bell, and that was that. Aunt Helen might only guess and would then remain reticent behind her gentle smile. Mummy . . . But you never considered

Mummy seriously in relation to your private life. Even if Aunt Cicely were to dig Mummy out and drive her down to see the picture in Brighton, she would probably just vaguely recognise that little man who was once at Ardyne and say that it was a small world or you never knew or something feckless.

Meanwhile, you wanted to get away from school. Oh, it was not just the embarrassing case of Jimsy! You had outlived school. You wanted to make another start where you could stand on your own feet and be Beth Ferrier for better or worse. One forenoon towards the end of her last term at Thurston Grange she was called to the headmistress's room.

"Ah, you, Ferrier! Sit down a moment. I've got something for you here."

The pretty, faded lady riffled among piled papers on her desk.

"Yes, certain results. No School Certificate for you, my dear, but we didn't try very hard, did we? On the other hand, you've got a pass—yes, let me see, yes—quite a good pass in the Oxford and Cambridge, and if you're only going in for nursing, of course . . ."

That little word 'only' rankled. For Beth her choice of career was a serious thing, another secret. It was what she wanted to do; it was a good, proud thing to do in expression of a private dedication. With merciless clarity the girl knew that the older woman looked at it through the spectacles of a snobbery. Lady doctors, yes; but lady nurses—my dear!

Mummy would object again: not because she had any considered objections to nursing but simply because she was by nature incapable of understanding why any female should want any sort of career of her own. And while Uncle Finlay and Aunt Helen were behind her, did that not horribly complicate the conflict with Mummy?

So it was back to Hove in late July, to suburban Hove on the hill, aloof in its mock Tudor villas and fine gardens from the fret of the Front and the big hotels: the Hove so closely linked with London by shining cars and expensive season tickets and electric trains. For Beth it was the intolerably dull, negative Hove of Cherry Gables, Mummy, Aunt Cicely and Billy where, she passionately felt, her soul would rot in the course of a winter.

As the train carried her from Victoria she realised with a pang that the issue of her future had never been settled with Mummy, thanks to Mummy's refusal to face a decision. Brisk Uncle Finlay had taken it all for granted and had arranged for her to enter the big Edinburgh hospital in September, and Mummy had been told. It was her maddening technique, however, to pretend that awkwardnesses did not exist and to refuse to have them brought into the open, and now the girl moodily looked forward to another of those sordid little bickerings, misunderstandings and reproaches; for Mummy was invincibly the innocent, outraged party in all these transactions.

The conflict came upon them quickly, late that evening. Aunt Cicely had taken Billy to the pictures to see one of those Wild West dramas that so greatly recompensed him for his in-born timidity, and mother and daughter sat out on the lawn on deck-chairs within the horns of a crescent-shaped bed of herbaceous plants.

Fitly enough, the air was clotted with the threat of thunder, the surly, brassy clouds lying heavy over the Downs and the sea. They had quickly exhausted their small stocks of re-miniscence, and confidences they had none, and there had been silence between them before Mummy herself raised the inevitable issue, apparently addressing a small garment she was knitting for Ketron's baby, expected in November.

"I thought we might have a holiday together this year, you and Billy and I. They say the Channel Islands are very nice in September. Of course, I couldn't dream of going with the crowds in August."

"But you forget, Mummy. I'm to start at the hospital on the second of September."

Beth schooled herself to speak quietly, watching her moves and controlling her tones with exquisite care.

"What! Are you still toying with that silly idea?"

"It's not toying, Mummy. Every girl has a job nowadays, and that's the one I want." She was still trying to be very careful, but her annoyance betrayed her. "What do you expect me to do? Sit here and turn into an old maid?"

"Of all the silly, schoolgirlish things to say! Of course, I know you don't care in the least what happens to Billy and me. You're just like your father. Pig-headed; must get everything your own way."

This, as Beth thought, was a queer and even sinister back-lash from the past. Having snapped it out, Mrs. Ferrier fell back on sentimentality.

"Ketron is coming home to have her baby, and I did think we might all be together for once in a while."

"Ketron coming home! Goody!" cried Beth naturally. "That would be nice for Christmas, with the baby."

"From what I see in the papers," observed Mummy sarcastically, "nurses spend Christmas feeding dirty old men and women with plum pudding. However, if you are determined to go your own selfish way," continued Mrs. Ferrier, gathering up her knitting, "I'm going inside. It looks like rain. See that the chairs are put away nicely."

As she folded the chairs and stacked them in the verandah Beth considered sadly the sorry shape that even an umbilical relationship could take. She could not know for certain, but she guessed now that Mummy had long ago accepted defeat when Uncle Finlay had claimed her for the New Year party. She guessed that Mummy was too lazy to be bothered with a difficult daughter, too shallow to care much about the losing of her. She would be content with Billy, whom she could wholly possess; and Ketron was coming home to be a real companion.

Beth stood on the verandah watching the preliminary cantrips of lightning over France, the livid light running along the lower edges of the clouds, prettifying them. There was nothing between them and her now. It was victory, much easier than she had expected, but Mummy had had the Pyrrhic triumph of divesting it wholly of glory, even decent happiness.

The next fortnight was a period of uneasy armistice, and Beth knew the reality of positive, ever-present unhappiness. She was unhappy to be conscious of guilt, even if that had been put upon her: unhappy because she was vaguely sorry for the mother she despised; unhappy to be leaving Billy to a fate she could not envisage. Even the vigour of Aunt Cicely could not pump oxygen into the collapsing body of the family life. It was a fortnight of small outings, tea parties, going to the pictures, shopping—a panoramic foretaste of the cost of surrender. And surrender was the critical impossibility. Beth knew that, even if she was prevailed upon to stay within the stasis of suburban life, nothing would stop her walking down to the Front one day and finding a job, even if it was only selling ices in a seaside café.

Thus she lost more sleep than was good for a young girl, being terrified by the knowledge that she must act on her own account to break the tension, and that her first word must inevitably start another scene with Mummy, all the more squalid for being final. She lost sleep simply by wondering, wondering, how she could initiate and then face the crisis. It was mortifying that Mummy's strength lay in her gift for doing nothing. It was hopeless to think of confiding in Aunt Cicely, who would make it all worse by blundering in with her clipped, half-baked decisions.

The solution came out of the blue, provided by Uncle Finlay in person, almost literally the god out of the car. He rang one day at lunchtime. Aunt Cicely answered the ring of the telephone bell and returned to the table, looking faintly pleased.

"Finlay," she answered her sister's inquiring glance. "He's coming for tea, driving down in another new car. Says he wants to talk about the arrangements for Beth."

"I wish he would mind his own business," snapped Mummy.

"Rot, Elaine," returned Aunt Cicely, but mildly. "I want to have a jolly good look at this new car of his. Trust Finlay! He always does himself well in the way of cars."

"And you'd better keep out of the way until I hear what he's got to say," Mrs. Ferrier turned on her daughter.

Beth was delighted. Fear and unhappiness slipped from her as does pain after the few black minutes in the dentist's chair. You trusted absolutely in Uncle Finlay's strength and singleness of purpose; you wickedly rejoiced to think how Mummy's peevish demurrers would wither away before his dynamic simplicity. That was really why she hated him.

He came at four o'clock, slipping into the drive at the wheel of a great blue car that almost vociferously proclaimed the elegant superiority of British automobile engineering; and Beth was out with Aunt Cicely to greet him.

"Hullo, Beth, my pet!" he hailed her, slipping out of the driving seat and bending to give her a smacking kiss on the cheek. "Bought your kilt yet? Hullo, Cicely! What do you think of my latest toy?"

"Finlay, Finlay!" crooned Aunt Cicely. "You've got an eye, haven't you? Can go?"

"Ninety on the best stretch down and still well within the collar, but simply terrific in traffic. Apart from stops I didn't need to change down once through the worst of South London."

"Pretty little thing," mused Aunt Cicely, her appraising head cocked to the side. "Well, Finlay, if you ever want to give me a birthday present you know what I'd like. But you'll want to have a word with Elaine. She's in the drawingroom. Tea in half an hour, Beth," she adroitly dismissed her niece.

Aunt Cicely was not in general a subtle woman, but she knew to a hair how the parties stood in the small battle now approaching. You could not live with Elaine for a week without knowing her to be a knot of petty resentments. She thought Elaine a damn' fool in the business of Beth and a career in nursing, but she had her loyalties, and it was not easy to sit and hear the bluff commonsense of Finlay Ferrier bulldozing through the female sensibilities, not easy to feel that his assumption of the *fait accompli* wasn't a thought highhanded. If only Elaine would speak up and not sit like a hurt old cat, nursing her grievances.

"For myself," she dared to intervene at one point. "I'm all

for a girl having a career, and if Beth's hell-bent on being a nurse, jolly good luck to her! I still don't see why she can't do her training in London and be near her own people."

"No, Cicely," Finlay Ferrier bowled her over flatly, and with his indestructible sincerity. "She'll get far and away the best training in Scotland. Nothing like it. Pick up a job anywhere when she's qualified. And Helen and I," he added in clumsy innocence, "are always at hand."

There was nothing you could do against such assumptions, and Elaine could only sit like a fool, saying nothing. On her behalf, and on Beth's, the sister and aunt, and not without cunning, made the fatal allowance.

"Well, I suppose we'll have to think about organising some uniform for the child."

"You needn't worry about that, Cicely," said Finlay cheerfully. "Those big Edinburgh hospitals have their own approved suppliers. I think you can trust Helen to look after all that."

"I suppose we can," admitted Cicely dryly. "Now, a cup of tea. Where's that girl?"

Beth joined the company with apprehension and found it impossible to rejoice in the wonderful things that were told her—how Uncle Finlay would drive her all the way to Scotland in the new car one day next week—"Got to run her in properly, anyhow," Uncle Finlay explained—and how she was to have a fortnight at Ardyne—"a nice party of young people," Uncle Finlay promised her—before the day when she would first don a nurse's uniform and start learning how to dust a room.

She went through the motions of delight and gratitude and Uncle Finlay was obviously much pleased with himself as organiser and foster-father, but Beth could not be happy. It seemed that Mummy, by contributing not a word out of her guarded world of resentment, could have the last word as between them after all.

Apart from Uncle Finlay, the only perfectly happy person about Cherry Gables that afternoon was young Billy who, returning from a Boy Scout outing as the uncle was departing

for London in the great car, was tipped a pound and told not
to spend it all in one shop, a jocular injunction the poor boy
took seriously and promised himself faithfully to obey.

4

The party was clamorous. Jimsy found that if he could
detach himself from a conversational group and stand apart
for a minute, the clamour was deafening to an intolerable
degree, like the noise of a panic in a monkey colony or a
quarrelling of macaws. The high, competitive voices of
American women, the whorls of scented cigarette smoke above
their fabulous hats, the reeks of gin and cosmetics, the shrieks
that declared with utter insincerity admiration or affection, the
clink or smashing of glasses, the guffaws of male laughter from
the ring of fans about a licensed wit—they made a confusion
that had his eyes smarting and his head aching.

He wished that it would stop, and that he could slip away
to his tiny, quiet apartment in a block high on the hills above
Los Angeles. In one of his reflective moods during their voyage
across the Pacific Nicky Font had counselled him.

" You're going to find Hollywood a strange place, Jimsy. I
suppose it represents the dream of every feather-headed girl in
the world, but it's tough. It's Number One all the time, little
man, and devil take the hindmost. It's a hell of vanity and
jealousy; it's as brittle with insincerity as one of those toffee
baskets they dish up as a sweet in India; the gushers are always
at your back with a naked knife, waiting to get you out of the
way. Aw, there's a lot of nice, intelligent, brilliant people in
Hollywood, but as a social phenomenon it's about as healthy as
a high-class bughouse for rich dipsomaniacs. Pass the bottle,
Jimsy, and note well how Hollywood got one, Niccols Font,
into a condition of self-disgust. No man to advise you, Jimsy,
but a word in your ear. Just try your goddamdest hard to be
absolutely yourself."

He could never be anything else. Making pictures had been

fun in Ceylon with Feng and Nicky and Munt on a glorified picnic; the factory conditions of the studios depressed him, and the social life outside them seemed to him to have a raucous rawness all its own. Oh, the waiting, waiting, waiting on the set till the lighting was right, the hot glare of artificial lighting despite the brilliance of the Californian sun outside, the huffs and even tantrums of stars! It was often that Jimsy, sitting apart on the chair of tubular steel that bore his own name across the back, waiting for Munt and his myrmidoms to announce that something decisive might now happen, would dream himself out of the madhouse and see rain-clouds over the Small Isles and feel again the brooding peace of the place where he had been a boy; or he could wish himself back at Ardyne, rowing Miss Beth and Master Billy across the bay to the island.

He could never be anything else but himself, and Hollywood would hardly let him be that, but now it was nearly at an end. The last linking shots had been taken, the editors had pieced and cut the many thousands of feet of celluloid Munt Kopaks required to make any picture, the run-through in the secrecy of the projection room had filled the studios with rumours of a new brilliance, another triumph for Transocean, an Oscar for Munt in prospect. And now he was giving this great, roaring party to celebrate the end of the job and to let all the colony and the newspapers know in unequivocal terms that another Kopaks masterpiece was almost ready for the preview.

Jimsy had been briefed as for a big studio scene. He was to take Feng Lee under his wing, speak for them both and play to the theme of the innocents in Hollywood. The outlines of their stories, he was earnestly advised by the write-up people, had already been circulated, but he was to embroider freely. One of these urgent men held to the idea that Jimsy should refuse to speak anything but Gaelic until it was pointed out to him, and he morosely accepted the fact, that Jimsy spoke very good English in the picture. . . .

"I was just thinkin' up somethin' on the wee *deoch-an-dorus* theme," he explained.

They were penned into a corner almost immediately, Jimsy and Feng Lee, by the hungry reporters of the strange ways of the world of Film: hard, abrupt, sallow men with the remorselessness of criminal detectives, the brittle, wary sob-sisters, watching for the weak spots, eager to be slick in debunking. Jimsy felt himself a man at bay; he had never known that the American reporter could dive so deep into privacies for a story.

"Say, Jimsy," said one, "what exactly is the lowdown on this boarding-out business?"

Jimsy explained it carefully as he had explained it to Nicky Font long ago.

"You mean to say, friend," drawled another, "you don't know who your Mum and Pop were?"

"No, I don't know."

"Gee! He doesn't know. What about the girl-friend?"

"She doesn't know either. Her mother was Chinese, but she thinks her father was Burmese. She was born in Singapore and educated in an American mission school."

The pencils scribbled fiercely and "Waal, that's one line on a story," said one of the inquisitors, adding "Guess she speaks good English?"

"She doesn't, in fact," said Jimsy calmly. "I don't know if that's a reflection on American education."

This sally was greeted by an appreciative guffaw.

"Wisecracker, eh?" they asked almost in chorus, agreeing among themselves that the kid sure had something. "Go on, Jimsy. . . . Spill the beans. . . . You and li'l Feng Lee now? How do you feel about the kid?"

"Feng Lee and I are good friends. We've got our work to do together, and we do it."

"Aw, tell that to the *Methodist Bugle*."

Again Jimsy felt penned and at the mercy of people who, kindly enough, worked according to a scale of values that were not his. He looked about him almost desperately as if he could plead with a look to a friend to come to the rescue. He was conscious of the small person of Feng Lee, puzzled but smiling, pressing to his side. Now and again she slipped her thin fingers under his.

The room beyond was still a confusion, a whirlpool of milling, chattering people under swirls of smoke, but suddenly Jimsy perceived that some sort of unusual commotion was interesting the mob by the buffet. A woman screamed, then a ring formed about something on the floor, then the something was carried out behind the curtains. One of the journalists detached himself from the ring about Jimsy and fought his way to the point of disturbance. He returned smiling.

"It's only Nicky Font, out for the count. More ticker trouble, I guess."

"He sure asks for it," observed one of the sob-sisters. "The next'll be the last if he don't let up."

"Nicky!" cried Jimsy. "I must see him. Please let me go," and he looked round the ring of his gaolers like a prisoner at bay.

"No, son," said he who had gone to investigate the trouble, but kindly. "He's out for the count, and Doc Schlesinger will have him half-way to the clinic by now. Your place is right here till we're through with you. Now, bud, give us a little spiel in this Gaelic lingo of yours."

It ended at length, the inquisition, and Jimsy felt wearier than ever, as if he had been physically pummelled. Feng Lee's hand in his, he made to lead her towards the buffet, but across their track there immediately loomed the figure of a man most beautifully dressed in London clothes, his face magnificently handsome even if it had been touched to the glow of sunburn with the aid of paint and powder. This splendid person grabbed at Feng Lee and pulled her close to his side, crying, for he was far from sober now:

"Come, pigeon, till I eat you."

"What can I get you to drink, Feng Lee?" asked Jimsy quietly.

"I'll get Miss Lee what she wants," asserted this man truculently. "Think you can hog the girl as well as the picture?"

"It would never have occurred to me," said Jimsy, adding with a touch of sarcasm, "Mr. Bond Royal."

That was the fine name their leading man had assumed.

"Whenever I hear it," Nicky Font had drawled on hearing whom the casting people had chosen for the part, "I just can't help think of an ad. for sassy notepaper in the *Woman's Home Journal*. The man's a phoney, to boot and to wit."

"Sure," Munt had agreed cheerfully, "but he's just got left to him that amount of good looks and box-office appeal to complete my picture. The kids are going to walk away with it anyway. Or did I forget to tell ya?"

"Must have. Was it not to Douglas Fairbanks, senr., when the stationery was new on the market?"

He was an Americanised Englishman, this Bond Royal, a good player of one given type in his day but now edging, to his private terror, into the penultimate stage of any actor's working life. The close student of the handsome, made-up face would have observed two fine slits down his cheeks, through which a cunning surgeon had extracted an excess of superficial fat. He had reached the stage when he could no longer distinguish as between living and acting in his behaviour, and now, with drink taken, Jimsy saw him to be in the snarling mood that had so often made him the intolerable autocrat of the studios.

Jimsy was at the buffet, asking for a blameless glass of iced White Rock, when one of the newspapermen tapped his arm. This was in person the gentlest of them all, in print the formidable Walt Becher of *Film Fact*, of whom it was said that his word could make or kill a picture.

"Sorry, Jimsy," he apologised in his pleasant Virginian voice. "You've sure had your fill of us guys to-night, but I wonder if you could give me one little message in that Gaelic of yours. Something for our readers, from you to them. They'll be tickled to death."

"Wait now," said Jimsy, amused. "Yes. What about *Na h-uile la gu math duit, a charaid?* Meaning, may all your days be fine, my friend."

"Attaboy! Can you write it for me in block letters?"

Jimsy did so and Walt Becher considered the result ruefully.

"Doesn't add up to the phonetics," he observed, "but that's grand. Thanks a lot, Jimsy!"

They were falling into quite serious talk about languages when they were hailed loudly from behind by a voice now hoarse with drink. It was Bond Royal, swinging in his gait but still holding the slight person of Feng Lee under his right arm.

"Say, Walt! Walt, old boy!" the ragged voice claimed priority. "Forget our pet dwarf for a minute and listen to me. Did I tell you about me and the traffic cop in Santa Ana? You want a story. . . ."

Walt Becher hesitated and then said slowly:

"Sure, you told me, Bond. That was the picture before last, wasn't it, old timer?"

The insult was deliberate, perfectly timed in its declaration in the whimsical drawl that is the foundation of all the satirical humour of North America. Jimsy could not have wished for a doughtier champion to return the insult to himself.

"What do you mean—old timer?"

Over the handsome face of Bond Royal had spread an ugly snarl. He almost threw Feng Lee behind him and swiped with his fist at Walt Becher's face. Walt dodged easily and, with his own open hand, caught his assailant a smack across the cheek, the crack of the blow like a pistol shot. Bond Royal fell back on his haunches amid a forest of quickly withdrawn legs.

Jimsy became aware that Feng Lee was again taking shelter by his side. Then he felt a hand on his shoulder.

"What a story! What a story!" Munt Kopaks was intoning raptly; then urgently, "Get the li'l girl to heck out of this before a real rough-house starts up."

A smooth studio car driven by Jimsy's negro friend, Joe, purred under the porch and swept them away along the lighted boulevards and down and up the eccentric hills of the city. Their apartments were in the same block, but they got out of the elevator on Jimsy's floor.

"Come in, Feng, and have a drink or something," he

suggested. "At least we can have a rest after that awful party."

"I hate that Bond," said Feng Lee. "I make tea."

While the girl worked in the kitchenette Jimsy put a call through to Munt Kopaks and anxiously asked after Nicky.

"None too good," returned the thick voice unhappily, "but Doc Schlesinger reckons to pull him through. Gee, we'll want the old duck back soon to get cracking on our next picture!"

"I'm not sure I want to make another picture, Munt," said Jimsy unhappily.

"Nuts!" cried the voice at the other end. "Say, Jimsy! Take li'l Feng Lee with you and go away for a vacation. There's a swell cottage of mine at Monterey you can have and welcome. Lie about the beach and do nothing for the next weeks, and you'll be back in a month, rarin' to get on location again. I've a yen about a picture in the Philippines. Sure you're tired, son. Go right away and sleep on it. Happy dreams."

Feng Lee came with the tea, placed the tray on a small table and, while he lolled in the chesterfield, knelt before it to do him honour in her native way. The little touch of domesticity was pleasing after the roaring insincerity of the party. She was a beautiful child, kneeling there, black hair above the pale face all perfectly set off by her tunic in dull red, its golden embroideries gleaming in the light of the single reading-lamp on a side table.

Suddenly that soft golden light was diluted by a livid flash from the outer air, and the peace within the room was shattered by the first crack of a summer thunderstorm. It seemed to fill the bowl in which the city lay with its crazed fury. Jimsy saw the quick, alarmed turn of Feng Lee's head, saw a frightened face lit up by a second flash. Then she was on the settee beside him, a frightened little girl burrowing close to him and hiding her head under the arm he put about her thin shoulders. She seemed very soft and light and sweet.

He was content to sit there protecting her tenderly but without passion. He sat and stared blankly at the cold blue flares and forks of the lightning. His head ached and a weight of frustration was upon him. He felt himself a failure, a fraud and, in some subtle way that evaded his self-analysis, a deserter from old truths he had once cherished. Clear in his morose mind was the conviction that he was, for good and all now, a waif, a bit of driftwood on the tides of circumstance. But "It's all right, Feng," he assured the girl. "It will pass away in a few minutes."

"I do not want to leave you," the muffled, light voice replied from his armpit. She snuggled closer, saying "I want to stay with you, Jeem-say, and be your small wife. You are so kind; I shall be so good."

And so she stayed.

5

Beth wished that she had come to see the picture alone. She felt that in going with Gillie she was getting two parts of her life dangerously confused.

It was nice to have Gillie for what the other girls at the hospital called her "steady," he at the University, she a student nurse. It was nice to have a big, strong, clever escort to pictures or plays or concerts on her nights out; nice just to have the reliable distraction from the conventual order of routine and the functional amenities of the nurses' home. But Jimsy was a secret, surprisingly important as she considered the past and the present. Remembering Thurston Grange, she had decided that Gillie must not share it lest he spoil a memory.

Yes, she should have come alone on one of her afternoons off or with one of the other girls. It was dreadful to have to sit in the second-best tier of the balcony and act as if it was as new and remote to her as it was to her companion. You wanted to cry out to Jimsy, to say that you remembered him just like that, to boast a little, to be happy in a special knowledge shared. The dreadful thing was the picture told much of the story as she had gathered it in bits and pieces at Ardyne— the boarded-out orphan, the page-boy, the little steward at sea in the great ship.

From that point she was learning, and she half-believed it must be true. Again you wanted to shout that Jimsy would never steal; you wanted to cry when you saw him, small and lonely, walking the streets of Colombo.

The rest was obviously romance: a story superimposed upon an experience. She could have laughed to see Jimsy on an elephant's back, Jimsy with a Chinese foster-sister, an alarmingly pretty girl. It was still Jimsy in every gesture and glance. It was as if they were playing together again in secret, building the little house on the islet in the bay before Ardyne long, long ago. She rejoiced wilfully in having secret knowledge Gillie could not be suffered to share.

They passed from wonder into the December night, looking with superior pity on those who queued for the last run in a chilling rain from the East. Princes Street was dead, the Castle only an idea above the swirling haar that was down almost to the level of the lamp standards; it was, except where an occasional shop window was aglow with lights to display female garments irrelevantly flimsy, a street existing as such on the strength of noisy trams, the occasional taxi and people in raincoats, their heads and umbrellas tilted against the rain. Gillie had his right forearm under Beth's left, his fingers locked in hers: the limit of familiarity she could allow him.

"It's not a bad picture," he shouted so that she might hear within the hood of her green raincoat. "Some of the travel stuff is magnificent. I expect that little chap on the elephant is really a bit of a squirt, but he gets away with it. Better than that awful old bounder, Bond Royal."

Beth had to choke back an indignant defence of Seumas Bell as a person and said instead "Weren't those scenes in Ceylon perfectly lovely? What joy to live where there is so much blossom about!"

"Oh, I expect there was a good deal of faking," observed Gillie with male superiority. "That camel bit seemed to me phoney."

From an island by the General Post Office they got a tram that, filled with the stenches of wet clothing, rocked them up and over the Bridges. They halted to part within the outer gates of the hospital. He held both her hands in his and looked with all the directness of his perfect manliness into her dark eyes.

"A kiss, dear. Just one."

"No, Gillie! *Please*," she protested with agitation.

He was sensitive enough to perceive that her refusal had this time some mysterious warrant, and he was dexterous enough simply to raise her right hand to his lips and kiss the back of her glove.

"You will some day, you know," he asserted gently. "But good night, Beth. Next Tuesday as usual. Happy dreams."

There would be no happy dreams for her that night, she knew, for her conscience was plaguing her. She was so innocent, and she seemed to herself to be involved in confusion and sin. The sense of guilt imposed on her long ago plagued her with that familiar sense of leading a double life. Oh, it was wonderful to be Uncle Finlay's favourite, and to be a bright, promising student nurse among so many other bright girls! It did not give her something which, without being able to define it, her spirit needed. Mummy was almost nothing now but an occasional writer of scatty, nearly indecipherable letters, all about the baby and that mysterious Ketron who had never returned to her soldier in Aden. And if there was always Gillie, strong and dependable and male, she still had to keep her secret from him.

Before going to bed she found a vacant desk in the library and pretended to write a letter, and she could never have done so for the tears that kept filling her eyes. She wrote a date and stared at the blank sheet and finally admitted to herself what really irked. So silly, so schoolgirlish! It was still true that what she really wanted was a Christmas card from Jimsy Bell as he had promised, the symbolic assurance that the real Beth Ferrier still survived, that the days of innocence endured. But it was only five days till Christmas now, and the Air Mail envelope with the American stamp had not come. The silence of it all, the blank negation, seemed insupportable.

Each morning was a frustration. There were plenty of cards

for her in the rack; her presents might be the richest any girl in the hospital would receive. The fragile envelope with the U.S. stamp, however, did not come, and it mattered to her more than she could ever have guessed it would. On Christmas Eve, with a gaiety somewhat forced, they decorated the wards with streamers and holly and mistletoe, and they set up the Christmas Tree from which the Registrar would distribute the gifts in the guise of Father Christmas. For Beth it was an automatic task, not onerous but devoid of joy. A sort of numbness was upon her, and the sentient part of her was elsewhere.

On Christmas morning there was but one delivery of mail, and she did not rush with the others to seize her share of it. She knew now that she had been forgotten or deliberately ignored by an old friend. It was all past, that old happiness of girlhood. She belonged now to the world that had shaped about her under Uncle Finlay's influence, the world in which a career of her own and Gillie and virtual separation from her own mother were the chief components.

Even that world was changing. Beth went through to Glasgow for Uncle Finlay's invariable New Year party, and she was shocked to see what had happened to Aunt Helen, that quiet, wise woman. That she had been poorly, as they say, Beth had been aware with the vagueness of youth, but she was frightened to see in her aunt's face that sign which she had already come to know so well, the yonderly look of those who face the approach of utter darkness, and her clinical knowledge was sufficient to let her know that within the body of the older woman there was a slow wasting beyond the power of surgery to arrest.

Uncle Finlay, of course, sought to be bright and to pretend that the days were quite as good as they used to be.

"Of course we'll have our party, Beth, your party. Your Aunt Helen would be angry if we didn't. She doesn't feel like being there, and that's an awful pity for you and me, but she keeps telling me we're to go ahead and enjoy ourselves. I've a notion I'll try to get her away after the holidays. Into the sunshine for a spell. I thought of the Union-Castle run to

South Africa and back. . . . Anyhow, Beth, she'll be angry if you don't enjoy yourself to-morrow."

The ghost of Aunt Helen, and then the strong immediacy of Gillie, who could only politely share her concern. He possessed her for the evening, and even in the conventions of the dance she could feel the urgency of his impulse to possess her person. She was much more subtly aware of the drive of his uncomplicated personality to master hers; and, being tired and feeling lonely, she could not find it in her to resist on any basis of reason.

At a late hour, when the others were shrieking in the delirium of the Eightsome Reel, they went together into a dimly lighted anteroom that had been set aside for harmless dalliance. With the grace of a strong panther Gillie let his body slip down on the settee they shared until his head rested on her arm, and he looked up into her face, not wholly unconscious of his own good looks and charm.

"You're looking lovely to-night, Beth. You're always so calm—and remote. Such nice dark hair, such lovely features." He toyed with the hands in her lap and wheedled. "That kiss, dear? Come and be kind."

The kiss was for her important. She had never wholly understood those many girls in the hospital, nice, jolly girls, for whom a kiss was the most trivial of exchanges in the traffic of the sexes. She understood the surrender to be a decision, a pledge. Now she bent her lips to Gillie's and felt his arm tightening about her neck, his body rising to meet hers.

CHAPTER EIGHT

Return Journey

JIMSY SAT by Nicky Font's bedside, the latter dying. The trouble was technically pneumonia, but they had told him that the feeble, abused heart could not last much longer in any case. This was the end of four years of friendship and work together, and Jimsy had never known before that one man could love another so greatly.

Nicky talked, and there was no use now being fussy and begging him to conserve his strength. Jimsy loved to listen to the old, drawling voice even in near-delirium.

"I am dying, Egypt, dying," it announced whimsically. "And that Jimsy, old horse, is a quote from the daddy of us all. I have immortal longings in me. Fortune and Antony part here. . . . Every line a quote and from the last scenes of just one play. What a guy! What a guy! Give me to drink mandragora —there he goes again, the Master!—but it won't be Scotch now. Queer that your country killed me, my best little friend. The glass, Jimsy. Give the Gods a laugh to see me drinking iced water on the threshold."

Jimsy had to hold the goblet between the frail weak hands and pull it away when the stuff started to overflow the pale-blue lips. The tired head sank back into the pillow on a sigh.

"I want to go home, Jimsy, back to New England, and let the Gods this knot intrinsicate of life at once untie. . . . Gee, do you think old Will once nearly died and recovered to recollect in tranquillity? What a guy! What a guy! Where was I, Jimsy boy?"

"New England."

"Sure, New England. That's the immortal longing now,

old horse. Up the North Shore from Boston there's a little old town and a harbour full of white schooners. They've got eyes painted round the hawse-holes, for they're mostly owned and manned by Papist Portuguese, and they go 'way, 'way out fishin' on the Banks, as you read in your Kipling when a boy. Now, Jimsy, it seems to me the swellest place that ever was, and I wanna go there for the last look-round. Sunset and evening star, and one clear call for me. But would you call Tennyson a poet when Shakespeare's around? No, sir. But his twilight mood kinda fits in with mine."

"We'll manage that, Nick," Jimsy assured his friend, afraid that his voice would break as he said it, " as soon as Schlesinger give us the okay for you to travel. I'll go with you, of course."

"You'll come with me, Jimsy! Say, isn't that swell? What a pal! But, Jimsy, boy, you can't go trapesin' across the American continent with a near-corpse. Your work, son."

"Don't worry, Nick," Jimsy said gently, and laid his hand on the pale one that lay so long and emaciated on the counterpane. "My work here is all done, especially now that Munt has left Transocean. I've had all I want out of Hollywood. I've saved; I'll be a well-to-do man when I get home. You see, Nick, I'm like yourself. I want to go East and finish my trip round the world and have another look at the place I came from. No, I'll see you home first. Probably I can get a sailing from Boston."

"Well, well, well! And little Feng Lee?"

"She left me a month ago," Jimsy almost laughed. "One of those South American boys over at Culver City for the Andes picture. No bones broken. She was a dear little creature."

"A lass unparallel'd," Nicky quoted again, but drowsily now.

"I'll go now, Nicky," said Jimsy, rising, "but I'll ring first thing in the morning to hear how you are, and I'll be down as soon as they'll let me. Try to sleep."

"Yes, sleep. A sleep and a forgetting." He seemed near to a ruminative sort of delirium. "Something about the ravell'd sleeve of care. Look it up for me, Jimsy. Will Shakespeare, my dear master. Unarm, Eros, the long day's task is done, and we must sleep."

So far as Jimsy Bell was concerned, the last words of Niccols Font were Shakespeare's. He rang the clinic in the morning to hear from Dr. Schlesinger that his friend had died at dawn; and the hurrying, honking life of the city, the fret and falsity of the studios seemed unsubstantial things beside the burden of his grief. Even as he had to help the attorney with Nicky's affairs and, alone in the dusty apartment, clear the papers of moment from under empty bottles and out of drawers crammed tight; even as he must cable a sister in that fishing port of New England and deal with a mortician in whom commercial briskness and a proper awe of the hereafter were surprisingly but convincingly fused, Jimsy was walking in space, in a realm without boundaries and sure resting places.

Preparing to take Nicky home, he was preparing to take his own farewell of the American continent. The cremation was the last ordeal. Munt Kopaks had arranged it all with his producer's instinct. There was a choir to sing Sullivan's setting of *The Long Day Closes*. The great ladies of the colony came heavily draped in black, as to the obsequies of an emperor; and the reporters, the sob-sisters and the flash-bulb photographers were there to record their movements, while the newsreel cameras whirred softly to record their entrances and exits. A minister of some Presbyterian order orated in the plangent convention of formal American oratory. . . .

"To-day we say Good-bye to a friend. We say Good-bye to a great artist. We say Good-bye and Godspeed to one whose every work in his artistic sphere was conceived in the Spirit for the uplifting of the human Soul. . . ."

And Jimsy Bell was not the only one there to know that the slim form within the draped coffin on the catafalque, so soon to sink into even physical destruction, would in life have been the first to start a belly-laugh at the echoing emptiness of it all. Rather give him Shakespeare with all the stops out, the great voice ranting Hamlet's unanswered questions.

Nevertheless, he took his friend home across the continent,

a handful of grey ashes in a crated marble urn in the freight car. Jimsy had thought it a pleasant idea that these ashes should be scattered on the waters of the Pacific, but a stiff letter from New England, signed Emily Rose Pasch, requested that they be returned for burial in the family grave in the old burying-ground above the Atlantic. It was difficult to realise that the writer was the sister of daft, delightful Nicky. There was much in it about the casket, the ashes, the remains, the deceased, a gloating over the terminology of sepulture. It implied disapproval of Nicky's way of life and of the means taken, without prior consultation, to dispose of his body. It ended with a reference to the advice of Pastor Boland and to the text, Job V and 7.

Jimsy hired a car in Boston to take him up the North Shore turnpike, and for all that the ashes of his friend were on the front seat beside the driver he was fascinated to see the great city and its academic suburbs give place so quickly to an unfenced landscape that seemed to him untidy, then to a series of townlets with broad, tree-lined streets and a white, high-steepled wooden church in the centre of each. It was a world away from California, and when they came down to the sea Jimsy knew that he was back once more within the Atlantic community. Though they faced eastwards, though architecture, speech and the design of the boats were all different and unique in their setting, those fishing harbours and small ship-yards were Scotland in reverse. Over all he discerned the neat narrowness of the Calvinistic tradition and the moroseness of a breed that traffics with the sea.

When they came to the port about which Niccols Font had played and dreamed as a child he was promptly informed, as a messenger who has been looked for, where he would find Widow Pasch. This was in a white house, in an unkempt lot on a bluff above the sea, that could have done with a lick of paint, Jimsy thought. He was received in a Victorian parlour by a dark woman it was difficult to believe could be Nicky's sister. Perhaps she was much older; perhaps a half-sister; perhaps she had aged quickly in austerity. A dark moustache had grown above her upper lip, and her voice was hard in the nasal Yankee way.

"I was expecting you, young man," she greeted Jimsy severely. "What have you done with the remains?"

"I stopped at the mortician's down the road," Jimsy hurried to justify himself. "Kearns was the name. I thought it best to leave the urn in his mortuary until I knew what you wanted."

"You got some sense, at least," Mrs. Pasch allowed. "Joe Kearns has my order to open the grave for the ceremony even if it's the first time a Font has had to be burned to a cinder before he could be buried among his own flesh and blood."

"That was all carefully discussed, Mrs. Pasch," Jimsy urged anxiously. "In fact, Nicky had instructed his lawyer. The climate out there, you know, and the long journey . . ."

"That may be. It's against Bible just the same. But I'll go and fetch you a cup of coffee. Guess you're peckish after the hike from Boston."

Jimsy was left to sit on the hard edge of a rocking-chair and consider the ship models, the stuffed seabirds under glass and the arrangements of shells on plush which, with ornate texts in frames crossed at the ends, adorned the chamber. Mrs. Pasch returned in course with a pot of strong coffee and warm waffles and maple syrup on a tray, and Jimsy found them good as he sat eating and being cross-examined.

"Did the attorney say what the estate might be?"

"Quite a lot, I think, Mrs. Pasch. At least a hundred and fifty thousand dollars. Nicky was one of the most brilliant script-writers in the business."

"Might have been double if he had left strong drink alone. Nothing good ever came out of the bottle, or Hollywood for that matter. Still," Mrs. Pasch allowed, "I will say that Niccols paid for my Em through high school and college. My Em's teachin' school at Brattle Creek right now."

"That must be a great satisfaction to you, ma'am."

"It is. My Em took after me, praise God, and a hundred

and fifty thousand bucks will sure help us both along, never mind how they were earned. But I guess you'll want to get right back to Boston, young man."

Jimsy hesitated, much taken aback, saying "I thought you might wish me to wait for the funeral."

"No call for you to wait, young man," declared Mrs. Pasch. "I reckon, seeing it's only his ashes, we can wait awhiles till I write the family and have the interment carried out in proper style. I guess you were at some sort of service when they reduced my brother, ashes to ashes."

"Yes, we had a choir, some fine music and a simple service."

"A bit of Popery, I'll be bound. That's not our way in New England, where we walk in fear of God and His judgments."

Her words apart, Mrs. Pasch's attitude made it clear to Jimsy that he would not be welcome at a family service in a windswept burying ground, with wizened yokels and red-faced fishermen in black crowded about a square hole in the ground. He was made clearly to understand that, in bringing his friend's ashes across thousands of miles of North America, he had taken part in a discreditable exploit, and that no limb of Satan from Hollywood could be suffered to mingle with the godly by the graveside.

So he made his way back to Boston, rejecting the sentimental impulse to stop at the Kearns establishment and look for the last time at an urn with a few handfuls of greyish powder under the ornate lid. It was a relief to be accepted within the vast anonymity of the city, but when he had booked in at the Bellevue and wandered out on the Common to pass the hour before the evening meal, the pangs of loneliness afflicted him with almost physical force. As he sat on a bench and watched the unfamiliar birds of America foraging for crumbs beneath and about it, his eyes filled and his throat tightened under the press of emotion. He felt himself another Nicky Font, a waif unwanted now—and now no Nicky to provide a wry running commentary on the processes of living.

That was all finished. He was done with the States and the

States with him. But it was without rancour on either side as it had been with Feng Lee and, blaming himself for falling into self-pity, Jimsy stirred himself to realise that he must now set about doing what it was in his heart to do. He thought in a flash of wonder that he could fly up to Gander to-morrow and come down over the peaks of Arran into the airport of Prestwick with the next dawn. Something of the Scotsman in him demurred to the expense, and what was there to take him home again in a hurry? Seven days at sea in a slow medium liner and time to think—that was what he wanted.

He rose and moved back to the hotel with the purpose of discovering where he would find the shipping office in the morning.

2

She felt herself in a pit, in a blackness of desolation, with only an odd grey cloud of steady thought passing overhead now and again and swiftly lost in the limbo of unhappiness that encompassed her.

"Turn over on your face, dearie," commanded Sister Kelly, and she obeyed the command she had herself so often given to others: so often that she had no faith in the ritual. The seat of her pyjama trousers was turned down, and she felt the prick and plunge of the needle. Sister Kelly was a fattening, middle-ageing Irishwoman, a surprising person to be in charge of nerve cases, but Beth admired her deftness with the hypodermic.

"Right down to the bone!" triumphed Sister Kelly as she wiped the puncture and covered her patient's person again. "Two or three shots like that and you'll be up whistling with the lark before the week's out."

"I won't, Sister. I don't want to whistle any more. I don't care. I just wish I could sleep away."

"Arrah! A strong, fine-looking girl like you. They all say that at first, the nerve patients," added Sister Kelly, "and they all live to forget they ever said it or felt like it. It's like the bad dream that can plague a healthy person half a day and is then just a thing to laugh at. Now, dearie, can I be getting you a cup of tea, or a book?"

"Nothing, Sister, thank you."

"Well, the injection will rest your mind. Lie quiet now till I come along with your lunch."

Tea, books, lunch, when she simply wished to be left alone with the very thing that frightened her. It was herself turning in and in upon herself, hating herself but enjoying going over and over each cog in the revolving wheel of self-disgust. It was her own hell, and she wanted to keep it to herself, for it was impossible to conceive that she could ever escape from it, and she would fight to deny another's entrance into it. Even the specialist, a surprising-looking person with a large, white face crowned by a russet fringe of hair about a bald pate, confessed frustration to the house physician at their evening colloquy.

"She knows enough about the technique to be stubborn, and she's enough of a lady by upbringing to be costive about her own affairs. She's not, by the way . . ."

"Oh, nothing like that, sir! First thing old Nellie Kelly went for. I really think it's just a fairly ordinary love affair gone wrong somehow."

"No love affair, Morris, is ordinary for the persons involved. Any relations?"

"There seems to be a mother and sister somewhere in the South of England, but she nearly hit the ceiling when I suggested she might want to see them. An uncle is her sort of guardian; seems to be a big shot in industry; but she doesn't want to see him either."

"Very well. Just so," the specialist mused. "Poor girl, and quite a dark beauty. We'll leave it to time just now. Keep the drugs going and tempt her with the nicest food you can raise. Pity there isn't a friend of her own sex we could tap."

"Not one among all the girls she trained with. They liked

her, but she was aloof. But they all know that she had a boy-friend—a ' steady ' as they say."

"Perhaps that's it, as you suggest, Morris."

Her unwillingness to see anybody out of the old life was more than petulance. It was part and parcel of the sense of guilt that was at the root of her sickness. If she had been a plain surgical case she would still not have wanted to see either Mummy or Ketron. That link had almost completely snapped one Easter at Hove when it became known that her husband was suing Ketron for divorce and Beth, hot-headed for justice as always, had defended him against the injured sneers of her mother and half-sister. Ketron had technically deserted him, keeping the child, and Beth could see nothing but slattern disloyalty in that.

It had been a first-class row among the three women, the fur and feathers flying among them in Aunt Cicely's genteel drawing-room, and Beth had almost enjoyed it. But it had had the inevitable outcome, Mummy siding with her stepdaughter against the daughter of her own body in that queer deviation from the normal produced by the sympathy of types rather than of individualities. They were all very stiff with each other until Beth left by the late afternoon train next day, knowing herself unpopular and herself not caring much how the people at Hove managed thereafter. No: that was unfair to Billy, now terrified by the prospect of facing his National Service and to Aunt Cecily who, having driven her down to the station, permitted herself a barking comment at the door of the coach.

"I'm out of this family quarrel of yours, Beth, you know, but if you biffed into them with some commonsense I'm not sorry. Frankly, for two pins I'd take up your half-sister by the seat of the pants and lam her backside good and hard. Pity is that my sainted sister thinks she's wonderful. Heavens, the poor ass is messing around in the most vulgar way with the band leader at the Royal Grand! Not very nice for one of the oldest inhabitants like me."

That was all of the past, however; it wrote itself off the

account now being paid with so much bitterness. Uncle Finlay was the one to worry about, the one you were frightened to meet; for Uncle Finlay knew at least something of how it had stood between her and Gillie and must have known from the papers what had happened to him, and Uncle Finlay was a man robbed of much of his spirit since Aunt Helen died. Beth was terrified of the exposure of her own melancholy to his.

Within the pit she must inhabit, turning over and over all the circumstances that had thrust her into it, her mind would keep coming round to the curious realisation that Aunt Helen had been at the very centre of the tangle of influences about her. That quiet, wise woman who had been the very spring of Uncle Finlay's bouncing conduct of life, who had come to seem so much more dear and reliable than Mummy. She had been perfectly the mature woman a young girl needs behind her, the quiet woman by the hearth who confers the sense of belonging. Beth could persuade herself that, had Helen Ferrier lived, she would have run to her knees with these present troubles and not be lying, isolated beyond succour, in a hospital room surrounded by those to whom, however kind, she could not confess a syllable of what ailed her.

The fault was her own. She should have confided in Aunt Helen long ago instead of evading the barbs of her little teasing jokes. But it had been one of the most foolish of her romantic illusions that her engagement to Gillie was a delightful secret they would reveal in good time. It was the bitterest of thoughts now that he had never taken her to meet his own people, as if she were a shopgirl to be ashamed of! Aunt Helen would have had something to say about that.

Then she had herself behaved like a shopgirl. He was so urgent and handsome; he had passed so brilliantly in his subject and won the scholarship to Princeton. He would be a year abroad at least and would then send for her or fly home to claim her. Just one short week-end of love. It was nothing nowadays. He wished to tell her all his love before he went.

Even in her extremity Beth was not burdened by any great

sense of moral guilt. She could recall now how the death of Aunt Helen and the squabble at Hove had seemed to leave her alone in the world to make her own choices, and she so much wished to make him happy, if that must be the way of it. The shock now was to know that it had not made her happy somehow. She had felt furtive and foolish in the small hotel at Dunbar, and for all that it was the month of May, the sea blue and the beeches blazing in fresh foliage, magic had eluded her and her surrenders had been half-hearted. As he drove her back to Edinburgh on the Sunday evening Gillie had rallied her, and she had thought to hear a little rub of irritation in his tone.

"I don't believe you enjoyed yourself, Beth. You were always a bit of a puritan, weren't you? "

Was it that he spoke out of extensive experience as a male with shopgirls and such? Poor Gillie! He was dead now, and she could be almost sorry for him in his fated capacity of he-man, conscious of charm and strength. But the last betrayal—that was what could not be borne. Again Beth pressed her face into the pillows and cried and cried like a baby.

The night sister, a gentle girl from the West Highlands, whose voice lilted the intonations she had heard in the speech of Jimsy Bell, found her in this state and patted her shoulder and then put her arm about her and lifted her into the sitting position.

"There now, dear. It's a lot of trouble you have on your mind, but you must help yourself to get better. Yes, yes, but you will! And here's your cup of malted milk, and you'll take the two doses to-night, doctor says."

"Tuinal again! " Beth protested. "Oh, I suppose they'll knock me out for an hour or two, and then I'll waken in the early morning and lie in pure hell for hours."

"What a way to talk! " said Sister mildly. "Rest you now, and I'll be taking a keek in every now and again to see if you're awake. Ring if you want me. There's whiles I think that when a girl is troubled in the mind she's best crying it out on another woman's bosom. We know," she added in a flash of illumination, "we know more about each other than the menfolk ever will."

"Bless, you, Sister, and how wise you are! "

Her colleague tidied the bedclothes and slipped in a fresh hot waterbottle with the quick professional skill they shared.

"There now. I'll leave the lamp, but you will rest better without it, if you can. That's the bell-push lying to your hand. Any time you want me, dear, even if it is only the trouble in the mind. *Oidche mhath! Beannachd leibh!* "

Good night and blessings upon you. As the drug started on its work Beth took to thinking drowsily of Jimsy Bell and Ardyne under the summer sun, and this so agreeably that she stretched out an arm and switched off the light. It was so interesting that Jimsy and her kind Sister were from the same part of the world, as if the circumstances of their upbringing gave them an understanding beyond the ordinary. Gentler, subtler folk than such as Gillie. . . . No, no! Not that! She struggled to keep her mind on a little picture, such as you might see on the television screen, of clean sea water dripping from Jimsy's oars and then the shallow hollows and small fountains on the surface as he feathered for the next dip of the blades, and the whirlpools they left behind.

There were days and days like that, the battle always raging: black cloud against yellow sunlight, despair monstrous above the flicker of hope and the passing longing for the recovery of self-respect. Tired, so tired of it all; still wishing every night that the ritual taking of sodium amatal were like putting one's head in the gas oven.

One evening the specialist, the circlet of russet hair, as of a Tudor king, hanging below the eaves of the black sombrero he favoured, was preparing to get the progress report from the houseman when the latter produced his wallet and proudly announced:

"I think we've got the clue to the trouble with the girl in Number Four." And he passed over a scrap of newspaper clipping, obviously from the *Scotsman*. "She asked Sister for her handbag, and while she was scrabbling for what she wanted, this floated out and down to the floor. Old Nellie Kelly ought to have been a policewoman. She simply put her great flat foot on the cutting, picked it up careless-like and palmed it. And it does look like what you want, sir."

"Let me see."

The great man slowly adjusted a pair of heavily-rimmed reading glasses and held the morsel of paper at arm's length, his comic features seeming to confess a faint distaste.

"I remember this," he announced at length. "I've met the father somewhere, probably at some ghastly dinner. General Manager of Loyal City Assurance. That's the man." He went on, half-quoting, half-commentating. "Crashed over Elizabeth Airport, New Jersey, did he—the son, I mean? Trying to establish the stalling-point of a new type of reconnaissance air-craft, was he, the damn' fool? And then, Morris, mark this well, he leaves behind a young wife, daughter of an airport official, after only a fortnight of married life. But not one ruddy word about the packet of nervous trouble he left behind in Edinburgh."

The specialist removed his outsize spectacles and handed the cutting across the table.

"See that it's slipped back into the handbag. She'll be look-ing for it in a moment of masochism one fine day."

"You do think it's a line, sir?" the houseman asked eagerly.

"A lawyer wouldn't regard it as proof, Morris, but good work by you and Sister Kelly. Now we've got the likely point of attack, something to work on. We know almost for certain the nature and degree of the probable shock. She's how old, did you say? Oh, yes—twenty-two, and she was never a fool. Yes, Morris, my son, we see just one other glimmer of light in our miserable careers of frustration. I *think* another ten days or so of the intensive treatment, and then we'll get her out to Lilywood. Mightn't be a bad idea to suggest that she could help with some of our more intractable cases. Oh, and may bountiful Jehovah be thanked that it's not a case for shock or deep insulin! I hate those techniques. I like to walk the whole road and back again with my unhappy victims. Now, the latest about that old bitch in Number Two . . ."

3

Jimsy Bell walked the length of the promenade at Brendan but could never escape the feeling of being looked at with curiosity. It was near the end of the summer season in that seaside resort, but there were still plenty of loitering trippers to stare, still plenty of their raw infants to stop in their tracks point a sticky finger and bawl "Heh, Maw! There's an awfy funny wee man."

His stature, an asset in Hollywood, unremarked in Liverpool and Glasgow, was here like one of the shows by the pierhead. He had taken care to buy himself in Glasgow two dark suits of inveterately British cut and a quiet trilby to replace the broad-brimmed Stetson he had needed under the Californian sun, but there could be no disguises in Brendan, where so many people had so much time to stand and stare, where the busy gossip of a small island community was even more pervasive than the passing, cruel curiosity of trippers.

Jimsy soon realised that he had made an error, begotten of American habit, in the very manner of his booking-in at the Brendan Arms. He had asked for a small suite of bedroom, sitting-room and bathroom, and he discovered—so much had he forgotten of the ways of his native land—that he might as well have rented the Marquis's castle a couple of miles down the coast from Ardyne. He did not know it, however, as perhaps he should have remembered, that the staff must look on the hirer of a private suite as a person exalted or romantic.

He was the talk of the staff dining-room on his very first night in Brendan, even as he was looking across the bay and seeing the Highland hills again, the light of evening putting every conceivable pastel shade of blue and green and tan upon them. The authority below stairs was Jackie, one of those posh university students who had taken a vacation job as a waiter and had been allotted the task of room service for the gentleman in 3 and 5.

"He's quite an ordinary sort of chap," Jackie protested above the rattle of questions from his female colleagues. "He's very quiet. I should think his accent is Highland, if anything. He's courteous and thoughtful. He just doesn't want to talk. That's all."

"Fine ham a haddie!" cried Annie Maclaverty, a rufous woman from the farming backlands and in charge of the hotel linen. "Fine ham a haddie! That's just you toffs hingin' thegither, all ladida and how do, old boy. There's somethin' queer about that yin: a wee nyaf like that with a private sweet. You mark my words."

Jackie, the student, was about to be funny, saying:

"I'll mark them up now, Annie. I've been marking your words for the last six weeks, and you've never come back for a check yet," when something like a yelp from wee Agnes Sproat, the scullery maid, and the clatter of cutlery on her plate indicated that she had been visited by a flash of illumination.

"I ken who he is!" she shouted her discovery through a mouthful of potato. "It's been on the tip of ma tongue ever since he came, but I juist couldny put a name to him. But I've got it noo. He's thon wee chap that played in thon film—ye remember the one about the boy and the big elephant in India or one of them places; he was a kinda orphant lost in the forest and there was an awfu' bonny wee Chinese lassie wi' him."

This caused a great raising of voices about the table, but Jackie's was the clearest.

"You're thinking of Sabu in *Elephant Boy*, Agnes, and the guest in 3 and 5 certainly isn't Sabu."

"I'm no' thinkin' of Sabu in *Elephant Boy*, Mr. Smart Alec," Agnes retorted with heat. "I seen that when I was a wee lassie. I'm thinkin' of this other pictcher wi' the Chinese lassie in it. I seen it the year I left school, and there's been mair like it by the same wee man since that. Cut my throat."

Agnes drew the back of her knife symbolically across her windpipe, and her intensity of conviction greatly impressed her colleagues.

"Ye're right, Agnes," pronounced Annie Maclaverty judicially above the babel. "The lassie's right. It a' comes back to me now. The same wee man was page boy at Ardyne the time Festus Ferrier died. Then he run away to sea or somethin'. The very man! Agnes is right, and," she added a thought weakly, "I thought masel' I kinda kent the face."

"*Kennst du das Land?*" murmured Jackie to the ceiling through the blur of cigarette smoke.

"And that's enough out of your trap," Annie snapped at him. "Seems you canny take a tellin'-off when you've had it."

"Annie, your class-consciousness is boring."

It was felt, however, that Jackie had lost in the battle of wits. The joint recollections of Agnes and Annie made a story sufficiently circumstantial to be convincing, and it spread like a discharge of oil over a tidal anchorage. It was carried that very evening to half a dozen homes of daily workers and so reached the dance halls and into public houses by the male staff off-duty. Next morning it was being told in shops and offices, and the drivers of tradesmen's vans took it into the remotest of the island's farm lands before evening. Brendan was sheltering a film star *incognito*; Brendan would tell the world.

The threat to his privacy came at Jimsy that night in the person of a dusty little journalist in the unfortunate sports jacket, rumpled grey flannel trousers and dirty cuffs under the shrunken arms of a pullover so sadly accepted as a uniform by so many of the rank and file of his trade. To the astonishment of Jackie, who thought he knew the right way to deal with the Press, Jimsy agreed to see him.

"Some poor little hick reporter after a story and his lineage. I owe these chaps something, after all. Send him up, and I'll give him a story to end all stories."

The shabby small man, one of his shoulders higher than another, was ushered into the room blinking uneasily. "Mr. Pettigrew," Jackie announced him.

"Come in, Mr. Pettigrew. Take a seat. What will you have to drink?"

Mr. Pettigrew had spent much of his professional life awaiting the pleasure of petty local councillors in the interests of a timid local newspaper with a circulation of some 800 copies, and he was overwhelmed by the friendly ease of one who might be about to give him a story of national dimensions. The phrase "a courteous and easy personality" passed through his mind. He admitted that he would enjoy a wee whisky.

"Jackie, a large whisky. Soda, Mr. Pettigrew? No, water. And bring me a small dry ginger. And now, Mr. Pettigrew, you want a story. Got your notebook there?"

It was comic when you came to think of it, the page boy from Ardyne dictating easily to the Press even through such a scruffy representative!

"I'm right in thinking that you are *the* Mr. Seumas Bell?" said Mr. Pettigrew in an effort to command the proceedings.

"Right first shot," Jimsy agreed; "once a page boy at Ardyne. The city newspapers will have it all in their libraries. Since then I've been round the world with Transocean and made three pretty big pictures, but—and please get this quite right—I have retired and do not intend to return to Hollywood."

"Is tha' a fac'?" gasped the interviewer, who used the glottal stop in moments of excitement. The pencil jotted down the Pitman symbols with more facility than the poor man's typewriter could ever handle English prose.

"Can I say what you intend to do now?" he persevered.

"You can't, for I don't know myself. You can say that I am here for a short holiday and to attend to some private business, and you can tell your buddies in the Glasgow offices that they needn't send down their special writers and star photographers, for I won't see them. This is exclusive to you, Mr. Pettigrew, and you've got to pay me back by refusing to give away my address."

"I'll try," said Mr. Pettigrew morosely, thinking of the nagging arrogance of most of those news editors on whom he depended for the best part of his living. "It would make a grand finish to the story if you'd only say something about your plans. It's not every day a young film star decides to chuck it up."

"No comment. I'm like the Garbo, I just want to be alone."

"That's a good line!" cried Mr. Pettigrew, almost coming to the fullness of life.

"Use it," Jimsy advised him curtly. "It's probably been used before. Now, I'm afraid I've got some phoning to do."

The little journalist swallowed his whisky so rapidly that he choked a little. It was not every day that he was treated to a drink, and a big one at that, by a person of eminence. With an awkwardness that Jimsy found embarrassingly pathetic he stuttered excessive thanks to his host, wrung his hand and almost backed out of the door in his sad clumsiness.

Jimsy then put a call through to the offices of Auchterlony & Blair, solicitors and notaries public, and asked to speak to the partner in charge of the sale of Ardyne as advertised in the *Glasgow Herald*. Next morning, hiring a taxi to take him barely four hundred yards for fear of the prominence now pressing upon him, he shook hands with Mr. Magnus Blair in a high room that smelt of old papers and leather bindings.

This was a dark man in early middle age who looked exactly what he was and had been, a Territorial officer of Gunners with memories of Sicily, the Rhine crossing and the Dortmund-Ems Canal.

"Sit down, Mr. Bell. I knew you were here. Things get around pretty quickly in a small place like this, I'm afraid."

"Too quickly for comfort," Jimsy grinned; "but you get hardened to it. It's just part of what the Americans call the pay-off. And I expect you are wondering why I should be interested in Ardyne?"

"Frankly, I was. A solicitor shouldn't say it but there aren't many private inquirers for big houses like that nowadays."

"It's quite simple. You see, Mr. Blair, coming to act in the movies was just an accident, and I'll never go back to it again. But it let me make a good deal of money, and I've saved it—in dollars at that. But I was brought up in the catering trade. I'm really interested in catering. And what was simply in my mind was that Ardyne, provided the price is right, would make a very nice little private hotel and a reasonably sound investment and give me something constructive to do at the same time."

"Yes, yes." Mr. Blair considered this proposition slowly. He opened his cigarette case and passed it to Jimsy. "Yes, I believe a good private hotel at that end of the island might do very well. As you know, Brendan's full of retired, well-to-do people, and a good many of them would be glad to pay well to be looked after well. In fact, there wouldn't be much difficulty in raising a small private company. . . ."

The possibilities still seemed to entrance Mr. Blair, and he figured rapidly on a pad.

"But the price?" Jimsy interrupted him, adding, "By the way, I'd want you to act for me as well as for the sellers."

Magnus Blair laughed and threw down his pencil, crying: "You ought to have been a lawyer yourself, Mr. Bell. But let me put it this way. If you come to me, wanting a five-roomed bungalow in a good position in Brendan, I'll sting you for at least four thousand five hundred. But if you are willing to take an early Edwardian mansion of sixteen rooms off my hands, you can deduct at least a thousand. And if you hold out on me —well, it's a choice between taking what I can get or tearing the roof off the place."

"So grim as that? Has it fallen into bad order, then?"

"Bad order! It's in perfect repair. Trust Finlay Ferrier for that. You know he lives there now."

"No, I've been such a long time away."

"Yes, he sort of lost heart after his wife died, and about a year ago he had a shock. He's not at all the great Finlay Ferrier he used to be. His niece looks after him now. . . . You'll remember Beth Ferrier? She's a trained nurse, and she also had a bit of a breakdown some time ago. Overwork, I believe. She was very keen on her job. But there they are now."

In the lawyer's office, talking business, Jimsy Bell was suddenly taken by a sense of the grotesque poetry of life, of whirling elements settling into a pattern after the unease of the years between. Not that, he reflected, the pattern was ever final except in the article of death, and then it would take God himself to say how the influences had worked in the main. He had to prod himself to follow Mr. Blair's new and bright idea.

"I tell you what, Mr. Bell. Why not run down and look at the place for yourself this afternoon?" His hand reached out for the instrument at his elbow. "We can have a yarn with Beth and fix it up now."

"No, no! Please, Mr. Blair. It's a little bit awkward, if you don't mind. I'd rather go—well, a little more slowly."

The old soldier of the long agony looked baffled but recovered himself to say: "Well, what if I ring Beth now and give her the gen, and then you can ring her from your hotel before lunch? You may be quite sure she knows you're here."

Then there was her voice along the line, richer and cooler now, but the intonations still those of the girl he had known. He felt she was chuckling.

"Yes, Mag Blair told me to expect a ring, but I would have been hurt if you hadn't rung in any case. Of course, Jimsy! Famous men like you! The news came in with the morning milk. And just fancy you being interested in Ardyne."

"Do you know, I think I've thought of Ardyne at least once a day since I left it."

"Jimsy, you make me blush. There's another nice thing about you; you haven't lost that adorable Highland accent. I thought Hollywood would have ironed it out and sent your voice up your nose."

"I carefully cherished one of my few assets, Miss Beth," he laughed.

"*Miss* Beth!" And he could hear the crackle of her spirit.

"Very well, and thank you, Beth." He took the hint.

"That's more sensible. But we could stand here for hours, letting the tear doonfa' over the dear, dead days. Look here, Jimsy. Will you please come to tea and wait for dinner to-day? I'll send the old shooting brake and Jock Jamieson to your hotel about three. Yes: the same old brake and the same old Jock, both mellowing a bit. No, no, no! We're not badly off for service. Good. Oh, goodie! Isn't it exciting? I'll be waiting for you in my best bib-and-tucker. Oh, Jimsy, this is gorgeous! And won't we talk and talk?"

4

He felt he must be as nervous as a girl preparing for her first big party, and he found himself giving thought even to his clothes. Not the blue suit; that seemed to reduce him to near nothing; the light-grey double-breasted flannel was the thing on this fine August day. A white shirt freshly laundered and a maroon tie; the dark tan shoes he had had made to order in Glasgow; no hat. He fidgeted in his sitting-room until the girl at the desk rang to say that the car from Ardyne was at the door.

It was the same old brake, indestructible, but as they shook hands with enthusiasm Jimsy saw the smears that the years had put upon Jock Jamieson. His hair was nearly white along the sides of his head, and his face was leaner than ever about a mouth that seemed to have sunk a little over shrunken gums. His person was smarter than of yore, however, and a neat serge suit, a clean collar and a black tie suggested something like a uniform.

"Jock!"

"Jimsy! I canny ca' ye Mr. Bell. I juist canny do it."

"Don't try." And when Jock held open the back door of the brake Jimsy laughed at him. "Put that parcel in the back seat. I'm going into my old pew beside you."

"Aye, aye," Jock continued sententiously as they started along the front. "So ye're a big man now but juist the same old sixpence. I'm proud of you, son."

"That's nice of you, Jock. And I'm grateful to you."

"To me! How that?"

"Oh, just for a word or two on the importance of personal dignity. Still a politician, Jock?"

"No, no. Nut what I was. Gettin' a bit old in the tooth and

shiftin' a wee bit to the Right; and to tell ye the truth, Finlay Ferrier, capitalist and a', gives me conditions that make ma work at the big house a pleasure—not like thon Festus, who killed near' everything he touched. There was juist three of us that beat him—you and me and Miss Beth. Thon's a rare lass."

"What about Billy?"

"I was juist goin' to tell ye. It might come up atween you and Miss Beth, and I wouldny like the lassie hurt. But the dirty truth is Master Billy's a waster. He was called up, and the Army didny keep him six weeks. So whit is he now? Shover-gardener to his Ma and his auntie, and just a dirty wee boozer in between."

"Poor little devil!" muttered Jimsy.

"Juist what his father and mother made him. But here we are," announced Jock, swinging the brake between the familiar stone pillars. "Just you have a good dekko at ma lawn; that's my labourer at it wi' the mower now. See the new rose garden. It's past its best for this summer, but it's a topper. And there's the best of the lot of them out on the steps, waitin' for ye."

It was Beth indeed, a young woman now, but somehow still seeming to trail the clouds of her inveterate girlhood; Beth slim in a cotton frock, its basic red setting off her darkness; Beth of the beautifully modelled, poised head; but now a Beth happy and friendly and bubbling with excitement.

"Jimsy!"

"Miss Beth!" He quickly corrected himself with a happy laugh. "Beth, I mean. What a pleasure to see you again!"

"And at Ardyne, too! Or are we just acting in a nice sentimental picture."

"I hope not. I don't think we are."

"Well, don't let's be clever. Look Jimsy! It's such a lovely day I've had the tea laid under the trees over there. Uncle Finlay will be with us as a special treat. He's terribly excited about your being here. He says there's something special he wants to tell you. You'll remember that he is apt to get excited."

"He couldn't be as excited as I am. There's so much I want to know about you."

"And I about you. Where on earth shall we start?"

As they walked together across the lawn Jimsy could appreciate the new degree of tidiness Finlay Ferrier had brought to the old place. The lawn, now being mowed afresh, was as a rich carpet of such a green as he had missed for many years. Down there on the edge of a slope and breaking the monotony of grass was the new rose garden, still ablaze with the beauties of the second growth. The putter-putt, putter-putt of the motor mower provided a domestic note of serenity in a scene loved and cared for. Before they settled down in the deck-chairs Jimsy turned to look back at the big house, its sandstone face serene in the afternoon light.

"It's a wonderful building of its period," he murmured.

"It may be," she said shortly, "but I can't understand why you should think of buying it."

"Oh, it's a good deal more than sentiment, I assure you, Beth, but we'll come round to that. Now, you start."

"From the year you stopped sending a Christmas card to a lonely student-nurse and nearly broke her heart?" she teased him.

"We'll come round to that too, if you like."

It was surprising how much two people, friendly and profoundly interested in each other, could exchange within the space of half an hour. Time was telescoped, and the saliences of the years were so few after all. But when Beth rose, saying that she must go in to bring out Uncle Finlay for his treat, both of them knew that they had treated themselves to narrative, often facetious, and that they were still edging nervously round the clot of speculations and velleities that were theirs alone.

Jimsy followed Beth across the lawn, and at the same time a young girl in proper servant's uniform came down the steps of the house and approached him, a vast silver tray with the tea-things firmly held by red hands at the ends of strong forearms. His trained eye rejoiced in the picture, and he saw it all as framed, and he chuckled to think that not all the ingenuity of Hollywood could reproduce it perfectly—against the green of

British grass and the mild sandstone frontage, the sturdy country girl in her black and white and the easy, uninhibited stride of Beth: the rare lass of Jock Jamieson's happy phrase.

The brake had been left by the door, and when Jimsy had got his parcel from the back seat he turned to see Finlay Ferrier come slowly down the steps on Beth's arm, a changed man; and he experienced the small flutter of concern such a reminder of time passing must always produce. There was that little twist about the mouth that he had seen in this man's brother years before; the feet shuffled slightly, and Jimsy helped Beth to give him a lift from the gravel to the grass. He was talkative in a jerky way.

"Yes, Bell," he insisted as they made their slow way towards the chairs, "I've been wanting to see you for a long time. Always wanted to tell you what happened after you had that bit of trouble in the big ship—that business about the watch. Mind you, I was angry with you at first, but Beth here kept ramming it down my throat that you weren't one to steal; and when I was in London once—Oh, it was a while after you disappeared!—I got hold of Charlie Catto of the B. & A., and I said to him: ' Charlie, I still want to know the truth about that boy, Jimsy Bell, you got set up as a steward in the *Canberra*, the wee fellow that was logged for pinching a watch.' "

"That was very kind of you, Mr. Ferrier," murmured Jimsy.

"No. It's just that I could never abide untidiness. Anyhow, just to tell you my story," resumed Finlay Ferrier, crumbs falling down his waistcoat as he munched at a sponge cake. "It was a good while before I got anything back from Charlie Catto, but this was a letter to say it was all cleared up. The passenger who laid the charge found the damn' thing at the foot of a trunk."

"I'm surprised he had the decency to admit it," said Jimsy tartly. "He was an unpleasant person."

Finlay Ferrier ignored the comment on his important narrative.

"Now, wait till I tell you what happened. It must have been a year after that, maybe two. Anyhow, one day I met Charlie

Catto in Leicester Square when I was in London on business. We were both going to the same dinner, as a matter of fact. And I said to him ' Charlie, do you remember the wee steward your people logged for pinching a watch?' 'Are you still harping on that?' says Charlie. 'He would have been re-instated and perhaps compensated if he hadn't skipped the ship at Colombo.' 'He didn't need it,' says I. 'Look!' And I pointed to a poster above the door of the Empire. 'That's the wee chap the B. & A. lost when they decided that the passenger is always right.' It was a picture of you, Bell, on that elephant, large as life. Now, that was a queer turn-up, wasn't it?"

"Extraordinary!" Jimsy agreed enthusiastically. "I'm glad that old mystery is cleared up."

He was thinking how odd it was that the man from Penang who had done him so much wrong had also done no good to the very near kin of his host and hostess, when Finlay Ferrier went on "Yes, Bell, I've been wanting to see you for a long time to tell you that story. Always wanted to tell you what I said to Charlie Catto. . . ."

It was pathetically plain that the poor, stricken man was ready to go over it all again. Meanwhile, Beth had opened the parcel Jimsy had brought with him for her: a huge box of chocolates and a carton of American cigarettes—all that he had been able to raise at short notice in Brendan and out of his luggage. Now, still talking, Finlay Ferrier kept feeling among the chocolates and popping them into his mouth like a greedy child but without its fear of discipline.

"Uncle Finlay!" commanded Beth at length, her tone pro-fessionally firm. "No more chocolates, please. So many won't agree with you, you know. In fact, dear, I think you'd better come inside and have a rest out of the sun. Come, now."

"Let me take your arm, Mr. Ferrier?" And Jimsy was on his feet.

"Very good of you, Bell. Poor little Beth gets the worst of it with a great lump of an old chap like me. Anyhow," he persisted as they made their slow way across the lawn, "it's been a pleasure to see you. You must come back soon, and we'll have another good yarn. You'll agree we had the laugh on Charlie Catto. . . ."

Jimsy sauntered on the gravel until Beth came out again, and they moved on to the lawn to walk slowly up and down, into the lengthening shadows of the trees under which they had sat at tea and back into the glow of late afternoon. The grass was all short and sweet-smelling now, Jock's assistant putting the fancy finishing touches to the borders of the great rose garden.

"What do you think of Uncle Finlay?" she asked abruptly.

"A change—rather frightening when you remember what a hearty, bustling man he was."

"That's the onset of senility, rather premature in his case. It's the most terrible thing, growing old! Do you know, Jimsy," she burst out, "if we were hard up, I could fill Ardyne with twenty old people: people with means, people who could pay good nursing-home fees? They're all just slightly silly and useless, and their daughters-in-law don't want them. Just with enough means left to keep them out of the public institutions and not let the side down."

"There's an idea there, you know," he said with interest.

"Not for me, thank you. They're so foolish, and they can be so dirty, and they're always pathetic. Give me a good old General Accidents ward every time. I don't want to be reminded every day of my life that it isn't worth living."

He was hurt by the edge of bitterness in her tone, and he hesitated before he spoke again, firmly.

"I don't agree with you. It is worth living, except in the quite exceptional case, for the good things to see and do between the bad spells. Don't think it's a line from one of my pictures, Beth, but I'd count life worth living for just quite a few afternoons like this."

"You're really a cunning rogue, Jimsy," she chuckled, "and when you lay on that nice Highland accent of yours you almost persuade me."

"I'm beginning to see that you need some persuasion," he said, crisply again.

They had returned to their chairs, which Jimsy had dragged forward into the embers of the sun, and the sturdy girl in uniform came across the lawn to take the tea things away. Jimsy rose to help her, saw that her grip on the silver handles was firm, smiled and said "You're having a busy day, aren't you?" to which the girl, blushing deep, returned "Thank you, sir. It's a pleasure."

"Jimsy Bell," teased Beth when the girl was out of earshot, "breaking little Dolly's heart! It's a shame. Now she's your doormat, and I'll never hear the end of you."

"Would she like a photograph, do you think?" he asked quite innocently.

"Would she like a photograph! She'd be on her knees before it every night and morning. You're the dream-lover, you know. But," Beth added mischievously, "it's not to be the one with Ma Palai. That's mine. It's on my dressing-table, if you want to know."

"All these years and in spite of——"

"All these years and in spite of lots of things."

"You honour me, Beth."

He spoke gravely, and he seemed to brood for a space, his eyes on the ground.

"I hope you don't think it was an act, my speaking to Dolly. I was once one of these people, remember; I may be again. I can't help it, but when I see a tired girl sagging under a tray in a café or a poor little *commis* being bullied by a head waiter, I want to dash in and help them out. It's in the blood. It's one of the strangest human situations, being in service. And that, to come to the point, is why I'm interested in Ardyne."

"Tell me."

He told her what he had told the lawyer in Rothesay, and she withheld her response, seeming to ponder profoundly.

"You don't seem to be impressed," he encouraged her.

"No." And her speech was jerky and harsh again. "I can't bear to think of you kowtowing to second-rate matrons from the suburbs of Glasgow. Perhaps it's foolish of me, but that's not my picture of Jimsy Bell. No! I'm not thinking of the film star, but whenever I've thought of you all these years—and there have been plenty of them, the Lord knows!—it's been of your dignity, your—what's the word?—integrity."

She seemed to him to be begging many questions, but he replied gently "I would have used exactly the same words of you."

"Sometimes I've thought," she added recklessly, "that we're just a couple of simpletons who got caught up in a mess created by my own father in the first place."

She rose abruptly and said that she must go indoors and look after her invalid and see to the dinner, and could he amuse himself for an hour; and Jimsy said that he would enjoy a walk around and a yarn with Jock Jamieson. The latter he avoided, in fact. It was nearer his mood to stroll along the shore road and turn over the first impressions of his return to Ardyne.

So pleasant it had been; so much he had been able to tell and hear that cleared the air; but it stuck in his mind that Beth and he had not yet reached the limit of their confidences. She was holding something back, as they said. They were involved together, and yet she hesitated to admit it, even to herself. In his innocence he concluded that she felt herself bound, so long as he might live, by her duty to Finlay Ferrier, her second and better father.

They took their dinner together quietly, however, keeping their concerns away from the candlelit table in what had been the library. She had changed into a dark dress, it might be midnight blue, and there was a string of large amber beads, almost blood-red, about her neck, her skin flawless as ivory in the soft, yellow light. The caterer in Jimsy appreciated the balance and quality of the meal: the small bowl of creamy tomato soup, the cold salmon with salad, green peas and potatoes all fresh from the garden, and a cheese soufflé light as thistledown. There was also a bottle of a musky Montrachet.

"Uncle Finlay insisted," Beth explained. "He actually wanted you to go down to the cellar and fish up a bottle of vintage port. I had to tell him that we still wished to enjoy the rest of the evening."

"There's plenty of light yet," said Jimsy, glancing through the windows. Encouraged by the wine, he asked: "Will you let me wallow in sentiment and row you out to the island?"

"A fond farewell," she said, the enigmatic edge of hardness again in her tone. "Let's have coffee outside and see what the weather's like first."

She picked a Paisley shawl from the back of her chair, and Jimsy helped to drape it about her, a vast square of cream silk with only an edging of the harness pattern in mild colours above the long white tassels. Dolly served them with coffee outside, and Jimsy had the poor girl blushing again with his involuntary smile. The night was mild, the on-shore wind fallen to nearly nothing, and the aftermath of sunset behind the islands had laid a film of gold on waters now resting at the turn of the tide. A pretty wagtail ran and dipped about the lawn.

"I suppose we'd better go while the light holds," Beth suggested. "I'll just run up and have a look at Uncle Finlay and get something warm for my shoulders. It will be cold on the water."

She came down again and handed him a heavy garment to carry over his arm to the jetty. There at the end of the running-line was the old boat, as trig as ever—"Uncle Finlay always fusses about that sort of thing," Beth explained—and when he had pulled it in he helped her into that lovely garment, the nurse's cloak, heavy blue outside and warm red within like a strange bird's nest. Again seeing the external world within the frames of a moving picture, he studied her posture in the stern-sheets as he shipped the oars, engaged her attention with a smile, and said:

"You look like Lord Ullin's daughter."

"She was drowned, wasn't she?"

The tone was at once dry and morose, and Jimsy felt that he had been snubbed for a clumsiness, but it made him all the more desperate to know what was at the root of her unease. He knew of women enough not to ask argumentative questions now but to keep rowing and pick a place on the shore of the island where, at this point of high tide, he could help her to land dryshod.

They walked by the old track, now seeming so short, to where they had played at building a house, and some of their work survived, a wall built up of rough stones across a gully in the rock and the outline of that primitive museum in which Beth had laid out her collections of wild flowers.

"Poor little children!" she murmured. "Shall we knock it down and call it a day?"

She had her right foot poised above one of the rough little walls, but he caught at her wrist and cried:

"No, please! It's the time to be sentimental and leave our little symbol alone." And his voice was urgent. "Time and the tides will deal with it. Neither your life nor mine is going to be so long as all that."

She pulled her arm away from his grasp and flared out at him.

"I'm sick of the way people keep talking about 'life.' What do they mean? So many years in this beastly world, or what happens to you while you are in it?"

"What happens to you, of course," Jimsy said quietly. Remembering the occasional tantrums of Nicky Font, he perceived for the first time the sure signs of the recent breakdown the lawyer had talked about. "A life may last only twenty years and yet have been full of enjoyment and value. A man can live to be ninety and still have been a curse to himself and everybody about him."

"But what if you know, when you're only twenty-two, that you've made an utter mess of things already, and that you're just fit for looking after an old man till he dies, and then—Heaven alone knows?"

"If you're talking about yourself, Beth, you're talking nonsense. Look here"—he touched her arm again—"you're dead tired. I have upset you by waiting so long and talking so much. Let's get up to the house and I'll go back to the hotel, and we'll start again when you have had a rest."

"No. I want to tell you now while I'm in the mood. I may never feel like this again. You've *got* to let me tell you."

"Very well. But understand: nothing you can tell me will affect me in the least. You see, I know all about you. You are you, Beth Ferrier. And you talk to me of dignity, integrity!"

"And who else in all this world can I talk to?" she asked.

The gloaming was closing about them, and the off-shore breezes were stirring. The tide, now beginning to ebb, slapped listlessly on the rocks almost at their feet. He arranged the slack of her cloak about her shoulders and became aware that her body was taut as when, a child, she braced herself to take punishment.

"It was a man." She began to speak bleakly, as if she recited a rehearsed piece. "I loved him or I thought I did, and I was sure he loved me. Then he was going to the States, and I went with him for a week-end. Then he was killed in a flying accident, and I discovered that he had married; and that must have been just about a month after he left me. Then you come back. . . ."

She was muddled in the mind, Jimmy perceived with alarm and pity, but he saw to the root of her trouble. It was the betrayal that she had found unbearable, and it distressed him that he could not, as they stood on an islet in the near-darkness, make more than a pass at opening the slow course of therapy that could alone drive out her private devils of guilt.

"Listen, Beth. You asked about a Christmas card that never came. That was because of my own private spasm of feeling guilty—and somehow responsible to you. Yes, it was a girl; yes, it was little Feng Lee. No passionate love about it, just affection and convenience, both of us lonely. It went on for nearly two years until it became merely convenient for us both to call it a day and part. And if you're going to talk about me coming home on the top of your trouble; if that is important, what about me bringing my own parcel of damaged goods back into your life?"

"It's not the same," she insisted unhappily.

"It's allee same same, as dear Nicky Font used to say." Jimsy tried to laugh. "I must tell you all about Nicky some day soon. But come, Beth. It's getting late and dark. Let me take your arm along the path."

The shooting-brake had been turned in front of the house, and as they came up across the lawn they could see, in the faint light of the side-lamps, that Jock Jamieson was busy with his duster on the metal parts.

"Jock wants to hurry me home and get back to his bed," Jimsy chuckled, "and I have kept you too late, tired you out."

He halted to face her earnestly.

"There's still a lot to talk about. I still owe you one pound, twelve and threepence, for instance. Can I ring you in the morning again?"

"Yes, please do," she whispered.

"And will you remember just this one thing, Beth? You needn't be lonely, any more, you know."

"Oh, Jimsy!" she cried. "What a kind, kind thing to say!" And she clutched for his hands and held them for a moment between hers and within the warmth of her cloak.

Then it was just the conventional good night of old friends in Jock's presence. The gravel spurted under the tyres, and the beams of the headlamps probed the dark places of the drive. It was fast going along the shore road and silent over the Firth on that side of the island, but when they came round the point it was to see Brendan and its bay aglow with festive light: the coloured lamps strung in loops along the promenade, the flares in front of picture houses and the riding lights of yachts, fire-flies hovering above black water. From somewhere behind the town came the metallic braying of mechanical music from some cheap little fair.

"Still goin' like a ruddy circus," observed Jock, breaking the silence between them. "It's a queer change from Ardyne, not five miles away. I must say, Jimsy, I like the quiet nowadays. I'll bet ye had a rare long chinwag wi' Miss Beth."

"We did. As the poet nearly said, we fairly tired the sun with talking."

"Aye, big changes," said Jock portentously, slowing down for the hotel entrance. "Still, and it's mebbe no business of mines, but thon's a rare lass. If you were thinkin' of hangin' up your hat, I mean. A rare lass."

"We'll have to be thinking of that, won't we, Jock?" retorted Jimsy cheerfully. "Thanks for the lift. See you to-morrow."

THE END